PARADOX

THE TRANSIENT TRILOGY BOOK #2

M.K. PARSONS

For those who are joined together with unbreakable bonds.

PROLOGUE

I don't have many memories of being five. Not too many people do, I suppose. In fact, I think I've only got one, but it's the clearest memory of my childhood.

Saving Roxy.

My mother hid her dark side from me. She wouldn't talk about the portal. If I asked, she would distract me with treats or diversions. Looking back, I think she thought of me as her plaything—a doll to dress up and take everywhere. To make her feel normal, to make her feel like she was good. But I knew there was something off about my mom, even at that age. I knew people were afraid of her and her portal.

Once, when I was supposed to be studying for my entrance exam to army school—Leona required all eight-year-old children in the citadel to enter military school—she caught me playing. More specifically, she caught me pretending Arabella Eisen was my mom.

She lost it. I don't mean a tantrum. I mean, she *lost* it. She threw things and raged as I cowered in a corner and cried. I was sure I'd be headed to that portal room and disappear like all the other people that went in, but never came out.

I was a little kid, and I was sure my mom was going to kill me.

She left me alone in my locked room for the rest of that day and night. Laying there, my stomach rolling with hunger, I decided I would never ever be like her. I would do whatever I had to do to be the *opposite* of her.

I was never surer of it than I was a few days later, hiding outside the portal room, watching her. Leona and Arabella were in the hallway arguing—well, my *mom* was arguing—and they didn't notice me sneak in with them as my mom swiped her key and the doors disappeared.

What I saw terrified me. The portal room seemed to go on forever, echoing and severe. The lack of furniture inside the room only granted the portal more authority. I could sense the room was a death room.

Afraid they would see me, I dove under a console inside the room and rolled up in a ball as my mother's voice got higher and more frenzied.

"You bewitched him," Leona said to Arabella, her voice a growl. "You forced him to love you instead of me."

"I didn't, Lee." Arabella shifted the weight of her baby to her hip and reached a palm to frame Leona's face. "That's not what love is. You can't force someone to love you. I'm sorry. I didn't realize how much you cared for him."

"You're not sorry!" Leona spat, pushing Arabella's hand away. "Don't lie to me. You wouldn't give him back to me if he begged you."

"Lee," Arabella said softly. "Eli and I are married. We have a baby. I don't want to hurt you, but he chose me. And I'd love it if you could accept this and move on. Find your own happiness. I hate for you to live like this."

"Don't patronize me," Leona snarled.

Then Eli stood in the doorway. He took slow steps toward the women.

"What's going on?" His voice sounded tentative, as if he was trying not to upset some delicate balance. "Leona, is everything okay?"

"I don't want your pity," Leona said, glaring. She backed up and pulled out her knife as if she thought he might hurt her. She pointed the edge of the knife at Eli. "You, of all people. You've led me on."

Eli glanced at Arabella. "What do you mean, Leona?"

"You made me believe you loved me. All along. You lied," Leona said, her voice demanding.

"I do care about you, Leona. We both do." Eli took a step toward her. I wanted to warn him to stay back. I could tell something was going to happen. I tried to wave to him. He didn't see me, but Arabella did. She motioned me back under the console.

Eli suddenly doubled over. His face turned purple and he struggled to breathe. My mother watched with satisfaction. I could tell she was hurting him with her mind. I knew she could do it, because she'd done it to me before.

"What are you doing, Lee?" Arabella's voice was breathless. Worried.

"I don't want to be made a fool of anymore." Leona stared at Eli.

"Please let him go, Leona," Arabella took a step toward her. Eli gasped and fell to his knees. "We are responsible to our abilities, Lee. We have to use them for good."

"Don't talk to me about good! You've never given me a choice. Either of you. Why couldn't you just ask me what I wanted?"

"What *do* you want, Leona?" Eli managed.

"It's too late!" She cried. "I wanted to be happy. I wanted my son to have a father. Was that so much to ask?"

"That's not too much to ask," Eli said. "But you never said anything. You can't blame me for what you never said, Leona. And you can't fault someone else for not feeling the same way."

"I can. And all of you will pay."

Eli doubled over in pain again. I watched the knife my mother still held. It flashed against the lights of the portal console as she held it out. Before they could react, she plunged it into Eli's chest with a maniacal cry. I saw the look of surprise on his face. The desperate glance toward Arabella, as if he couldn't leave her and their baby unprotected.

"Morris," he whispered to her, his voice gurgling as blood spilled over and ran down his chin. He fell to the floor, completely still.

I'd never seen anyone killed before. At least, not violently. I'd seen plenty of people hauled away to the portal, but I'd never seen the blood dripping off the end of the knife. Now I knew blood had a smell. I'd never seen a grown man's body lying on the floor, motionless. Now I knew what *lifeless* meant.

Arabella cried out in pain, as if the knife had wounded her, too, and she fell to her knees beside her husband. Roxy grabbed her mom around the neck and whimpered.

I stared hard at Eli. I wanted to go to him. I wanted to be brave enough to put my hands on him and try to heal him. Maybe I could make all the blood and death and hatred go away. Maybe I could fix it. I had done it before, with a dying dog I found in the gardens. But I was too scared of my mom to try to save Eli.

When Leona turned around to the console, calling the portal to life, somehow Arabella composed herself. She put her baby on the chair and stared hard at me, showing me the compass on the chain around Roxy's neck, indicating I should follow the direction it would lead me. I had to find courage. I didn't have a choice. I was the only one who could get Roxy to safety. My mom would kill her, I was sure of it. Arabella was sure of it.

It was up to me.

I wanted to be paralyzed with fear when my mom pushed Arabella into all that light and heat. But I took my opportunity instead. I grabbed Roxy and ran.

It was storming that night. I hated thunderstorms. But I knew the only thing I could do for Roxy and her parents was follow the compass. I pushed open the door and headed into the night.

When Roxy got too heavy for me, I set her on the ground and took her hand. Rain soaked our hair and clothes as I led her through the dark, with trees snaking up toward the sky and trying to block the way of the rain. I cringed at every crack of thunder and blinding flash. Roxy stared at me, frowning.

The compass stopped directing me, so I pulled her under a bush behind the Military School. Rain seeped through leaves and drenched us. The wind whispered to me, telling me I would lose her. I would be found and my mother would kill us.

But seconds or minutes or hours later, a man's face appeared. He seemed kind. "What happened?"

"She killed them," I said. "She killed them both."

His eyes closed for a moment as if it hurt him to hear the news. But he nodded and reached for Roxy.

Roxy didn't smile, but she went willingly to the stranger. As she wrapped her arms around him, she looked back at me.

"Will you be okay?" The man asked. I considered his question, but when I saw that Roxy was safe, and Leona wouldn't be able to hurt her, I was okay. I nodded.

"Thank you," he said before he and Roxy disappeared into the night.

I never forgot that night. I think it was what saved me from becoming like my mother. The kind stranger in the storm was my hope. If he could beat the influence of Leona, maybe we all could.

Maybe even her son could choose a different path.

ONE

Teaching people how to be free was harder than setting them free in the first place.

I thought it so many times in that first year of managing New York City. Now, listening to the council discuss strategies for speaking to the factions about reunification, and signing endless documents about our new system of law, I was more sure than ever.

"Governor Koenig," said an older man with a long mustache he kept fingering. He was interrupting me as I explained—again—my plan to get Ohio to open its borders and extend its protection against marauders who wandered the broken nation, killing people struggling to survive and stealing what little they had. "You are too young to remember what happened the last time we tried to get everyone on the same page. You're asking for another civil war, like the one we had after the blackout."

"We have to do something. We can't just stand by, attached to this country. We're a part of it whether we want to be or not, and it's in our best interests to see that it gets back together."

"Why? Why can't we just stay separate? It's worked well enough for us until now." A woman, still dressed in Leona-approved costume, folded her hands on the table and sighed as if I was a nagging fly buzzing around her, trying to disturb her peaceful existence.

"How can you say that?" I stood up, leaning on the glass of the levitating table in the center of the room. I looked around the room, making sure I met the eyes of each council member in turn. I had learned it was the only way to get through to them. By intimidation.

I didn't like how closely intimidation resembled domination.

She continued. "We aren't some faction struggling to survive. We have technology unheard of in the rest of the world. We have resources; we have trade with several countries. Most of all, we have the portal."

I sighed. "We are not using that portal to control anybody. That's what Leona did, and that's why she's a fugitive now. Fear doesn't make peace."

"I think it does," she said, though she didn't look at me as she spoke.

"I don't want this city to be secure because we step on everyone else to do it. I want us to be united. I want the whole country to be united. That's when we'll really know what freedom is. That's when everyone will be safe."

"But that's impossible!" Several people stood up and everyone started murmuring to each other. "It can't be done."

"It was done once. When the country began. Why can't it happen again?"

I hoped they didn't call my bluff and ask for details. Leona had made sure I had several gaping holes in my American history education.

I saw all the blank looks around the table and realized none of them knew any more than I did about the origins of the United States of America. Most of us hadn't been alive before it had fallen.

"Look, I know we can't just march out in a crusade and convince everyone to pull together. But we can work on them, little by little, and encourage friendships and alliances. We can offer them our help in exchange for theirs."

They sat back down and appeared to mull over my words.

"You ultimately hope to make an alliance with Ohio?" The oldest man at the table spoke. I nodded, and gestured once again to the detailed plans I had already laid out in virtual form in front of each of them.

"It will work," I promised. "I will make it work. You have to trust me."

They were all quiet, so Greer called for the secret vote. When the tally came up on my virtual screen, I saw I had won their support.

By a very narrow margin.

"Thank you," I said as they started to stand and some left the room. We were meeting in Leona's old throne room, converted to a theater of seats for every representative in the new government to have a personal area with a computer data center.

I knew my day was just getting started. The doors were opened and the citizens started flooding in. They made a line from my table all the way to the arched doorways and out to the main hall. They were there with their grievances and petitions. Without a solid law, every matter had to be weighed and decided on separately. We needed a court system. We needed judges and lawyers. But first, we needed a code of laws. And I didn't think we were ever going to be able to agree on it.

A couple stood in front of me. The first thing I noticed was her flamboyant Leona-approved costume. She looked like a Victorian clown. Her arms were wrapped around her chest and he, who wore plain clothes not unlike my own, glared at me, his hands on his hips.

"We want our marriage annulled. Leona forced us to get married."

"You both feel this way?" I considered them. They weren't the first to ask for an annulment. We had been taking them on a case-by-case basis.

I looked at her when I asked the question. She gave a short nod, but she wouldn't look me in the eye. I brought up their marriage document.

"You both signed this document, agreeing to live together as a married couple. You had the choice to go against Leona. I think you should live by your decision and make it work."

I remembered Roxy in the bunker, insisting that the kids live by their choices. It had worked for them. Maybe it would work for our city, too.

"You can't force us to stay married! If you do, you're the same as your mother." The man leaned over my center. I could tell he was trying to bully me.

"Speak respectfully or you will leave, sir. Shall I call security?"

He hesitated, but finally shook his head and looked away.

"I am not Leona," I continued. "I believe in everyone following the rules and being responsible. If you want to end your marriage, you will have to get a divorce."

"But that will take forever," the woman said, her voice weary.

"Then maybe you should put the time and effort into coming to an understanding. Especially if you have a family. My advice is that you try to make it work. You may be surprised by what happens."

They left quickly. He was in a huff and her feet dragged as if I'd added to the burden. I felt harsh. Unrealistic. Part of me wanted to give the people what they wanted and make their lives easier, but a bigger part of me just knew, however it had gotten into my brain, that people had to be called to account in order to grow. It was part of the process of learning to be free.

Later that evening, I stood in my personal conference room at the citadel, alone, for once. It wouldn't last long. It never did. I went to the window and spoke a word. The computer program that ran the palace lifted the ridged glass and gave me a view of the street below. I saw New York's bustling maglev traffic, the sidewalks packed with people who now understood freedom.

But how did they manage to go on without Roxy?

I thought about the night I'd taken her to Morris when she was a baby. I thought about the night I'd kissed her on top of the Croton Reservoir in 1874. I thought about that first night I found her walking on Broadway. The night everything in my life changed. The first time I had looked into her eyes, I saw the stars. I had seen the spark of life and hope that was lacking in me. In my family. She was shining, brilliant. And I knew I needed her. I saw all the pages of my story, and I knew she went all the way to the end.

So, now, trying to live without her, while I dealt with the endless process of freeing a city, was torture. In fact, I wouldn't wish it on my worst enemy. Not that my enemy would know anything about it. My mother only ever loved herself.

I shook my head in disbelief. Why was I—Levi Koenig—son of one of the worst human beings in history, elected to take her place? Why would the city give me her palace, her position, her resources? Didn't anyone wonder if I might take all that power and resume the tyranny my mother had begun?

"You aren't your mom, Levi. Anyone can see that," Greer always said when I voiced the question.

I intended to prove it. As soon as I figured out how to live without Roxy.

It had been over a year since Leona had thrown herself into the portal to escape justice. It felt like ten years. The realization hit me again. Roxy had left me. I hadn't seen her, heard from her or recognized her voice in my head for so many excruciatingly long months.

I heard Greer speak behind me. "Roxy's one girl. You got millions to think about." He stepped up to the window beside me. "I'm right, aren't I? You're thinking about her again."

I didn't answer. He knew the truth.

"She's not coming back. I think that's obvious by now. You can't be staring out the window all day wondering where she is or what she's doing, if she's thinking about you, or if you could have done something different to make her stay. You can't change the past. The present needs you focused. This city and country need healing and you happen to be a healer."

I looked back out the window. I'd asked Greer to keep me honest, and part of me was grateful for his admonition. But it didn't seem like asking too much to think about her once in a while. "They seem like they're doing okay."

Even though we both knew the people were far from okay, in a sense I was right. Technology was booming. Maglevs zoomed with new independence over the improved SmartStreets that no longer tracked citizens. Jetpacks hadn't been used much since before the blackout, but now HoverWings, lightweight jetpacks recently patented out of New York, had caused the skies to fill with busy commuters. I had tried one of the packs when the patent was first tested at the citadel. I couldn't deny the rush of adrenaline and the heady experience of conquering gravity with technology.

I watched a Domestic Service Robot cheerfully maintain traffic control in front of the citadel gates. His blank smiling face reminded me of the old DSR's Roxy had kept in the bunker—Arty and Henderson.

"Remember the way Roxy used to yell at Arty?" A smile pulled at the corners of my mouth without my permission.

Greer smiled. "How could I forget?"

"Governor Koenig," a woman's voice called from the center of the room. I turned to view the realistic image projection of the computer that ran the citadel—another of my inventions. Her name was CORI—Cognitive Organizational Relational Interface.

"Speak, Cori."

"There has been an incident in the kitchens. A staff member has been injured. Emergency support has been alerted."

"Thank you, Cori. I'll go right now and see if I can help."

"As you wish, Governor."

The computer projection vanished as a robotic vehicle came from beneath the glass floor and glided quickly to my side. It was a transparent platform with two handles on either side to grasp. I stood on it, grabbed the holds and felt myself whisked away.

In seconds I arrived at the grand hallway connecting the upper floors with the main foyer. The vehicle deftly adjusted, lifting me over the iron railing and lowering me safely to the ground, slowing only when it was inches away from impact. The breeze from the ride blew against my face, exhilarating me. I could almost forget why I wasn't happy. Opulence surrounded me; I had hundreds of staff that still operated with the mindset of servants. As I passed by, they lowered their head in respect or saluted me.

But the riches I'd inherited from my mother came with too high a price.

I was piloted down the hallway toward the kitchens, where I hopped off the lift and entered the large main room. It was easy to find the source of the trouble. I only needed to follow the scent of blood.

I'd always been good at that.

The crowd parted for me as if they somehow knew my secret. They didn't, though. I'd made sure of it. I didn't hesitate to use my gift when it was necessary, but I didn't want everyone reading about it in the live news flashes on the SmartPavement.

Medics leaned over a young woman as they tried to staunch the frenzied flow of blood from a large gash on her forehead.

I looked at the head chef. He wrung his hands and stared at me, as if he expected me to blame him for the accident. As if he might be portaled for speaking.

"I don't know what happened," he said, trembling. "I told her to get me a butcher's knife from the QuickWash, but when she opened the door … it was like the knife jumped out and attacked her! I keep them so sharp … I didn't want anyone to get hurt, Your Excellency."

I shook my head. "Governor. And I believe you. Just stand back."

The blood was flowing fast, and the girl's face was pallid, her lips white. She had minutes to live.

"You can do something, can't you, Highness? She's such a beautiful girl. She's been through so much. It would be a shame for her to die like this."

"Take her to the emergency lift," I said, removing my jacket and placing it over her as they loaded her on the hovering gurney. I pushed her to the lift, holding up a hand to stop anyone else from joining me.

"Take me to my rooms, Cori," I called to the computer.

I rushed the gurney down the hall and pushed her through the door that had dematerialized in anticipation of my arrival. I pressed the button to replace the door and secure it before I turned back to the girl, whose long blonde hair was matted with blood that still oozed freely. I took a deep breath and focused all my energy on the long, jagged gash. Familiar burning ignited and my fingers found their eerie glow. I traced the path of the wound with my thumb, and watched in satisfaction as the angry red slit became a faint scar. The color returned to her face and she opened her eyes. She stared at me in surprise.

"Governor?" She held a hand to her head, confused. "How did I get here?"

I smiled as she sat up and dropped her head in respect. She wobbled, so I put my hand on her shoulder to steady her.

"Careful. You might want to rest for a few minutes before you try to stand."

"No, I should go ... sorry to disturb you," she said, peeking at me with a troubled kind of awe.

"Do you remember hurting your head?" I gently tugged on a strand of hair hardened with dried blood. She reached up to her head and patted the scar.

"Y—Yes." The clarity returned to her eyes. "The butcher's knife ... it flew out of the QuickWash. How ... I didn't expect to wake up." She eyed me with curiosity.

I shrugged. "I have a knack for getting people out of trouble."

"I guess," she said in confusion. She seemed to catch herself and quickly bowed. "Thank you."

I couldn't deny I enjoyed the appreciation. I smiled back. "No need to thank me. Has the dishwashing unit ever malfunctioned before?"

"No, sir. I can't explain it. Someone serviced it yesterday, in fact."

This caught my attention. "Who serviced it?"

She shook her head and looked at her hands in her lap. "I had never seen him before."

"Why do you keep looking down?" I lifted her chin with a

finger. She still avoided my gaze.

It took her a moment to answer. "I was taught not to make eye contact. When I was brought here to be a servant."

Her words brought back a host of disturbing memories. I could guess how she had been treated, and why I saw the guarded shadows in her features.

"You mean a slave." I frowned. "You're free now. You can look me in the eye. And you don't have to work here."

She smiled, though it was weak, and I wasn't sure she completely meant it. I wondered if she was smiling because she was afraid of me and thought I wanted her to smile. Regardless, I felt kind of breathless at how pretty she was.

"I don't have anyone. The citadel is my only home."

"I can't believe we haven't met before," I said.

"We have met before," she said, and watched me for my reaction.

I was speechless. I was surprised I'd forget such a beautiful face. "I'm sorry, I know a decent governor would know this, but tell me your name."

"Madeline. Madeline Thomas."

I nodded. The name fit her.

"When did we meet?"

She shrugged. "A few times in the corridors. You smiled and said hello."

I knew she wasn't telling me the whole story. She kept something back from the exchange. But I accepted her answer. She had a right to her secrets, even if I was curious.

A tiny seed of hope burrowed into my spirit. It was not anything crazy, like believing in some kind of life without Roxy, but I welcomed the emotion, whatever it meant.

When she dared to meet my gaze, she was thoughtful. "I can see you're carrying burdens."

I had no idea how she knew. But it was a relief to hear someone say it. I felt understood for the first time since I'd become governor. Maybe for the first time in my life.

"You miss her."

She looked away, as if embarrassed she had seen my secret wound. My mind was reclaimed by Roxy's image and the reality of her absence. I swallowed hard.

"So you're a dishwasher and a mind reader," I joked to cover the emotion.

"Your relationship with Roxy Eisen isn't exactly a secret," she said with a shrug. Again, I didn't know what to say in response. I had that feeling again—that she was holding something back.

"I should go," Madeline said and took a step back, but it took her another moment to move toward the door. I wasn't sure I wanted her to leave, which surprised me. But I didn't stop her.

When she left, Greer was waiting in the hallway. He watched her go—her head down once again—and then looked at me with a thoughtful expression.

"What?" I said, defensive.

"Nothing." He shrugged. "Just been awhile since I saw you smile at anything, even if it was a wimpy little excuse for a smile."

"I smile. All the time."

He nodded. "I suppose that's true enough. But smiling because you want your people to trust you and smiling because you're happy are two very different things."

I couldn't disagree. "It seems kind of pathetic to still be thinking about her so much when she hasn't been here for a year."

"It *is* pathetic," he teased. "But I *do* think you'll get over her." He stood up and put his hands on my shoulders, giving me a shake. "If you make up your mind to stop thinking about her, it will get a little easier every day. I promise. I've been there."

"I don't know how to explain it," I replied, rubbing my hands over my face. "It's like I lost a limb. I'm stumbling around, feeling like a fool. I don't want to be this way. But I don't *work* without her."

"You just need to find a new way of working."

Greer refused to pity me, and I was glad for it.

"Maybe Madeline Thomas could help you find yourself a new

way."

TWO

Through blinding snow, I saw a dark form walking away, and somehow I knew it was her. I could sense her essence, there in the darkness that was my brain. My dark made her light shine brighter.

I called to her, louder and louder until my throat burned and tears froze on my cheeks. She didn't turn around. I tried to hear her mind, but she closed it off. I could sense the invisible wall between us, an impossible fortress. The harder I tried to catch up, the farther away she seemed.

Exhaustion finally won. I leaned over, resting my hands on my knees and coughing breaths. I yelled in frustration.

When I stood up, she was inches from my face. Her features were as icy cold as the snowdrifts around our feet. Her dark eyes seemed empty. Soulless. Her arms shot out and grabbed me around the neck.

"Governor, wake up."

I coughed out of reflex, glad to discover I was not actually being choked by zombie Roxy. I was in my bed at the citadel. A soldier who must have been posted outside my room spoke through the com, effectively dispelling the effects of the dream. I sat up.

"Are you alright?" He asked.

My chest was still tight, but I could breathe. "Yes." I sighed and leaned over the side of my bed.

I closed my eyes, breathing slowly as the burning in my chest subsided. As I considered trying to go back to sleep, sudden white light invaded the monitor that gave me a view of the soldier and the hallway outside my room.

Gooseflesh appeared over my skin, along with a feeling like static electricity. I could feel energy humming from the other side of a magnetically sealed door. I picked up my laser pistol and went to the control panel to open the door.

The door dematerialized and I stepped out into the light. Perspective seemed altered; the ceilings were elongated and the hallway stretched so far I couldn't see where it ended.

I heard laughter, harsh and mocking.

"Who's there?"

No one answered my call. I was sure I was still dreaming. It was the only explanation. I must have dreamed the part when the soldier woke me up.

I held out my laser pistol and stepped into the light. The laughter got louder.

When I turned I saw an eight-foot white apparition standing at the end of the hall, glowing in the dark, its back to me. A thick white mantle shrouded a bowed head, disproportionally large. Its arms lifted at the sides. It cut in and out like a weak radio signal.

I stared at it for a long time, unable to grasp what it was or why it was in the citadel. Time seemed to stop as I waited for the figure to turn around and look me in the eye.

Finally, I caught on. I was looking at a hologram, though I had no idea where the projection was coming from. I'd never seen anything so realistic, even in cutting edge virtual tech. And for no particular reason at all, I knew the message was coming from Joe. Something about the spectacle had his name written all over it.

The signal seemed to gain strength. It turned, slowly, the space between us devoured by its imposing presence.

I searched for features, but inside the shroud there was only black. Even though I couldn't see, I knew instinctively it watched me.

I tried to appear indifferent, as if I was not impressed by the display. I stared into the hollow blackness where eyes should have been and waited for the projection to reveal its purpose.

"I have a message for Roxy Eisen." A voice spoke in a rumbling tone that made the marble floors vibrate beneath my feet.

"She's not here," I said, shrugging. Inwardly, my heart seemed to jump into my throat at the mention of her name.

"I suggest you do whatever it takes to find her. Tell her our business is just getting started."

"What business?" I scoffed. "Identify yourself."

A rush of air blew from the empty black space of the shroud. The entire wall of crystal windows blew out with a deafening crash, and I felt the force of the gust against me. I tried to plant my feet on the floor. As the wind grew stronger, I finally had to drop my pistol and grasp the corner of the doorway that led in to my room. I saw my pistol fly off into the night along with every other unsecured item in the hallway.

With difficulty, I reached inside my room and pulled myself inside. I sealed it and leaned against the wall, breathing hard.

"Cori!"

The computer-generated face appeared as a ghostly image before me. "Governor, Koenig, how can I help you?"

"First tell me if I'm dreaming, then let's get that thing out of the hallway!"

"You are awake, sir. An unusual energy was detected, but it has been contained. Security is scanning the citadel as a precaution. I regret to report three officers who tried to enter the hallway have died."

I slammed my fist into the wall. "This doesn't make any sense."

Cori continued to watch me with her falsely empathetic expression, her hands folded in front of her.

"It said it was going after Roxy," I told my computer system.

"Yes, sir."

"If it's going after Roxy, I'm going after Roxy, too."

"Not advisable at this time, sir."

I laughed. "Because of the danger of the mission or the danger of finding Roxy when she doesn't want to be found?"

Cori didn't smile. Even when she did smile on rare occasions, it was more creepy than genuine. "Sir, I was referring to the danger of the mission."

"I don't care. I need you to inform Greer about our travel plans and then locate Lon from the bunker."

"Yes, sir."

I knew the circumstances were less than ideal, and I knew Roxy would not be happy about me showing up wherever she was hiding out. Even so, my heart beat faster at the thought of seeing her again.

Soon.

"How in the world can we just take off and find Roxy? I get you're worried, but we don't have real evidence of a threat. We also have no idea where she is. How do you know we won't lead this thing right to her?" Greer stood in front of me with his arms folded across his chest. I frowned as his logic threatened my decision.

"I'm not leaving it to chance. If whoever did this found me through all the citadel security, they will find her, too."

Greer remained unconvinced. "What if it was just a specter? What if someone from the past is messing with you? Like I said, someone might be trying to get *you* to reveal where Roxy is. Maybe she's safer staying hidden."

I considered his words. I did. And he had a valid point. But the truth remained. I wasn't going to lose this chance, this excuse to find her.

"Greer, I don't have any way to prove it, but I'm sure that message was from Joe. And if that's the case, you know she's safer with me."

Greer sighed, resigned. "I guess we're going to see Lon."

An hour later we were at the maglev pad on the roof of the

citadel. The royal maglev my mother had used was a hybrid that could be used for street traffic or as an aircraft. I had helped design it. It rose out from under the pad where it was stored, buffed and glimmering in the sun. I hated the bright purple and silver. It hadn't been long enough for other people to buy many of the new maglevs, so most were still brown.

"I need to have this eyesore recolored."

We hummed down from the top of the citadel on a magnetite ramp and joined the other traffic circling Bryant Park. Cori had located Lon, who now lived in New Jersey, in his family's home that had been unoccupied since his parents had joined the rebellion seventeen years before and sacrificed their lives.

I had time to observe my city as we traveled over the river. People seemed to be recovering from the dark years my mother had stolen. They wore comfortable clothes now, though the style still marked by fanciful Victorian fashion. The anxious expressions I used to see every day were replaced by cautious smiles. There was light in their eyes that hadn't been there before.

Hope.

But was all that hope riding on my ability to be a good leader? And did I have it in me to be what I needed to be if I didn't come home with Roxy?

I felt Greer watching me. I pretended to be intensely interested in something floating in the Hudson River.

"It's a fuel cell," Greer said. "Don't be acting like you aren't thinking about her again. Nothing more commonplace than an old fuel cell."

"You have to admit, fuel cell tech is cool." Fuel cells bolstered the solar energy we harvested from the transparent cells that covered the entire city, also providing a layer of UV protection. The fuel cells used water energy to back up the solars.

"Very cool." He kept staring at me, and I heard all the things he didn't bother to say again.

Lon was right where I would have expected him to be when we

found the old house on a quiet street in Jersey. He was in front of an elaborate computer base that covered most of the space in the front room. He came to the door to let us in, barely greeting us before he went back to his chair.

The windows were open, allowing a comfortable cool breeze that contained an element of peace lacking in the citadel climate control system. Lon had a half-eaten bowl of oatmeal in his hand, and took infrequent bites while he divided his attention between three separate SmartScreens. He handled figures that suspended mid-air above his head and read data that scrolled independently.

Greer had given Lon a position in the new government. His job was to keep an eye on the government systems as we transitioned from the old regime. He ensured everyone worked toward the common goal. From the look of it, he took his job seriously.

I saw an old tire swing in the backyard through the kitchen window beyond the front room. It dangled limp and idle in the breeze, hanging from an oak easily a hundred years old. Had Lon swung on it as a child? Had his dad put it up, anticipating the day he'd be old enough to take a ride?

Lon apparently noticed what had my attention and guessed what I was thinking. "I went to the bunker before I was three. I don't remember ever playing out there."

The matter-of-fact truth of his words irritated me. My mother specialized in stealing childhoods. Breaking up families. She forced people apart until it became their way to be dependent on her and independent of each other. So many kids, like Lon, didn't even remember what they were missing by being controlled.

"Levi?" Greer nudged me with his elbow.

I stared hard at him. "If I ever have kids, they're going to have a tire swing."

"Sure," Greer said, nodding, though I got the feeling he thought I was nuts.

I turned back to Lon. "We need to find Roxy."

THREE

Lon regarded me with his trademark expressionless expression. I had never figured out whether it meant he thought I was an idiot or he was just completely unexcitable. Maybe it was a little of both.

"This is where you say you'll be happy to help me," I prompted him.

He pushed his glasses higher on his nose and sighed thoughtfully. "What makes you think I can help you find her?"

"Because you have to," I said, my voice sounding harsher than I intended. "She's in danger."

"I don't remember Roxy asking you to keep her safe." Greer said as if I was a loose cannon that might explode. That gave me the very uncomfortable feeling that I was acting like my mother.

"It's my fault she's in danger," I said.

"How?" Lon folded his hands in his lap and regarded me evenly. "Did you do something to Roxy we don't know about?"

"My mother did."

Greer shrugged. "So? You think you have to make amends for what someone else did?"

I was irritated that they were turning my noble rescue mission into a psychotherapy session. "In this case, yeah, I do."

It was simple to me. My mom had broken the city. She had broken Roxy. The responsibility was with me and my gift to fix everything.

"See, I don't have a problem with you making this a better place," Greer continued. "But you aren't the one who messed it up. You don't answer for Leona just because she won't. It doesn't work like that."

"Fine," I said, annoyed. "Maybe you're right. But I don't have time to think about that right now. *I have to save Roxy.*"

They both nodded, if hesitantly, and turned to the computers. Lon tapped a few icons in the air and a virtual surround of a blizzard came up. He turned back to me and gestured. "She's there."

"You knew where she was?" It made me angry. I had no idea where the girl I loved more than anything had been for the past year, and Lon kept regular tabs on her.

"Did you think I would let her get away without putting a marker on her ID tat?" He looked at me as if he was disappointed in me for thinking it. "She's in a remote area up in Canada. It would be hard for anyone to find her if they didn't know where to look."

"You can't count on her being willing to be found, Levi." Greer tried to be honest with me, but it didn't matter. I would convince her. I would do anything to persuade her to stay with me.

And I would never let her out of my sight again.

"Getting there won't be easy." Lon refused to be optimistic, even when I opened the arsenal file from the archives and showed them all the tools and weapons I had at my disposal.

"Come on!" I pointed to a jet pack in the projection. "We can go anywhere with those."

He adjusted his glasses. "Do you know how easy it would be to shoot you down in a jet pack?"

I sighed. "Seriously, it's like you don't even want to save her."

"Don't go there," Greer warned me. "Lon and I grew up with Roxy. She's like a sister. There's no doubt here we care about Roxy, even if it's not the same way you do." Greer shifted his stance and continued in a quieter tone. "I'm just trying to help you be realistic. Trying to cross into Canada isn't going to be a picnic in the forest. It's closed off and guarded by the Canadian army. They don't want States people coming through."

"I know," I said. I did know. I'd been in countless virtual meetings with the president of Canada. They had their own problems of survival and marauding. They didn't want us bringing ours into the mix, and I couldn't blame them.

"There's a way," Lon assured me as he brought up a 9D image of the border between the Divided States and Canada. The image surrounded us and blocked out the house so completely that it felt like we were really there. I almost felt the chill of the breeze.

Lon highlighted the border lines and marked where we were standing.

"Ohio?" I was doubtful. Most of Ohio was surrounded by a cement wall as thick as it was high, and it was fitted with every kind of explosive technology available. When Ohio had disengaged from the Eastern Divided States, they'd turned on their fence and not let another soul in or out. Anyone flying low over their borders was shot down, no questions asked.

"I've had a few virtual conferences with Ohio. They won't be interested in helping me," I assured him.

"If you could get across the wall, you could get to Lake Erie. There are several small islands. You could take a jetpack that becomes a small SmartBoat, get across the lake undetected, and travel up to the Hudson Bay Lowlands where Roxy has been for several months," Lon said.

"But how is that easier than bypassing Ohio? Either way we have to try to get into Canada."

"Canada has an alliance with Ohio. They trust the wall, so there are no guards along that section of Lake Erie," Lon explained.

"Assuming we can get through Ohio. Which is a big assumption."

Lon shrugged. "I'll be here with tech support if you need it."

I drummed my fingers on the desk. "Are we going to be dealing with ice and snow up north?"

Lon adjusted the images and we were quickly pulled away from the border and back to the ground in the north.

"The ice is starting to break up. If we don't hit any late winter storms, it might be okay," Greer pointed out the evidences of spring in the snow-covered climate. "We better bring plenty of cold-weather gear, though."

"Check the arsenal and see what you can find. We leave in three days."

If they questioned my judgment they didn't say so. I left the house, trying to be confident. But I had no idea how we were going to get past that wall in Ohio.

Still pondering the options when I arrived back at the citadel, I headed out of the lift without looking and collided with something soft that smelled really good.

Madeline Thomas and the large vase of flowers she held went sprawling on the marble floor. The vase shattered on the hard surface. She quickly got back up and tried to start cleaning up, but she lost her footing on the slippery mess and fell again.

I caught her arm. "Hey, how about we leave the mess for someone else before you permanently damage yourself."

"I'm sorry," she said. I heard panic.

"Don't worry about it, Madeline," I said. "It's just a vase."

She glanced at my hand on her arm with a fearful expression, so I let her go. She stepped back.

"You're upset," she said, and then took another step back like she hadn't mean to speak her thoughts.

I hadn't realized I was being so obvious. "I'd call it determined beyond reason, but facing an impossible obstacle."

She waited for me to explain what I meant. I realized I really did want to tell her. Everything.

"Walk with me in the gardens?" I held out my arm.

"Shouldn't I do something about this mess? I don't want anyone to get hurt." Her voice faltered, as if the thought of walking with me terrified her.

I pressed my WristCom. "Mess in Section 5, Cori."

"Yes, Governor. A DSR has been dispatched."

I smiled at Madeline. "Ready?"

She shrugged and nodded. We began walking toward the large archway that led to the gardens.

It was chilly outside. I took off my uniform jacket and put it around her shoulders. "Sorry, I should have let you get a coat."

"Don't be." She fingered a white blossom clinging to a trellis. "I love the gardens. And I don't get cold easily."

"Good." It did something to me, watching her push locks of hair behind her ear. I cleared my throat. "I'd like to talk to you. About my dilemma."

She turned. "I'd like to hear about it."

I told her about the incident in the hall. I thought she would either think I was crazy or be scared away, but she just watched me.

"Do you think the person controlling the apparition was responsible for the knife in the QuickWash?" she asked.

I hadn't considered it, but it made sense. "I don't know why they would target you." It made me worry about all the people I was leaving behind.

"I think Roxy's in the most danger," I said. "I need to get up to Hudson Bay and find her before whoever was responsible for that apparition gets to her. And somehow I have to get across Ohio to do it."

"You can't. They'll shoot you," she said immediately. "My cousin tried to sneak over the wall from New England. It can't be done. They don't want visitors, even important ones."

"What happened to your cousin?" I could predict the answer. She shook her head and looked down.

"I'm sorry."

I thought the discussion was over, but as I moved to go back inside, she stopped me.

"I think I can help you."

FOUR

"There's a section of wall they don't guard well because of the terrain. It's nearly impossible to scale without being electrocuted." Madeline explained, her voice taking on an edge of excitement.

I nodded, feeling a spark of hope. "Go on."

"I may be able to disarm the fence in that spot." She rubbed her plain servant's tunic between her fingers.

I guess my surprise at her admission showed in my face.

"I know it's hard to believe," she said as I hesitated. "I'm good with electricity. This will sound weird, but I see it as an art. I wonder about the possibilities of using it and I have a few new ideas about it. I had an apprenticeship before I was brought to the palace to serve."

"Let me guess," I said dully. "Someone in your family ticked off my mother and she took out her revenge on you."

Madeline looked away, hesitating. "My father wouldn't divorce my mother to marry someone else on Leona's court. She was angry at the defiance and punished me to hurt him."

"What happened to your parents?"

Madeline quickly looked away and tears filled her eyes.

I didn't make her speak the words. "Whether you like being here or not, you should be doing what you're good at. I'd like you to come along with us and get us over that wall if you're willing.

And when we get back, I'd like to set you up with the electrical supervisor in the citadel so you can pick up where you left off."

She actually looked me in the eyes for a brief second. Then she nodded.

"Go to the archives and get whatever supplies you think you'll need. Just ask Greer to give you an approval code. If there's something that isn't there, you can get it at the printing station in the servant's hall. Dress warmly. Winter isn't over where we're headed."

She hurried away. I watched her, struck again by her beauty. I frowned and lowered my gaze. It felt all wrong to look at her. I was pulled toward another, and it would always be her, as long as we were both alive. Maybe even after that.

"We need an official reason for this trip," Greer said as we pulled supplies from the archives. I could tell he still had plenty of misgivings. "I can't very well put 'indulging the governor's obsession with Roxy Eisen' as a reason for using three employees of the palace and expensive supplies to climb the Ohio wall and head up to the wilderness of Canada."

"Tell the council I'm going to Ohio to make an alliance with them," I said impatiently as I sorted through a line of laser rifles.

"Hey, *Leona*, this isn't all about you," Greer replied. "You're a governor, not a king, and you answer to your people." He pulled a solar tent from a shelf. "I'm not lying for you. Are you going to try to make friends?"

"It's a good idea." I avoided answering his question as I took his basic solar tent and threw it back on the shelf, reaching toward the back for a bigger model with more functions. He made a face at me and threw it on the pile.

"Shoulda known we'd need the one fit for a *king*."

Ohio would make a powerful ally in our quest to restore the unity of the country, but it would be a hard sell. They had re-established the original constitution of the United States and they held to it rigidly. The leaders had no interest in modifying their ideals to fit a new age. And they didn't have to, since they had sixty-foot electrified cement walls.

Greer called my bluff and managed to schedule a meeting with President Edan Avihu in Ohio. Since hotels were a thing of the past, before the blackout and civil war, we were given explicit instructions to set up our camp at the Eastern gate when we arrived in Ohio. The message said we would be protected from marauders. We would wait there for his visit.

Citadel servants piled our supplies in a maglev van and the kitchens packed us enough food to sustain us several months if needed. I set up the force field lock on my room and headed down the hall to the lift, my gaze falling on several burn marks that marred the marble floor as a reminder of my meeting with the hologram.

I walked faster after that.

FIVE

When I saw the walls of Ohio from the air, as we flew close to their territory border in our hybrid maglev, there was a sick feeling in the pit of my stomach.

We stowed the hybrid in an ancient dilapidated barn. I tried to hide it under old tarps I found. "Where's invisibility wrap when you need it? Hopefully the marauders won't find it, or we'll have a long walk home."

We hiked into Ohio until we came to the walls. We made our camp where Avihu had instructed. A guard aimed a gun at us from a window in the wall. I entered the code into a text on my WristCom, sent to let them know we were supposed to be there. The guard closed the window and a sound like a huge air lock and metal grinding became our official welcome.

We set up the solar camp as we waited. Madeline started a fire while Greer complained about the "grandeur" of the model I'd chosen.

"What are we going to do with all this space?" He said as he gathered freeze dried meals for our supper. "All we needed was a three-person with a heater. We could fit at least fifteen people in here. Did you bring an extra fuel cell for all the heat this thing is going to need to crank out?"

"We won't need an extra fuel cell. And there are *four* of us," I corrected as I watched the wall, hoping to see signs that our meeting would occur quickly. I prayed the president didn't leave us out here for a week just to show us who was in charge. I was well aware who had the upper hand.

"Whatever," Greer said with a sigh as he passed out our instantly-heated food. This would be our last easy meal. We were leaving most of our extra food in the van to keep our packs light. I sat by the fire with mine and made myself eat.

Madeline didn't have much to say. She ate her meal mostly in silence, and she excused herself to her cot when the sun was just setting.

Avihu came the second day just after noon. We were sitting by the fire drinking coffee—New York City had the only coffee supplies left in the East—when we heard the lock disengage. The president and four armed guards stiffly made their way toward our camp.

"I guess we look dangerous."

I met him on the edge of our camp and shook his hand when he extended it. I could see the distrust in his expression before he spoke a word.

"President Avihu," I said, trying to smile like a dignitary. "Thank you for seeing me."

"Governor Koenig," he acknowledged. "What is this about? Peace talks are scheduled for summer."

I nodded and smiled, making sure he heard my confidence when I spoke. "I hoped we might strike a deal to become allies in the peace talks."

He grunted. His arms were crossed over his chest and the thick strap of his very large Marlin Laser Rifle. "I think it's a little early in the game to trust anyone, especially the son of Leona."

He sounded like he was familiar with Leona. He watched me with curiosity, probably interested in how I would to respond.

I didn't argue with him, but I displayed my own rifle by leaning on it. "I agree, sir. Which is why I've come with the backing of my council to make an offer of friendship to you."

He sighed. He was older than me by at least thirty years. He had enough experience to know better than to trust an unproven kid who'd been a convenient choice, rather than a smart one, for leadership.

"What do you want from me? You must have an agenda, so out with it." He waved his hand impatiently in the air.

I felt humiliation, but I made sure he didn't see it. "I'm interested in peace. I wouldn't have said so if I didn't mean it. But I also need to come through your wall and journey up to Lake Erie."

He nodded as if he had suspected as much, scoffing like I'd suggested I blow up the entire state. "And why should I let you do that? Canada trusts us to keep people out."

I dared to take a step closer. "I'm not a threat. I have a friend living up in the Hudson Bay area, and I believe she is in danger. I have to get to her."

"Doesn't she have a communicator?" He was already turning back toward the gate, as if the conversation wasn't worth his time.

"She doesn't want to be found," I trailed him, jogging to keep up pace with their group. "But she doesn't realize the danger."

"Let me give you some free advice, son. If you use your position to advance your personal interests, you show everyone watching what your weaknesses are. Go home and learn how to lead your city." He turned just after he walked through the gate and motioned for the guards to close it. As it rumbled across, he spoke. "I can't open the wall for a runaway that doesn't want to be found. Go home."

"Canada is only accessible by way of Lake Erie," I argued.

"The answer is no," he said before the immense gate clanged into place and we were alone outside the wall. I heard the hum of electricity a moment later.

I turned and shrugged helplessly at Greer and Madeline. But Madeline wasn't there.

"Where'd she go?" I hit the button on my WristCom when Greer shrugged. "Find Madeline."

A moment later I heard her voice. "I'm here, Governor."

"Levi," I corrected. "Where are you?"

"Inside the wall."

I shot Greer a look and he chuckled. "We need to keep our eye on that one, don't we, Gov?"

"Are you okay, Madeline?"

"Yes, sir. I was able to sneak through a door about two hundred feet from where you are when the president disabled the electricity."

"Good thinking. But how do we get in?"

"I'm working on the control panel right now. I can get it down for ten seconds when you're ready. But be ready to run. It won't take the guards long to get here from the main gate."

It wasn't a perfect solution, but I decided to trust her judgment. We packed up the supplies and minimized the solar tent. Five minutes later we were jogging down along the wall to the door she had found. I couldn't believe she'd found it, actually. The crack was nearly seamless. She must have known to look for it.

"Whenever you're ready, Madeline," I spoke quietly into my com.

Immediately the hum cut out with a jolt and the heavy door jerked open. As soon as we were inside, Madeline was already running, motioning us to follow. I glanced back and saw four guards at a distance, starting after us. One was pulling out a SmartGrenade, which was designed to seek out an enemy like a missile and blow them up.

We ran faster. We caught up with Madeline and raced downhill toward the water. We could see it, but we were still a good two miles from the edge. I heard the whiz of the grenade and turned with my rifle. I shot it out of the air, but it was close when it exploded. Greer went down.

The guards were closing in. Greer tried to get up but he quickly fell back down, holding his bleeding thigh and yelling in pain.

"Keep running!" I yelled to Madeline as I grabbed a small package from my backpack and expanded it by voice command. A second later it unfolded into a jetpack. I hauled Greer up and attached him to the vest as he switched it on. I grabbed hold of him and we took off.

"Aren't you glad I brought this?" I yelled over the whir of the motor.

As we came upon Madeline, I let go of Greer, hoping he had the strength to hold me while I grabbed her. I caught her, but as her weight lifted off the ground, the pack faltered.

"I don't think this thing was made for three people," Greer shouted as we clung to one another. It dragged us along the ground for the last mile, but we were outrunning the guards. When we reached the water's edge I gave the voice command for the jet pack to change into a boat.

It transformed and we climbed in, sliding along the sand haphazardly until it found the water and took off. Greer flopped down on the bottom of the boat. He reached into his supply pack and found a bandage to wind around his leg and then he laid back and closed his eyes. I engaged the inflatable nylon barrier surrounded with invisibility wrap. No one would see our passage.

The soldiers who were chasing us stopped when we got to the water.

"They turned around," Madeline observed.

"We're out of their territory," I said, but I couldn't shake the feeling that they had let us escape. That the chase was for show. Maybe Avihu was a little softer than he let on.

"So we're safe?" She sat up, hugging her knees. Now that nothing else had my attention, I looked at Madeline again. It was hard not to. She was a kind of beauty that seemed too perfect to be real. Her proportions, her features, every part of her seemed to have been carefully chiseled.

I wondered what her experience as a servant had been like, but I was afraid to ask her. Servants walked a fine line. Leona couldn't stand anyone more beautiful than she was, and she would single them out and make them regret their good looks. But at the same time, she despised people for having flawed appearances. She would subject her slaves to procedures and surgeries to make them "acceptable" in her eyes.

I avoided the topic and answered her question. "We're safe as long as Canada doesn't see us. Which they won't, since the cloak is on."

"High tech," Madeline said.

I shrugged. "Pays to be the governor of New York City, and to have inherited all Leona's toys."

"I can see that. From what I have heard, you invented many of them."

"Maybe," I said, not attempting to hide my grin.

We were sitting close in the small boat. We had a long ride to go, as well. We floated across the water, quietly enough to hear the waves lapping around us and seagulls calling overhead. With nothing else to do, we spent the time talking. I started out talking about tech, the portal and visiting 1874, but inevitably, I ended up spilling the whole story of what had happened, starting with the night I gave Roxy the cow.

"It's easy to see how much you care for her," Madeline answered.

I shrugged, feeling weird about bringing it up in the first place. "It doesn't do me any good since she obviously doesn't feel the same way." My voice had taken on that morose tone that I hated hearing in myself, the one that had made Greer crazy for the past year.

"I don't understand why she left," I continued, my gaze involuntarily dropping to Madeline's lips. I didn't realize I had done it until I saw her eyes get a little wider.

"From what you've told me, it doesn't sound like she left because of you," she said. "Put yourself in her place. Would you be able to make rational decisions about your future with everyone's voices crowding into your mind?"

"She only reads my thoughts," I argued. "It's just emotions with everyone else."

Madeline shrugged. "I would think emotions would be an even

bigger burden to bear."

I didn't have a response. It sounded familiar, like something Roxy had tried to explain to me.

Madeline hesitated and her eyes met mine with a silent question. It reminded me what it was like not knowing a girl's every thought. I liked wondering what she was thinking. Judging by what it had been like inside Roxy's mind, I knew Madeline was probably thinking more complicated thoughts than I was.

Greer groaned, stealing Madeline's attention. "Shouldn't you help him?"

"The wound is wrapped," I said, but I saw the blood had soaked through the bandage.

"I mean, shouldn't you do your thing … like you did for me?"

It dawned on me what she meant. I had been waiting, used to hiding my gift from the general public. But Madeline already knew what I could do. I nodded and reached for Greer's leg, holding it firmly as I closed my eyes and focused on the energy transfer.

After a moment, she touched my arm. "Be careful."

I looked down and saw that the leg was healed, and Greer was sitting up. I felt the tired, nauseated response.

"Thanks," Greer said.

"How did you know I should be careful?" I asked Madeline curiously.

"I don't know," she said. "I could just tell you were getting weaker."

"I was. Thanks for the reminder. Sometimes it's hard to come out of the zone." My eyes tried to close and I fought to keep them open.

"If you need to rest, Greer and I can keep watch," she said.

"Thanks."

I was asleep within seconds of lying down.

SIX

When I woke up, the sun had set and stars were shining over us. Greer and Madeline were talking in soft voices until they noticed I was awake.

"Thanks for the help, Gov," Greer said as I sat up.

I yawned, trying to stretch in the cramped space. "Thank Madeline. She reminded me to do it."

Greer narrowed his eyes at me, then winked at her. "Thanks for not letting him kill me while he was flirting with you, Madeline."

"Hey, nobody was flirting," I argued.

"How are we going to get out of the water and past the guards?" Madeline asked, probably to change the subject. She adjusted her position, causing her leg to brush against mine. She glanced at me with pink cheeks.

"Quietly," I replied, trying not to focus on the contact.

We would have to hide in the shadows and move past the area where they monitored citizenships. "If they don't see the boat, we should be okay."

We reached the shore without attracting attention. Greer stowed the boat pack along with the solar tent in his backpack and we crept through the woods.

We hiked for some time until we hit farmland, and made camp

at the edge of the woods. I asked Greer for the tent.

"That thing is going to give us away," he complained. "It could fit an army."

Though the air was chilly, being so far north in early spring, the tent was warm and dry, even without building a fire. We ate from our provisions and fell asleep on our cots before the sun had finished setting.

We hiked north, took another boat ride across the Georgian Bay, and hiked again until we met snowy hills. The blast of the chill met my face as we set northward toward Hudson Bay. After bartering in Sunbury for provisions and snow gear, we made the last trek of the journey. With every step, my heart seemed to beat faster. I knew Roxy would be mad. I had no reason to believe she wouldn't reject me and leave me again. But I was giddy at the thought of seeing her face and hearing her familiar voice in my head again. If I could just touch her, know she was alive and well, maybe I could move on.

The thought kept me going all the way, even after we walked into a blizzard and I got separated from Greer and Madeline. Lost in the white out, I tried to use my WristCom to check my location and map out the rest of the hike, but the tech seemed as confused as I was.

Hours after I had lost sight of them, I wandered in the snow. Part of me warned that I should stay in one place and wait out the weather, but I couldn't be still. Something called me on. It wouldn't let me stop. All I saw, all around me, was white. The snow drifted, making me glad for my snowshoes. I wandered on, feeling numb in spite of my self-warming snowsuit. My mind was a blur of white.

It jarred me when I saw a form in the distance. I didn't know what it was, but I headed toward it like it was a lighthouse and I was a ship lost in a storm.

It seemed to take an eternity to reach the point where I could make sense of the scene. My hopes plunged when I recognized it was nothing more than a dead polar bear.

Deep red stained the snow around the animal, a sharp contrast to the bluish white of the snow.

I saw the knife wound. I knew what kind of knife would make such a clean cut.

My stomach felt like it jumped up into my throat, so I couldn't speak. I called with my mind instead.

Roxy, are you here?

The wind continued to howl a mournful sound that matched the one inside my brain. I stood still and closed my eyes, willing her to speak to me.

Here.

It was only one word. I couldn't tell if she was happy to see me or angry I had come, or too close to freezing to death to say anything else. I ran as fast as my cumbersome snow shoes would allow, falling into several heavy drifts before I reached the polar bear. It was quickly becoming buried in the heavy blanket of snow. I grabbed large handfuls of skin and fur and tried to haul the heavy bear to the side. I couldn't make the heavy corpse move along the ground, but I managed to cause it to fall back a couple inches, so I kneeled beside it and dug with my hands until I felt something solid and semi-warm.

I heaved Roxy into my lap. She was unconscious and her lips were blue. I was frantic to rip off my gloves and look for someplace I might uncover her skin. My hands reached under her layers of clothes and found the smooth skin of her abdomen. I felt the vibration in my fingers and saw the glow beneath her clothes.

When I looked back at her face, she glared at me, her lips rosy and her eyes clear. She was covered in blood, but as far as I could tell it was from taking refuge beneath the dead bear.

As a wave of glee took over, I pulled her to me. She didn't resist, but I felt her hesitancy.

"You're alive. You're okay." I kissed her forehead and her cheeks around her thick scarf.

"I didn't need your help," she said, her voice muffled. I smiled as I pulled my gloves back over my hands.

"I know. I just happened by and I figured since I was here, I might as well give you a hand. You can go back to snuggling with your bear now if you want."

She tried to pinch me but the affect was lost with my layers of clothes.

"Take me home, Rox. I'm cold." I pulled her up with me.

"You are not. There's a heater in your coat."

"There's a heater in your coat, too, but your skin was like ice." I remembered the softness of her skin and was tempted to touch it again. She narrowed her eyes.

"The core heater gave out so I've been making do with animal skins and pine boughs," she admitted. "And I was just surprised by the storm. The bear would have warmed me up and I would have gotten back to my pod if you hadn't come along."

"Roxy," I started to lecture, but she gave me a look that made me stop. "Take me to your shelter quickly before I decide to be chivalrous and give you my coat."

She started moving.

We walked the distance of about a half mile. The snow was still falling, but visibility was better. I saw where she had been living.

"A survival pod?"

"I didn't need anything fancy. It was a cheap trade," she said with a shrug as she unzipped the small pod that hung from a tree like a cocoon. She climbed in, not looking back to see if I followed.

I climbed in and zipped out the howling wind. I turned to look around. The pod was the size of a small closet. Most of it was her sleeping space. There was a small shelf where a fabric safe flat heater warmed the hidden coils that went throughout the skin of the cocoon. She had a canteen and a solar powered semi-pc, which was a transparent card that acted as a basic computer. I felt a twinge of anger. She could have communicated with me at any time in the last months, but I had to risk my neck in Ohio and walk through a blizzard to get to her.

"Get over it," she said sullenly.

She took off her wet coat and hung it on a hook by the heater. I did the same with mine. I saw her teeth chattering and realized her clothes were soaked from sweat, blood and snow, but she couldn't take them off because I was there.

We sat huddled on the cushion that was her bed. After an awkward moment, as she wrapped her arms around her legs and shivered, I decided to risk her ire by pointing out the obvious.

"We need to take these wet things off, Roxy. There's no sense getting your bed sopping wet. I'm mature enough to look away."

She nodded without looking at me and began to pull off her thermal shirt and black overpants, and the leggings she wore beneath. I looked away until she had pulled a blanket around herself and averted her eyes so I could undress. I did, quickly, and set my wet clothes next to hers on the rack beside the heater.

I cast a glance her way and saw she had extended a second blanket toward me without looking. I took it and wrapped it around myself.

I sat next to her, which in my defense, was the only place to sit. In fact, I had to push against the outer wall just to avoid sitting *on* her.

"Cozy," I said, smiling at her. She shrugged.

"It's not the citadel, but it's got what I need."

"I didn't ask for the citadel," I reminded her. "Someone had to lead."

"Whatever."

"Don't be like that," I said with a twinge of irritation in my tone. Hadn't I just saved her life and wasn't I there to rescue her? The least she could do was show a little appreciation. "I've missed you so much. The whole way here Greer and Madeline had to hear exactly how much."

She frowned, not looking at me. "Madeline?"

I shrugged. Madeline might be the most beautiful girl I'd ever seen, but she wasn't Roxy.

"The most beautiful girl you've ever seen?" Roxy pushed the

wet strands of dark hair out of her face.

I sighed. "In an angelic sort of way, I guess. She's a servant in the citadel kitchen, but when we get back she's going to be promoted. She has a helpful knack for electricity. She got us through Ohio."

Roxy's eyebrows furrowed, making her eyes dark. I could hear her mind's argument, but she didn't comment. She couldn't blame me for spending time with other girls, and we both knew it.

"She's not you." I reached for her fingers, surprised when she let me hold her hand. Her expression softened to a resignation.

"It's good you found someone," she said. "A girl like that could be everything you need to do your job as governor."

My mind rebelled against her words, but she went on, and said the thing I didn't want her to say as she gently tugged her hand out of mine.

"You should bond with her."

I hadn't heard the phrase in a long time. Roxy and the bunker kids had called a physical relationship between the guys and girls "bonding." Roxy's version required complete commitment. My mother had forced people to marry or denied them permission at her whim, insisting everyone follow her rules of abstinence. Bonding was Roxy's way of reinventing the original idea of marriage that had been so twisted in our society. It had been her plan to keep the drama down in the crowded bunker, and for the most part, it had seemed to work.

"Madeline likes your ideas about relationships."

"I'm so relieved to be validated by your angel," she said, her voice oozing sarcasm. "Why haven't you bonded with her if she's so amazing?"

"She's just a friend, Roxy. I just met her! And even if I'd known her forever, I couldn't feel that way about anyone but you."

She met my eyes briefly, but she didn't say another word.

Sleeping together in the space meant for one person meant undeniable discomfort. But I didn't mind the sore neck muscles. I could say, no matter what else happened in my life, that I'd held Roxy Eisen in my arms for an entire night. I'd heard her soft breathing and watched her vulnerability. I'd visited her dreams, coming to me unhindered and unfiltered while she lowered the guard she held in place when she was awake.

She dreamed of me. We sat together, peaceful, hand-in-hand on a bench in a version of our city I'd never seen before. Her face was older. More of life was written in the lines. But she was more beautiful than I could describe. And her smile told me I had won her heart, and we would never be apart again.

It was rough letting go of the vision. I wanted to live there forever.

SEVEN

Greer and Madeline showed up the next day. We were sitting outside the cocoon by the fire while we roasted meat for our meal when we saw them approaching. Roxy stared hard at the fire, as if she was uninterested, but I heard her silent anxiety.

I wanted her to be open to Madeline, and be happy to see Greer. But Roxy had been away from people for a long time, and it was a big step to interact again. She would have to take on the burden of their feelings.

I felt a wave of protectiveness as they approached. I wanted Madeline to know Roxy as I knew her. I wanted everyone to see Roxy's heart. It wasn't hard and cold as she tried to make it seem. It was warm with concern for others. Everyone needed to understand the truth.

If I'm so concerned about others, why have I spent the past year alone?

I looked her in the eye. *Because you care too much.*

That's why we're no good for each other, Roxy's mind whispered to mine. *You want everyone to know the real me, but I don't even want you to know. Why are you so sure you have me figured out?*

I shook my head without looking at her. *Rox, if you saw it the way I do, you'd understand.*

Why don't you call me "Rox" again, loser? See what happens.

I greeted Greer and Madeline as I stood to grab more sticks from Roxy's firewood pile. Roxy stayed where she was, her arms around her knees.

"I'm so glad we found you," Madeline said as they came to stand by the fire. "We were beginning to think you might have been lost in the storm."

"We're fine," I said, trying not to sound nervous as I stepped out of the way so they could see Roxy. She stood, embarrassed.

Greer whooped. He took two giant steps around the fire and swept Roxy into his arms. She laughed a little, as if she couldn't help it, and hugged him back.

"Hi, Greer." I heard her silent greeting, too. *I've missed you. I'm glad you're here.*

"Howdy, Cap'n!" He swung her around a few times. "You are looking good! Just like a snow angel."

She gave him a half-smile before she faced Madeline.

"Madeline, right?"

"Yes," Madeline stepped forward and held Roxy's hand. "It's an honor. On behalf of our city, thank you."

"It wasn't just me. Everyone helped out." Roxy shrugged.

I watched Roxy size Madeline up. I had never given specific thought to why Madeline was pretty, but Roxy analyzed the soft features framed by strands of blonde hair peeking from the hood of Madeline's jacket, and how the snow only added to the effect of Madeline's creamy complexion and warm brown eyes. I heard jealousy permeate Roxy's mind before she could attempt to mask it.

I also noticed that Madeline seemed to sense what Roxy was feeling. She took a step back and looked at the ground, as a servant who had forgotten her place.

"Don't do that, Madeline," I said, tugging on her jacket.

Roxy cleared her throat. "So are you going to tell me why you're here in the middle of nowhere making me regret I took that stupid com along?"

I was glad for the invitation. "I had a visitor."

"Not the good kind, I take it."

I huffed. "When it comes to my family, it's never the good kind."

Her expression changed, and she forgot to veil her thoughts. *Joe?*

I tried not to be hurt, because I knew she would hear me. But I didn't get what it was about Joe. He was a monster who was out to kill her, yet she still got a little excited just thinking about him.

"It's not on purpose, believe me," she said. "What did he say?"

Madeline was confused. "What's not on purpose?"

"They talk with their minds," Greer explained. "It's creepy, but you get used to it."

"Yes, Governor Koenig told me." She hesitated. "What isn't on purpose?"

"Joe seems to have a mind control ability." I avoided Roxy's frown. "He tried to kill her, more than once, and she walked right into it like she was helping him get the job done."

"It was stupid. It's over. I don't want to hear about it, mudsill," Roxy muttered.

"I never said it was your fault," I replied with a sigh. "A year of solitude has really improved your people skills, Roxy."

"Shut up."

Madeline watched Roxy as if she was an oddity in a holding field in the archives that needed to be studied and understood. I almost wished her luck.

"You're the ones that found me. I'm not the one imposing here," Roxy said, scrunching into a ball next to the fire and staring into the flames. "So what did the mudsill say to you?"

I sat down next to her and held a skewer of meat close to the fire. "It was a hologram, probably because he's not man enough to face me, but I'm almost sure it was from Joe. Who else would put on a show and threaten you?"

"Leona?" Roxy shrugged.

"I don't think it was Leona." I couldn't explain why, but I was almost sure the message had come from Joe.

"It could have been both of them." Greer added.

"Whoever it was, they came as an eight foot apparition that tore apart the hallway outside my bedroom and killed a few guards," I explained to Roxy.

She didn't answer me. Typical.

"I'm going to go set up the solar tent and generator." Greer grabbed the packs and walked about ten feet away from the fire to unwrap and install the tent.

"You have a solar tent?" Roxy looked up in interest, though she tried to hide it.

"You have to stay in your cocoon," I said in a clipped voice, though I meant it as a joke. In truth, I wasn't interested in ever sleeping apart from Roxy again.

"Of course you'll stay with us," Madeline said.

"Maybe I prefer my cocoon," Roxy answered, but I knew she didn't mean it. The thought of space to move around and supplies she didn't have to forage for herself was tempting. Maybe she wasn't as cut out for solitary living as she thought she was.

She glared at me.

"So Joe threatened you. What does that have to do with me? It's not like he's going to find me up here. I've been here a year and I can count on one hand how many times I've seen people." Roxy tested the meat she was roasting and decided it was done. She handed it to Madeline without looking at her.

"Thank you," Madeline said as she accepted the meat.

"The message was for you, Roxy." I reached for my own cooked meat. I took a bite, enjoying the taste until I couldn't place it and wondered if I was eating polar bear.

"It's venison, idiot," Roxy scoffed. "What was the message?"

"He said he was coming for you. And he didn't mean with a horse and carriage so you could ride off into the sunset."

I probably deserved getting my arm punched.

"If he wants revenge so badly, why has it taken so long? Why now?" Roxy acted as if the information was nothing more than irritating and disruptive to her day.

"I didn't ask, since I was trying not to be blown out of a third story window."

She watched the meat she'd skewered darken and drip fat into the fire. It sizzled on the hot coals.

"Roxy," I said, knowing she wasn't going to like what I said. "You have to come back with us."

"I don't," she replied. "And I'm not."

"We came all this way to bring you home," Madeline said softly. "We're concerned."

"What would I do if I went back to the city?" Roxy's voice almost bore a hint of vulnerability as she stared off into the whiteness. *I'd just be more of a target there.*

"You need to be where I can keep an eye on you." I was unwilling to hear any arguments.

I'm not going with you. Let it go.

EIGHT

The wind started howling about two in the morning. I turned restlessly on my cot as Greer slept peacefully on his. The girls were on the other side of a heavy canvas curtain, but I could hear Roxy's soft snoring. It kept me awake, not because it was annoying, but because I wanted to be with her. Beyond the curtain was too far away.

I fell into a light sleep for a few moments, only to be jostled awake by an eerie voice. It took me a minute to recognize it hadn't been audible. It came from Roxy's mind.

"Ro-xy," the soft whisper sang into our collective consciousness. I heard her sit up with a gasp.

"I'm closing in. Your days are numbered."

It was Joe's voice. I had no idea how he'd managed to infiltrate her mind, but it was obvious the man had access to future tech, to say the least. I pushed back the curtain until I could see her white face.

"Believe me now?" I asked.

She nodded, but there was nothing sweet about the victory.

"Joe, you moron, why don't you come out in the open and then we'll see how big you talk," I said to thin air, in case he was still listening.

I got off my cot and went to the fold-out table where I had left

50

my WristCom. I buzzed Lon. He answered a moment later in a sleep-heavy voice.

"Sorry to wake you up," I said. "But Joe just tried to contact Roxy telepathically. Can you find our location and see if there are any vitals near us?"

"Sure," Lon said. We heard clicking as he worked at his computer. He must have been sleeping in the room with his system.

"Nothing within twenty miles," he said after a moment. "But I see some kind of aura that doesn't look familiar. Not a life form, but it must be whatever energy source he is using to create the connection. It's fading now. I'll keep an eye on it and let you know if anything changes."

"Thanks, Lon," Roxy spoke beside me. "It's good to hear your voice."

"You too, Roxy. I'm glad you're safe." The com went silent.

Roxy reached for a small round device on the table. She turned it over, confused.

"Is that yours?" I asked.

She shook her head. "I've never seen it before."

"I don't think it was here before," I took it and examined it. The outer shell was plain and unmarked by brand or model, but the inside revealed sophisticated wireless workings. "It's tech I've never seen, but I think it's a recording device."

She took it back and felt along the side with her index finger. She found a button on the side and pressed it. We heard unfamiliar garble, and then a distant voice.

"*Not everything is as it seems. Perspective must be found in the portal. I hate to ask it of both of you, but you need to follow Leona.*"

Roxy dropped the com and stared at me in disbelief. Her voice trembled. "Levi, that's Mom."

I could only nod in response. I felt dizzy considering the implications.

She sat down on a small fold-up stool by the table. I crouched next to her and ran my hand along her leg. "You okay?"

She nodded, but her lip quivered and she wouldn't look at me. She thought a thousand things at the same time and pushed my hand away. "You said she was dead."

"I watched her die in my arms." I remembered the scene, how Arabella's blood trickled from the blackened hole in her head; how it fell to the pavement and dripped into the water of the reservoir, which still churned, alive with white hot light. "I tried to heal her, but I couldn't do anything for her."

She gasped for air and waged war on her tears. The fight for control made her angry. "Why do the people I care about the most keep dying? Over and over again!"

"I wish I knew," I reached over again, and this time she let me put my hands on the sides of her knees.

At dawn, Lon called again. "There's something about five miles north of you. It's not a life sign, but it's the same energy form."

"Thanks, Lon," I switched off the communicator. "Greer, I'm going to check it out. Watch the girls."

Greer nodded, but not before both Roxy and Madeline protested.

"You're not going out there alone," Roxy argued. "And we don't need to sit here in the tent and be protected by the big strong boys."

"You aren't coming with me," I replied, feeling just as stubborn and unreasonable.

"Why don't Greer and I go?" Madeline was quiet, as if she was afraid we'd both turn on her. "You can stay here and keep an eye on each other."

I didn't miss the glance Greer and Madeline shared.

"It's sunny. I think the weather will hold. We'll be back in no time." Greer looked out at the bright sun reflecting off the snow. "Bundle up, Thomas. That's not the warm kind of sunshine." He turned back to me. "We'll gather some more firewood from the survival pod and bring it back before we go."

"Thanks," I said. We watched them head across the snowbank to a grove of naked trees where Roxy's survival pod hung. I couldn't help considering the ways we might spend the time we had alone when Madeline and Greer left on their mission. I raised my eyebrows at Roxy.

"Back off," she warned before I had a chance to imagine the scenarios. "I haven't changed my mind about that. In fact, I'm surer than ever I don't want us any more tangled up than we already are."

"You think holding me at arm's length is going to solve anything?" I turned my attention to adjusting the settings on the control panel for the tent's heating and lighting.

"I didn't invite you here," she reminded me. When I didn't respond, she picked up the small recorder and played the message again. I watched her while she considered it. She went to the data center and started pulling things up in the space in front of her. She sorted through articles and documents.

"I came to help you, Roxy."

"Why do you care so much?" She continued her almost frantic motions as she searched the information. I listened to the busy jumble of voices in her mind. It amazed me how many layers of thoughts Roxy had, all the time. Did every girl think so deeply about everything?

"What do I have that Madeline doesn't?" she continued, ignoring my musing.

"You aren't like Madeline. Or anyone else," I said.

"According to this obituary, Sarah Thorn didn't die until 1877," Roxy said. *Sarah Thorn* was the name her mother had gone by in 1874 New York.

"Next year." I wasn't sure how it could be true. I knew what I had seen, and Arabella Eisen was dead. "Maybe the info isn't accurate."

"Maybe," she said, but I knew she wanted to believe it was possible. I didn't blame her.

"Morris has died plenty of times," she mumbled.

I stood and went to stand behind her. Close behind her. I

reached my hand around her and waved off the computer. My hands fell to her arms, and slid down until my fingers touched hers.

She held her breath. Why did I have the power to steal her breath but not her permission to love her?

"You have Madeline," she reminded me in a strained voice. "You don't need me, Levi."

"Madeline is great. I only met her a few days ago, but she seems like the perfect girl. Sometimes I wish I did feel that way about her. It would make everything easier."

Out of habit, I listened to her internal response, hoping I'd made her jealous, but her mind was silent. It was becoming obvious that Roxy had learned to block me out.

"You never used to hide your feelings from me," I said, my fingers sliding between hers.

"I didn't know how."

"But you do now?"

She shrugged. "Mom told me to learn how to control it."

I nodded. "I'm glad. I'll help if I can."

"I don't need your help," she answered, but her tone was anything but confident.

I took another step closer and leaned my head on her shoulder. My cheek brushed against hers.

"You're a mudsill," she whispered.

"I know." I noticed she didn't move away. "Humor me. When I hold you it gives me the illusion that I can protect you."

"I never asked you to protect me."

"I never asked for your permission. This is what you don't get, Roxy, and I don't know how else to explain it to you. Asking me not to care about you or try to protect you is like asking me to hold my breath. It wouldn't last long or I'd die."

"You wouldn't die," she said in a sulky voice. "You'd just pass out."

I heard a faint trail of her thoughts that I took as an invitation to turn her around to face me.

Stop, her voice pleaded, but in every other way she reached for me. *I don't want to be hurt.*

I would never hurt you.

I reached for her face, studying every detail as if my life depended on its memory. I leaned close enough to see the gray flecks in the storm of her eyes.

She started to speak, but only managed a soft sigh.

I love you. I was embarrassed by my unplanned thought. But how could I hide it from her? It was my truest truth.

"Oh, I'm sorry," Madeline said, standing at the tent opening. I looked up as Roxy moved away. Madeline's arms were full of twigs. "Greer thought the firewood might stay dry a little better inside."

Madeline turned quickly to leave.

"It's okay, Madeline," I smiled, even though I knew it was weak. "Let me help you."

She stepped inside and let me take the bundle, but she avoided my eyes and went straight to her task of stowing the wood by the heater. I felt Roxy's hard stare on my back.

You can't have both of us. That seems to be the story of our lives, doesn't it?

She disappeared behind the curtain.

Pick her, mudsill.

NINE

"It's hard to believe it's spring in New York," I mused as I stared out at the blizzard through the plastic solar window. "Has it been like this all winter?"

Roxy was reading on her cot and didn't answer.

"I think it's safe to say Madeline and Greer had to make other arrangements for the night. Looks like it's just the two of us."

She still said nothing, by voice or thought. My words made the space inside the tent hum with tension.

Quite a bit of tension.

I turned back to my cot, and sat down to check messages on my WristCom. I wasn't able to have constant access to the server as I was used to, but I could still get messages downloaded within a few hours from when they were sent. Greer had sent a text saying they were safe and camping in a cave to wait out the storm. News from Lon made me uneasy. A skirmish in the Nationalist territory of Ohio had locked it down even more than usual, and there was to be a summit in New York in November. I would be expected to play host to the factions, because New York was the most civilized place to host it, and because no other leaders wanted to do it.

What did one do to put a country back together? The only political system I'd ever known was a dictatorship. It was not the first time I'd felt frustrated by the lack of leadership in the factions around New York. The Eastern Divided States generally stuck together against invaders, but it was a survival world in most of the region, and there was little in the way of organized government. Not to mention the fact that no one trusted anyone beyond their own village or family group. Marauders were a constant plague to the struggling society since the blackout and the war. But wasn't the task of helping my city recover enough of a burden? Why couldn't someone else step up to unite the states? How could the son of a tyrant teach people to get along?

Roxy huffed. I pulled back the curtain and looked at her. She was still reading.

"What?"

She didn't say anything at first, and I took the opportunity to realize that while the tent was cavernous compared to her pod, it wasn't exactly a large space, and with the curtain that separated us out of the way, we weren't exactly a great distance from each other.

We were also undeniably and completely alone.

"Your thoughts about the country and the factions reminds me of us," Roxy said suddenly, not lifting her eyes from the pages of her book.

"I don't know about that." I shook my head. "I think we're on the same page for the things that really matter."

She shrugged and pretended it didn't matter one way or the other. "In the time we've known each other, how many times have we actually been in total agreement over a decision?"

I knew the answer to that question, or at least I knew what she would say, so I avoided the topic. "What are you reading? Is that an actual book?"

I stood and swiped the book out of her hands to look at the title. It was definitely old. "Where'd you find this?"

"You mean where did I find the stash of books Leona buried while she distracted people with tech?"

"Is it really Leona's fault that no one reads books anymore?" I was skeptical as I flipped through the pages. "Why carry a book when you can fit any information into a virtual library on your

WristCom and project it anywhere and anytime?"

"You wouldn't understand."

"So make me understand."

"I grew up reading my mother's books, and it makes me feel close to her." She held out her hand for me to return the book. I moved it out of her reach.

"*The Life and Times of Nathan Hale.* Who's that? Old boyfriend? Should I be jealous?" I tossed the book back on her bed.

"Nathan Hale. Revolutionary War." She gave me a disdainful expression.

I shrugged. "Doesn't ring a bell."

"Hung for treason by the British army?"

That sounded familiar. "You know my mom wasn't big on educating me in the history of American freedom. I read a few of the banned files, but it was a while back."

She had returned to her reading and didn't appear interested in what I said. I wanted to get her attention—in fact, I felt a little desperate for it—so I tried again.

"That was New York City, right? I think there's a statue of him in the archives."

She nodded and sat up. "He was twenty-one years old. Almost the same age as you. All he had to do to save his life was sign a document pledging allegiance to the king."

I sat down on her cot. "He was a patriot. He was loyal to America." I shrugged, not sure why it mattered more than our silent dance.

She scooted away from me. "Don't you see? There *was* no America yet. It was still just an idea. A sliver of hope they had about somehow breaking free from their king and country. And Nathan Hale was willing to give up the rest of his life for that idea. Can you imagine making that decision, and then knowing that everyone around you wants you dead for your beliefs?"

I considered her words. "Nathan Hale reminds me of Roxy Eisen." My fingers trailed the side of her leg in an almost thoughtless gesture of affection.

She tensed. When she met my gaze, it occurred to me what I was doing. But I wanted her to know what I felt.

A clank disrupted the background noise of the howling wind. I tried to figure out where it had come from. My eyes fell on the small, flat heat panels extending around the tent walls. I put a hand on the closest one.

"I think the heat converter just went out."

"So much for high tech," Roxy said.

I went to the control box and checked the battery life of the fuel cells that powered the heat panels. "Dead."

"Why don't you try healing it?"

I made a face at her. "I think the blizzard and the solar tent are trying to tell us something."

"That it's cold?" She offered evenly.

I pulled out the instructions for the solar tent and quickly saw the oversight I'd made. Greer had been right. "I was supposed to bring an extra fuel cell for this model."

"Way to plan ahead."

"Fortunately, I know how to recharge a fuel cell using snow and salt. Because I'm smart like that. But it will take a few hours. Don't worry; I'll come back in a minute to keep you warm." I hesitated. "And let's not tell Greer this happened."

She shrugged and pulled her blanket up around her. I set up the recharge before I returned to her cot. The icy chill was setting in. I ignored her disparaging glance as I got close to her warmth and stole half her solar blanket.

"You and Nathan Hale are cut from the same cloth," I told her, though I knew she didn't want to hear it. She shook her head and tossed the book aside.

"It's making me crazy."

"What?" I thought the answer was probably me, but I asked anyway.

"That he died not knowing what he'd accomplished. He had no idea whether America would come to be, or what that freedom would mean. Even to us, after our freedom slipped away. What if he wasn't even sure he was doing the right thing? I wish I could go back and tell him he hadn't given everything for nothing, and that his sacrifice would mean something."

I didn't know what to say. She felt strongly about reassuring a guy who'd been dead for three hundred years. That was Roxy, and it was part of the reason I couldn't get over her.

"Stop it," she said in a whisper that was almost swallowed up by the howling of the wind around the tent.

"Stop what?"

"Thinking about me."

"Impossible. I gave up long ago."

I felt a surge of confidence and moved closer to her, hoping she wouldn't push me away. My hands found the sides of her waist. She shook her head in a pleading sort of way, but her hands were warm on my arms and in that moment, being close to her warmth was the only thing in all of time and space I wanted. I pulled myself up next to her and held her close to me. I buried my head in the warm and wonderful place where her neck met her shoulder.

"Levi," she said. I think she meant it to be an admonition, but her saying my name was anything but discouraging.

"Tell me to go away," I said with my lips close to hers, my breath sharing the same space as hers. "But not because you're afraid. Tell me to go away because you don't want this."

Her eyes glinted steel at the challenge. She didn't want me to think she was afraid. Eons, masquerading as seconds, passed while I waited for her answer.

"I can't."

And then we were kissing. Our thoughts raced together in a jumble of words and emotions until I couldn't separate hers from mine. Wherever any of the thoughts might have originated, we both decided in that moment that we had waited too long for this and neither one of us was going to be the one to prevent the situation from escalating into a new place we had never been before.

And escalate it did.

TEN

The next morning, I woke up alone in Roxy's cot. I sat up and looked around, but she was nowhere inside the tent.

I found her outside, sitting in the snow. Her arms were wrapped around her knees and she shivered.

"What are you doing?" She wasn't wearing snow pants over her leggings and her coat wasn't closed. I crouched next to her. I tried to read her, but her emotions were completely veiled.

"It was a mistake."

I realized, no matter how much she had hidden, that I knew she would say it. "No it wasn't."

She glared at me. "I was weak. I'm sorry it happened."

"I'm not sorry," I said. "And it doesn't make you weak. You're a girl and I'm a guy and that's how it works."

She turned angrily, but I sensed her anger wasn't directed at me. She was mad at herself. She pushed her fingers into her temples. "All those years, I told everyone in that bunker they had to promise to stay together if they wanted to do what we did. I made them promise *me*. Then what do I do in one moment of weakness?"

I was confused. "Roxy, you know I'm not going anywhere, right? I'm yours. Always. I promise. You won't be able to get rid of me if you try."

She blinked back tears. We both knew that my commitment

wasn't the one in question. I couldn't promise enough for both of us.

I considered what she was saying. Had we made a mistake? Had I pushed her to do something she wasn't ready to do?

My mother had never given me any instruction on sex, other than the stringent rules she established for all citizens. I had followed her rules, for the most part and especially after I saw how Roxy's bunker rules worked. But it had more to do with me being perpetually distracted by Roxy than me thinking it was the sensible decision. And being alone with Roxy in a cold tent had made the choice a no-brainer for me.

"Sometimes it's hard to know what's right and what's wrong," I said quietly. And I meant it. It was the story of my life since I'd inherited my mother's power and her citadel. Who was I to know what was right and wrong for an entire city full of people, much less a country that needed to be patched back together? I couldn't even figure out what was best for the most important relationship in my life.

I moved closer and crouched beside her. I slipped my arm around her waist, worried that she was cold.

"How am I going to face Greer? He's going to think I'm a total hypocrite." She didn't move away from me.

I shrugged. "I'm not sure this is any of Greer's business."

She shook her head, still not looking at me.

"I don't expect you to change all your opinions overnight, Roxy, and I don't think the reasons behind your beliefs are wrong. You wouldn't be Roxy if you weren't hesitant, but if you think you're going to get away from me again, expect to be frustrated." I waited until she lifted her gaze to look at me. "I don't take bonding lightly, either."

"I know," she replied quietly.

I wished I could erase the doubt from the edges of her expression. "It's going to be okay, you know. I promise."

Roxy assumed it would be obvious to Madeline and Greer what

had happened when they got back to the tent. I heard them outside, laughing at something. Roxy wondered if they were mocking us.

"How did you fare in the storm?" Greer asked as they reached the campfire where we were heating food.

"Fine," I said, before Roxy could answer. "You find anything?"

"A transmitter," Madeline said, handing it to me. It was a mess, probably because they had torn it out with their hands, but it was tech I'd never seen. I turned it over and tried to make sense of the wiring and origin of the parts.

Greer shook his head when I gave him an inquisitive glance. "I don't know what to tell you, boss. We've never seen anything like it. I sent Lon an image to see what he could dig up." Greer snapped his fingers. "That's another thing. Lon says someone came through the portal."

"Came through to our time? From 1876?"

"No one's got a clue. But the portal console logged an opening when the chamber was mostly empty. A scientist and a guard were killed, and someone definitely went to lengths to distort the security feed."

"It has to be my mother," I said. "And whoever put that transmitter here, whether it was Leona or Joe or someone else, they'll come looking for it." I gave Roxy a stare, mentally warning her she wasn't going to like what I had to say next. "We should go."

As I expected, Roxy started to argue, but her reasoning was weak. The transmitter was a tangible sign of danger, and she couldn't stay there by herself any longer.

"I have to help you find Leona," she said, resigned. A strange look passed over her face and she closed her eyes, holding her forehead.

"Are you okay?" Madeline put a hand on her shoulder. Roxy worked hard to change her expression.

And stay on her feet.

"I'm fine. Let's just go."

A dark foreboding seeped into my brain. It was a murky,

swampy thought I wanted to push away. Ignore. But I couldn't. I couldn't shake the feeling that I had just witnessed a potential problem.

And one I wouldn't like at all.

ELEVEN

"Did something happen with you two last night?"

I should have known Greer would get right to the point the first chance he had. Roxy had walked on ahead, as if walking separately from the three of us meant that she was making the decision to leave by herself. Madeline tried to keep up with her for a while, but eventually she gave up and walked alone, staring at the ground. Greer and I hung back, keeping a watch for wild animals or suspicious activity.

"Yeah." I didn't know what else to say. I had told Roxy it was none of Greer's business, but considering Roxy's worries about how he would take it, I was probably alone in that opinion. Yet it didn't seem like my secret to share. Besides, Roxy would hear every thought I tried to put into words anyway.

"She's listening?"

"Yes."

I didn't realize until I held it back that I did want to talk about it and with someone that had some sense in their head. Greer would know it wasn't a mistake, right? He might wonder about the timing of it, but he would be happy at the turn in our relationship. He'd be on my side.

Or would he? Maybe he would be disappointed with Roxy, as she feared.

"Sometimes my brain hurts thinking about things, you know?" I sighed.

Roxy was right about one thing—bonding changed things. There was no way to go back to the way it was before. We had been altered by our mutual decision, whether we regretted it or considered what we'd given each other a gift.

I would be spared from any further consideration once we got back across the river. Something was happening along the Ohio wall, about half a mile off shore. Laser fire ripped through the calm of the forest and commands were shouted. Roxy's mind responded to the fear and determination of an impending battle, because it momentarily caused her to drop the defensive veil she'd put up between our minds.

"Someone must have tried to get over the wall," I said as we crept along the edge of the shore. "You all head into the woods and take the long way around so you're clear of the wall. I'm just going to see what's happening." I ignored the silent opposition from Roxy and stared at Greer as I spoke.

"I'll go with you," he said without hesitating.

Roxy came to stand in front of me, her face turning red with the fierceness I loved, spilling up out of the well she kept close to her heart. "What do you think you're doing?"

"I'm the governor of New York City, for better or worse. I'm officially on a delegation to work toward reunification. I can't just let it go. I have to see if there's something I can do to stop it."

"You're just going to get killed, *Governor*," she whispered severely.

"I'll do my best not to," I said before I brought up my own laser rifle and followed Greer along the edge of trees opposite the wall. Roxy started to follow us, but a siren near them started to blare. Madeline pulled her back among the trees so they wouldn't be spotted, but they both held up their weapons, ready to help if needed.

Greer and I slowly approached as the laser fire started to dissipate. Ohio border guards kept their rifles trained on a group of unarmed civilians with children in tow. By their ragamuffin appearance, I could tell they had walked a long way and were seeking shelter behind the wall. In fact, they were willing to risk dying to get it. I held up my hands to the guards and moved between the group of refugees and the wall.

"I'm Governor Levi Koenig of New York City! Stop your fire!"

They regarded me with suspicion, but no one fired on us.

"Tell your friends to turn around and walk away," the commander called from the loudspeaker. "We have orders to shoot to kill if anyone gets near the door. No questions asked."

"Please!" one of the women called out in a voice brimming with desperation. Next to her, a man carried an unconscious young girl. I saw blood staining her thin and dirty canvas dress. "My baby needs medics! You have to help us!"

"We aren't trying to attack you," a man spoke behind her. "We're not a threat. We just need help."

"Rules are rules." The commander motioned his men to be ready to fire. "No one gets in or out of Ohio's borders without specific approval from President Avihu."

"Let me speak to him." I tried to sound more authoritative than I felt. They didn't need to know how intimidated I felt. "He knows me."

They hesitated, but after talking amongst themselves, a decision was quickly made. "All requests for leniency must be sent by electronic means at least three weeks prior to physical meeting."

"We don't have any way to send a request!" the mother cried desperately. "Please help her!"

The only answer was another warning round of gunfire that spit rocks and dirt up at our legs. I herded the group back from the wall and into the cover of the trees. I kept them moving until we were out of view of the guards.

The woman was sobbing by that time. She took the child and kneeled on the ground, cradling the tiny head of black curls to her chest. "She's going to die."

I surveyed the group warily. "What is your name?"

"Talia Stevens. My daughter is Juliet. Please help us."

I didn't like that there was no way to proceed without all of them watching. But I couldn't let the little one die. "Give her to me, Talia."

She stopped crying, but she hesitated. "Why?"

"Don't worry. Just trust me." I took the child, who was barely breathing, and motioned to the rest of the group. "Go into the woods and find firewood and anything edible. My team can help you find water as well. We'll make a fire and camp here for the night."

To my surprise, no one argued. The weary travelers followed Roxy, Madeline and Greer without hesitation. It was a strange feeling, having people obey me. Unnerving. I knew my mother had achieved that unquestioning loyalty and I hoped I wasn't receiving it for the same reason she did.

Talia cried as Juliet gave a soft shudder. I needed to hurry. She was taking her final breaths.

I laid her across my lap, placing one hand on her leg where the blood still flowed, and the other on her clammy forehead. The energy flowed quickly, and within seconds Juliet started to move.

Talia gasped. "You healed her!"

She reached for her daughter when the little girl sat up, staring at me inquisitively. I smiled, but I had a hard time keeping my eyes open. She had been very near to death, so the healing had drained me of most of my energy.

"Take her with the rest and find her some water and food," I said, and waited until Talia had complied before I leaned back against a tree and closed my eyes.

I must have slept through the entire evening and night, because dawn was breaking the next time I woke. I saw I'd been moved close to a campfire, and I'd been covered with a solar blanket. There was no sign of the travelers.

"Where'd they go?" I rubbed my eyes. My voice was raspy.

Greer turned a stick in the ashes of the fire, cooking what seemed to be a skinned squirrel. "They were going to try to sneak into Canada. I gave them the solar camp pack and told them where to go. They didn't want to stick around here. There is a group of marauders that has been ransacking camps in this region. They take everything and leave no survivors, according to the rumors."

"Did you give the travelers our provisions?"

"Yeah. We don't have time, anyway. Roxy was out scouting during the night and she spotted a well-armed camp nearby. We need to get back to the van and get out of here."

"I hope the van's still there," I said, stretching and reaching for the remaining canteen of water.

"Where's Roxy now?" I stood up, turning a full circle as I looked for either of the girls.

"She's alright. They both headed toward the shed where we left the maglev. I said I'd wait with you until you were strong enough to move. We'll catch up."

I stood up. "Let's go. I don't want to risk the girls being found."

Greer chuckled. "Now, Gov, you gotta admit Roxy Eisen knows how to survive. And Madeline can handle herself as well, she proved that to me when we were out looking for that transmitter and we got caught in the blizzard. Sit yourself down and have some breakfast first.

I made a face. "I wouldn't exactly call that breakfast."

"Food doesn't have to be rich and expensive to give you strength for the road," he said with a shrug as he ripped off a piece of meat and handed it to me.

I made a face, but I ate every bite of my awful-tasting portion of varmint, just to show him I wasn't the spoiled rich prince he seemed to think I was.

"You wanna tell me what happened with you two now?" Greer didn't look at me as he chewed on his own portion of meat.

"I don't know. Maybe it's better to lay it to rest."

He didn't say any more on the subject. And the more I didn't talk about what happened with Roxy, the more I was sure I didn't want to talk about it.

Maybe it was better to pretend it never happened.

TWELVE

We caught up with the girls by noon. When we were sure we were out of Ohio's patrolling range, I used the tracker on my WristCom to find the maglev.

The barn was no more or less dilapidated than it had been when we left it.

"Do you think it's still there?" Madeline asked as we stood in front of the door. I was afraid to open it up and see. Maglevs outside of major cities were unheard of. And the closest city that had been rebuilt after the war was Philadelphia. We were over three hundred miles away.

Two hours in a maglev flying home could become a week-long survival journey.

"I guess there's no way to know except to open it up." Greer threw open the old doors. They protested with moans and creaks as we took a collective breath and peered into the darkness. Greer was the first to walk in.

"Maglev's here. But the tarp isn't over it," Greer said. He went closer and with a touch of his thumb, opened the lower hatch where we had stored the food and water. "Supplies are gone."

I went to the side door and touched the fingerprint sensor. "I don't know how they got it open. It should stay locked without a citadel fingerprint."

"I'll tell you how." Greer was on the far side. I walked around and saw what he was looking at.

"They blew a hole in the steel framework." I rubbed my finger along the blackened, curled edges of steel and frayed carbon coating.

"Is it fixable?" Roxy asked as she and Madeline peered around the edge.

I sighed. "We'll have to see what part of the engine is affected, and find a way to get the hole patched."

"I can take a look at the electrical system," Madeline offered.

"Thanks," I answered and glanced at Greer and Roxy. "Why don't you two do a sweep and make sure they aren't waiting to ambush us," I suggested as I walked forward.

Roxy eyed me with suspicion, but kept her mind veiled as she followed Greer out of the building.

Madeline sat down in front of the control console and tried to turn on the computer system. She didn't speak at first. Suddenly, as I was prying away bits of burnt steel, I heard her small voice.

"What do you really think, Levi?"

"I think we're motivated enough," I said as I slid under the van to investigate the engine. "If we don't get the flying function working, we'll be walking. There aren't maglev streets outside the cities."

"That would be a long, dangerous walk."

We were quiet the first couple hours we worked together. But as Madeline made headway with the system, she got more talkative. I had a hard time not being distracted by her enthusiasm for all things electrical.

"Levi, this maglev is completely amazing! Why aren't all maglevs this sophisticated? The wiring is so intricate—and with such attention to the tiniest detail. But it flows, almost like a dance. So much fluid motion. It's beautiful."

I couldn't help laughing. "I honestly have never heard you talk this much. And I've never heard anyone talk about electricity like that before."

"I'm sorry," she said, grunting as she tried to maneuver herself completely under the front seat console. "I didn't mean to say those things out loud."

I chuckled again. "It's okay. I like listening to you."

And I did. I didn't tell her it was especially because *I* was the one who had wired the citadel maglevs into hybrids.

"In my experience, it usually freaks people out," she said. I could tell she was smiling.

"You can't scare me, Thomas." I tried to use my laser pistol to solder joints back together, but gave up when I almost burned my hand off.

Fortunately, Madeline didn't notice. "I bet I could scare you. Sometimes, when I'm working on a system like this, I imagine it as a painting, and then wish I knew how to paint so I could capture what I see in my mind. What do you think of that?"

"I think the world needs you to learn how to paint."

She went quiet for a few minutes after I said that. I thought the conversation was over, but she spoke again, her voice softer. "I would love to learn to paint." I could almost see her shaking her head, though I couldn't see her from my position under the wreckage. "No. That would be crazy. Only important people have time to do things like that."

I wondered if she was fishing for a compliment, but when she said nothing more, I began to think she really meant it. She really saw herself that way.

"You know, Madeline, you're a free woman now. You can do whatever you want with your life."

"I know," she said quickly. Too quickly. I wished she would say more, but she didn't.

In the silence that followed, I had an uncomfortable feeling. It was a sort of itch that I couldn't scratch, but in my mind, not on my skin. Something about Madeline's excitement over the tech in the maglev reminded me of someone. Someone I hadn't seen in a very long time.

I tried to grasp the memories that floated just out of my reach. I had been so young, the images seemed like projections on a screen.

No, they *were* projections. They were virtual video files I had found as a child, encrypted on my mother's computer system. I had seen a young Leona, before she was a mother. Her beauty was flawless—the kind that made a person want to stare, that nearly satisfied the soul's need for perfection. Her enthusiasm radiated out of every part of her features. She had laughed with glee as Arabella stood at the writing board. Not a virtual board, but the old kind. The old transparent kind that used markers and had to be erased by hand. Every inch of space was taken up with scientific formulas.

"Hold on, Lee," Arabella laughed. *"We need the science before we can build it. Work with me!"*

Leona sighed dramatically. "Don't you just want to build it? Let it pour out of our spirits all over the floor over there and turn into something spectacular, something that will make people remember us for generations to come?"

"Yes, Lee, sure I do, but first we need the plan!" Arabella replied in happy exasperation. *"That's what I'm for. To pull you down from the clouds and make all your beautiful dreams come true."*

"Keep recording this, Eli," Leona pointed toward the camera. *"This moment will go down in history. We're going to save the world, and we're going to do it with art. Art disguised as tech."*

"I have no doubt you'll pull it off, Leona." Eli answered from behind the camera with a chuckle.

"What are you thinking about?" Madeline's question brought me out of the memory.

I didn't answer for a moment. "I was just thinking that you reminded me of someone."

"Someone good, I hope."

I didn't answer.

We worked the rest of the day until we lost the light. Without any supplies and with the threat of marauders, we slept in shifts and conserved the remaining water. At least Roxy didn't complain about me sleeping close.

As soon as dawn broke, Madeline and I were back at work. I

got the engine running and she got the computer working around noon.

"The only thing left is this gaping hole in the floor. We'll have to patch it somehow before we can fly it, but I think we're ready to test it out," I was saying when we heard Greer and Roxy shouting from outside.

Roxy threw open the door. "Huge pack of marauders heading our way!"

"Get in!" I propelled myself into the cabin and started programming the computer. "I guess this is our test drive. Grab something and hold on!"

The computer was still booting when the first of the marauders turned the corner and came into the barn. Roxy and Greer pointed laser rifles out the window and held them off as I pressed buttons frantically, trying to get it to start.

Finally, I heard a familiar voice. "Welcome, Governor. Please select your desired program."

"Fly, Cori! Get us home NOW!"

"As you wish, Governor," she answered congenially. The maglev turned and barreled through the crowd of scavengers.

Immediately, it became obvious that we were all going to fall to our deaths if we didn't find a way to restrain ourselves. I held on to the bare steel frame and pulled open a cargo hold, praying the marauders hadn't taken the emergency supplies as well.

Everything was in its place. I pulled out lengths of cord and shoved the end over several of the steel frames a few times and tied it off. I helped Roxy and Madeline sit inside the makeshift swings I had made, then Greer caught on and made his own with more cord I handed him. Finally, I made a sling for myself. When the maglev got up in the air and began sailing smoothly toward home, I had the thought for the first time in a while that we were actually going to make it.

The maglev made it home. We had to stop once to make a few more repairs, but we managed to patch it enough to get us back to the citadel by nightfall.

I wanted to crawl into bed and sleep for a week, but I knew it wasn't going to happen. After I cleaned up, servants brought me a tray of food that I polished off in minutes. Nothing had ever smelled or tasted so good. I headed for the iron staircase that led to my mother's most prized possession. A few city engineers and a scientist went into the portal chamber as I stepped on to the moving circular staircase and looked up.

When I entered, Lon was at the main console with a deep frown.

"What happened?" I had to step close to be heard above the commotion of the portal.

"Massive solar storm kicked up during the night. The portal didn't react well. It activated and starting pulling everything in. We lost a couple techs before we were able to put a temporary shield in place."

"Did the cap fail?"

"No," Lon said, to my relief. "But the way it's sparking and carrying on, I wouldn't be surprised if the wormhole has been altered."

"That means we don't know for sure what happened to those techs."

"We can only hope they're safe somewhere."

I called in a few commands and studied the specs, though I doubted I would see anything the scientists and engineers had missed.

"It looks like the basic structure was demagnetized by the storm. Can we reverse it or reboot it?"

"We can try to isolate it in a magnetic field and then turn off the field. I've done it before with good results. But we won't know if it worked unless someone goes in."

"I'm not sending anyone in there without a good reason," I said, closing my computer windows and shaking my head. "If I knew the earth would stay in place without this portal, I'd be tempted to blow it up and never give it another thought."

Lon nodded without emotion.

"Did you figure out who came through?"

He looked at me. "It was Leona. I cleaned up the static on the feed."

"I figured as much. I assume you have patrols out?"

"Yes. So far no sign of her."

"I'll see what I can do." I watched them for a few minutes, but with my brain so exhausted, I gave up and headed for my room. I needed sleep.

"Call me if anything changes," I said before I left. "Oh, and Lon, we brought her home. She wouldn't come into the citadel, but she's here in the city."

He nodded again, his face remaining passive, but I thought I saw something more in his expression.

"I'll message her when I'm finished here," he said, looking back at his screens.

I went to my rooms. After a shower and before I slept, I checked my messages, wondering if Roxy had let me know where she was.

She hadn't. But I figured she had gone to the bunker, and I thought she would be safe there. I sent Greer a text asking him to keep an eye on her and make sure Leona or Joe didn't find her.

There was a message waiting from Madeline, thanking me for the chance to help with the mission and for her new position at the citadel.

I thought about her as I turned into my pillow and sighed.

Madeline would never be Roxy. So she would never be what I wanted.

Several weeks passed. I worked with Greer to organize peace talks and fix the wormhole. I saw very little of Roxy, which bothered me more than I told anyone, even Greer. When I texted her, she replied in general terms, one or two words. We had no sign of Joe or Leona. My mother must have escaped again through the portal, or she had left the city. Arabella's message on the mysterious com came to mind, but what could I do? We couldn't risk going through the portal until we knew it was safe.

One warm night in early June, I woke around three in the morning with an uneasy feeling. I sat up and listened. Nothing seemed out of place. No alarms blared; no one stirred outside my door. But I knew something was wrong, and I knew it had to do with Roxy.

I checked the tracker on her com—hoping she was actually wearing it—and messaged her. She didn't answer, but the tracker said she was at the bunker. I dressed and summoned a maglev. I checked Greer's tracker, but he must have taken it offline. Why wasn't he watching Roxy?

The feeling of unease grew as I set the maglev to head to the bunker on emergency speed. I stood on Lafayette Street, outside the bunker, under a minute later. I pressed my palm to the hidden security device, sensing something was very wrong.

Please be okay.

I ran through the corridor and pushed aside the heavy steel door that had been left open. I heard voices, and Roxy's mind was angry.

I forced open the door to her room and found Joe leaning over her. Roxy had her back to the brick wall. Joe turned when I entered, giving her the opportunity to slam into him, knocking him down. I pulled my pistol and aimed it at his head.

"What are you doing here, Brant? Do you realize how stupid you were to come here?"

He only chuckled, so I kicked him.

While he grimaced on the floor, I glanced at Roxy. *Is he controlling you?*

She found my gaze and shook her head. *He hasn't tried it yet.*

You can read his thoughts?

I can read everyone's thoughts.

This was news. I stared at her until Joe sat back up and spit in my direction.

"You're going to regret that, Koenig."

"I won't. I'll do it again if you move."

"I didn't come through the portal to see Roxy," Joe said with a shrug. "I just couldn't resist. How could I pass up the chance to be with my favorite girl?" He brushed his fingers along her leg. She jerked away. I threw my fist at him so hard his head snapped back and hit the cement block wall. While he tried to stay conscious, I heard Roxy's internal struggle.

Fight it, she thought to herself. *He can't make you do anything you don't want to do.*

Joe kept her gaze captive while he held out his hand for her gun, which she held at her side. I stepped between them and pushed him back. He was taller than me, and more solid. I fought an almost overwhelming feeling of inferiority.

He's better than me.

My ridiculous thought gave Roxy motivation to break the connection with him.

Get it together, Koenig. Let's just get him in the archives.

I nodded and made my mind go blank except for the task of restraining Joe in the maglev and putting a restriction force around him. He stared at us with a half-grin. If he was worried about his predicament, he didn't let on. What was he planning? I looked at Roxy for answers, but she shook his head.

He's not letting me read him now. I think he's just playing games.

When we got to the citadel, I had a security team take him to a holding cell below, warning them to be careful.

Just as I was thinking it was over, we heard shouts above the foyer on the balcony next to the portal chamber.

"What's going on?" I spoke into my WristCom. I didn't want to hear the answer.

"Levi," Roxy said as she grabbed my arm. She was looking up.

I unwillingly lifted my gaze, already sure of what I would see. Leona stood in front of the portal chamber with two citadel rifles pointed at the guards.

"Lower your weapons," one of the soldiers, Beth, instructed, but she couldn't keep her voice from wavering.

"Get out of my way," Leona hissed. She shot one and then the other. The white blasts hit Beth in the chest and the guy in the leg. They both fell, leaving the chamber door Leona's only remaining obstacle between herself and the portal. She took one of their keys and waved in front of the sensor. The door dematerialized.

She turned, glancing over the railing, and smirked at us. Then she disappeared into the chamber.

"Governor," someone spoke into my WristCom. "Joe Brant has escaped from the archives."

"How?" I looked at Roxy in disbelief.

"I don't know, sir. He convinced three armed guards to hand him their weapons and release his restriction field. They put me in one while he walked out the door."

We took the iron stairs up to the portal balcony, running even though the staircase moved upward quickly enough on its own. We stood on either side of the door as I tried to calculate where my mother was standing.

"I'm in the chamber. Hurry!" We heard her say as she worked at the console, flipping images mid-air and adjusting the ratios and specs of the delicate balance of the portal's gravitational power.

I went in, my gun pointed at her. "Stop what you're doing, Leona. You aren't going through the portal. You're under arrest. You'll have a public trial that's long overdue."

"Levi," she said, gushing as if I had just welcomed her back with open arms. She came to me, ignoring the weapon and putting her hands on my shoulders. "Look at you. My son, the leader of a city. I trust you will rule with as much heart as I have."

"I'm not ruling anyone," I said, nudging her back with my rifle. "And neither are you. Put down the weapon and stand back."

She laughed. The sound tried to convince me she was sweet and kind, but I knew the truth. I remembered every horror she had inflicted on the people of my city. None of us would forget.

"Your time is up," I said before I lifted my com. "I need security backup in the chamber. Immediately!"

"Levi, be sensible. You're not really going to do anything to me. You can't kill your mother, even if you have the misguided notion she has done something wrong."

"You're not *my* mother, and I'd be happy to kill you, like you just killed her," Roxy said, squeezing the trigger of her rifle as she gestured to the body of the female guard, slumped in the doorway.

"Her name was Beth," I said. "Do you even remember her? Do you even care that her life is over because of you?"

My words did nothing to the amused expression Leona wore. I was considering pulling the trigger myself when a force from behind lifted me off my feet and threw me against the wall. Roxy was thrown against the other wall.

Joe grabbed our rifles as Leona activated the portal. They jumped through, and everything went still.

I dragged myself up and across the room to Roxy.

"They can't be trusted with history," she said, holding her head.

I touched a cut on her chin and watched it vanish. "I know."

We turned toward the portal. It sparked, giving off more than the usual warmth. I felt sunburned standing in front of it.

"Do you think they made it through?" she asked.

I shook my head. "I guess we're about to find out."

THIRTEEN

I pulled portal suits from the storage, throwing one Roxy's way. After we changed into two of the protective outfits we had brought back from 1874, I went to the printing station and entered a request for historical clothing from the Victorian era. With almost immediate speed, the clothes were ready. I handed Roxy hers.

She looked at it with distaste. *There are little blue flowers all over it.* I hadn't ordered anything specific, but I thought she would look pretty in it. My thought only made her snarl.

"I don't have a corset," she said, as if it would excuse her from wearing it.

"I think it's there. Underneath the dress," I said, lifting the skirt to reveal the corset and bracing in case she hit me. She sighed and grabbed the stack of clothing with vicious flair.

"It always comes down to corsets," she seethed.

I eyed the guard, Beth, again. How many people had my mother killed because they were in her way? As much as I tried to forget where I had come from, it would always be part of me. I couldn't escape my genetic code. It was bound to my molecules. A murderous tyrant would always be one generation removed from me.

"Ready." Roxy stood up, all sweetness and pretty flowered-ness as she grabbed an extra laser pistol and jammed it under her petticoats. I smiled as she stomped to the red line.

"Give me a minute." I hadn't forgotten the jolt involved with jumping into the portal. I needed a few deep breaths.

"It's better just to jump and get it over with," she said.

"Just be patient," I said as I went back to rummage in the storage unit. I hit the com on the wall as I walked by.

"Locate Greer," I said.

"Locating Greer." Cori's voice filled the portal room. "Greer cannot be located. Would you like to leave a message, Governor?"

"Yes. Private message. 'Greer, Leona and Joe went through the portal. Roxy and I are following, so I guess that means you're in charge.'"

"Your message will be delivered."

I pulled out heavy duty electrical cord and went back to Roxy. I put my arm next to hers and wrapped the cord tightly around both of our arms.

"What in the world, Levi?"

"I'm not risking losing you in there."

She rolled her eyes and shrugged, but I got the impression she thought it was a good idea.

"Remember to hold your breath. We're coming up in water."

"I remember," she said, staring into the brightness as if she was mesmerized by the light. I pressed buttons on the console, hoping to isolate the wormhole and keep us from flying into the black hole, but there was no way of preventing whatever would happen.

"On the count of three," I said, but before I could start counting, she pulled us in.

The first time I had traveled the portal, I had known nothing. My mind had shut down as quickly as I was sucked into the light, and I didn't wake up until I breathed mouthfuls of water in the 1874 reservoir.

When I had returned from 1874, the trip had been more like a dream. I was on a mission to get back to Roxy, and I was reeling from not saving Arabella Eisen. My mind had been stuck in think mode, and it frustrated me how long it seemed to take to float through the years until time decided to pull me back.

This time, I was prepared for anything. Anything, that is, except what happened.

When we jumped, the electrical storm from the sun still had the portal lit up, blasting magnetic energy everywhere like a toddler with paint. It leaked all over us, making a mess of us, throwing the wormhole into a spin that tossed us around so violently I felt like I'd been through a mixer and I was one of the pieces that flew up and hit the wall.

Only it was the ground instead of a wall. I moaned and tried to lift my head. If it wasn't confusing enough being spat out of a wormhole like a rotten piece of meat, I quickly realized I had no idea where we were.

The wormhole had always been a fixed arc between the same point in New York City, but two hundred years apart. We were supposed to be soaking wet and hauling ourselves out of the disgruntled waves of the public water supply.

Instead, we were in a small field surrounded by forest. We were dry. There was no sign of humanity anywhere.

"What in the world is that banging?" Roxy groaned, sitting up and holding both sides of her head like she was trying to put it back in place. She leaned forward, violently losing whatever had been in her stomach.

"You okay?" I untied our wrists and put a hand on her shoulder. She wiped her mouth with her arm and nodded.

We heard the blasts again, coming from somewhere off to the west. It didn't seem very far away.

"Come on," I pulled her up and took a quick survey of her person. The last time we took a ride in the portal she'd broken most of the bones in her body. This time, wearing the protective suit, she'd fared much better.

The suits hadn't done much to protect our clothes. They were shredded in several places and burned.

We ran across the field and into the forest, until it stopped abruptly at the edge of water.

"Wait," Roxy pointed down the shoreline. We were on a high bank with a good view of the surroundings. "It's Manhattan. This is the Hudson River."

She was right, but it was hard to make sense of the different version of the island. This couldn't be 1874—or 1876—as I'd expected. We were in the center of the city, right where the reservoir—and the entire city landscape—should be.

Another blast interrupted my thoughts. Roxy pulled me down as an incredibly loud whine screamed in our ears.

"That's canon fire," I said in disbelief as I looked behind us and saw the black cannonball fly into a tree, splintering wood and sending shards into the air around us.

I looked down. A ship floated lazily down the Hudson, occasionally blasting toward Manhattan or New Jersey. Uniformed officers stood on the deck, laughing and drinking as if it was a party and not an attack. I stared at their uniforms in surprise.

"Uh, Roxy, we aren't in 1876."

"No kidding," she huffed. "Try a hundred years before that. Those are British officers."

My first impulse was to drag her right back to the spot we'd come through the portal and find a way out. But Roxy shook me off.

"Check it out," she pointed at the deck of the ship.

"No. Way."

"Looks like we aren't the only ones who took a detour in the storm," Roxy said.

Somehow it wasn't a surprise to see Leona standing regally at the helm of the ship, wearing her half-smile. The one she reserved for happy moments of wreaking havoc and devastation on unsuspecting people.

She was dressed to fit the part. I heard Roxy's brain take a detailed account of the exquisite red gown, complete with wide hip extenders and a plunging neckline. Leona's red hair was covered with a tall white wig.

"Do you get the impression she's not at all surprised to be in this time?" I sighed and rubbed my face with my hands. "This is not good."

"This is *so* not good." Roxy agreed.

As the ship passed by, on to the north, we walked back to the field where the portal had dumped us.

When we pushed back the brush, Greer and Madeline were staring up at us, dazed and shredded and trying to get up out of the dirt.

"What are you doing here?" I held out a hand to Madeline. I looked for injuries, but they must have remembered to wear protective suits under their clothes, because they seemed okay.

"Welcome to the portal," Roxy said evenly. "Why are you here?"

Roxy glared at Madeline. I felt the animosity, and it confused me until I recognized the emotion she forgot to hide. I didn't have a single clue why she was jealous, but I liked the feeling. I twisted my mouth and scratched my nose so I wouldn't smile.

"Where are we?" Greer turned in a full circle, his hands on the hips of his nineteenth century clothes. "This isn't right."

"It's the right place, but a hundred years earlier," I explained.

He did the math. "1776? Isn't that—?"

"The Revolutionary War," Roxy confirmed.

"Whoo-ee," Greer said under his breath.

"It gets worse." I sighed. "My mother's here and it appears she has overtaken a British warship."

Beside me, Roxy held her stomach and grimaced.

"Are you sick?" I felt her forehead.

"Must have been the portal," she mumbled. "I haven't felt right since we came through."

I helped her lean back against a rock and put my hand on her stomach. Blue energy surged.

"Better?"

She shrugged. "I guess."

I stared at her with doubt.

"I think it's better now." She stood up and dusted off her clothes. She gave the outfit a second glance, and gestured to the rest of us.

"These clothes aren't going to work."

I nodded. "We're a hundred years ahead in style."

"That and we're ripped and dirty enough to be homeless," Greer tried to hold together a gaping hole in the sleeve of his shirt.

"We *are* homeless," Madeline said.

"I suppose we should walk into the city and see what we can find." I started to walk, and they all fell in step.

We headed south in the New York from the past—through tall trees, marshes and swamps where buildings and streets should be. The only evidence of inhabitants was the occasional Native American wigwam. The residents disappeared into their huts when we passed by.

Eventually we found the settled part of the island. We wandered through the streets of colonial New York City as the citizens cast not-so-subtle glances of disgust or curiosity.

We ended up on Pearl Street by the water's edge. Ships were docking and boxes of goods were being unloaded. Men haggled over prices, adjusting their longer jackets over fitted waistcoats and cotton breeches, pushing wigs back on sweaty brows.

I felt very out of place in trousers and suspenders. "If anyone questions us, we just came in on a boat from overseas," I said to the others under my breath. "There was a fire on board. We haven't had an opportunity to buy clothes."

"Do you think that will work?" Roxy was skeptical.

A crowd gathered along the riverfront, so we stopped. Uniformed men came out of a tavern, and tension filled the air. British officers standing near the tavern eyed the group of men with suspicion.

"That's George Washington," Roxy said in a whisper.

The tall man in the middle did look familiar, though younger than I would have expected. I gulped, only able to think about our appearance.

They're just clothes. Roxy nudged me with her elbow.

It's not just that, I answered. *I don't want to mess with history. We need to lie low, especially around the first president of America.*

She shrugged. We turned our attention back to the events unfolding. George Washington stood a head taller than the men around him, with kind but wary eyes and dark hair, powdered to appear gray. He turned and laid eyes on us. Specifically, he saw our clothes. He started walking toward us.

Blast it. Our cover's blown.

Maybe he's just saying hello.

"I say, young people, what sort of fashion is this?"

He smiled while my heart thumped in my chest. I held out my hand. "Levi Koenig. Pleased to meet you, sir. We've heard about you."

I felt Roxy's eyes on me. *That's an understatement.*

The men who had followed Washington across the street seemed impatient for him to get back to their business. They kept eyeing the British soldiers, but Washington didn't move away from us. He shook my hand with some amusement.

"Mr. Koenig, you do not appear to hail from our fair city."

"Born and raised," I said, too quickly. Roxy elbowed me and I remembered our cover story. Washington raised an eyebrow, but didn't press further.

"What's going on here?" I asked, thinking too late that my speech probably didn't sound native, either. Roxy's mental critiques of my behavior didn't help, so I told her to shut up.

"We had a meeting with General Howe." Washington directed his words to the larger crowd, though I noticed he still kept his voice low enough so the British wouldn't hear him. "He seeks to speak of clemency."

The crowd started murmuring. Arguing. I realized how divided the New York citizens were on the subject of independence.

"I hope you told him to take his clemency and bury it in the privy!" a man shouted from behind us.

A British soldier straightened and took several steps toward our group.

These people smell bad. Roxy made a face at me. *No wonder I can't stop gagging.*

She looked peaked. I dug around in my pocket and handed her a handkerchief to cover her nose and mouth.

"I declined his offer." Washington pulled on his gloves. He stole a glance at the British and began walking briskly. He motioned for us to join him.

"You boys have enlisted, I assume?" He gestured to Greer and me.

"We haven't yet," I said, glancing at Greer. "We were planning on it as soon as we had the chance."

He hesitated. "And will you be fighting for the king?"

I looked back, seeing that the crowd had been left behind to sort out their differences. I looked back at the general.

"We'll be fighting for freedom, sir."

He nodded. I wondered if he just felt sorry for us, but he waved again for us to follow. "Come along, then. We are going to headquarters. My man can get you both on the register. We are short on uniforms. He'll give you money so you and the ladies can buy more comfortable clothes."

Comfortable for whom? Roxy thought.

"Allow me to introduce my wife, Roxanne," I said, placing a hand on her back. Washington seemed either indifferent or suspicious, I couldn't tell. He gave her a quick nod and moved on.

We fell behind the soldiers and Roxy jabbed me in the side.

"What are you doing?" she whispered. "First of all—wife? Really? We're going to go there again? And second of all—you aren't joining the army."

I didn't look at her. "I'd be the only guy in his twenties not fighting for one cause or the other. I can't blend in by standing around and expecting people to take care of us. If we have to be stuck here, I will pull my weight. And as for being your husband, it's the best way I know to take care of you in this time. Deal with it."

"Soldiers die, Levi."

"If you haven't noticed, we're in 1776!" I caught a few looks from the other men when I raised my voice, so I continued in a quieter tone. "It's the only thing I can do. And I'm not going to stand by and watch you get hurt. You're sick."

She snarled. "I'm fine! I never asked you to take care of me."

I was irritated and my first impulse was to take it out on her. But what would it prove? I didn't know how *not* to try to keep her safe, especially after what had happened between us, but she wouldn't be Roxy if she didn't fight it.

"How will getting yourself impaled by a British bayonet help me?" She huffed. "If you join up, I will, too."

I sighed, frustrated. I stopped walking and caught her hand, turning her to face me. We had walked into woods, and as the rest of the group moved down the path into the trees, we were quickly alone.

"Roxy, be reasonable."

"When am I ever reasonable?"

"I don't want you to fight," I said plainly. "Not because I don't think you can do it, but because I don't want anything to happen to you."

She started to argue, but something stopped her. She looked away.

"What?"

"Lucy said something in 1874," she said. "She told me that sometimes we do things, not because we understand why, but because they make someone else more comfortable."

I nodded and kicked at some pebbles on the side of the path, feeling a little guilty as well. "Lucy was a wise girl."

She didn't say anything else, so I took her hands and squeezed them until she looked at me. I swallowed my pride before I spoke. "We have to be willing to let each other make choices. I'm sorry if it sounded like I was trying to control you. But please let me take care of you. Until we figure out what's wrong with you."

"Nothing's wrong with me," she mumbled, but after a moment she gave me a short nod.

I knew it was the closest thing to an agreement I was going to get.

FOURTEEN

Even though the trip wasn't planned and I had plenty of work to do elsewhere in time, there was something undeniably cool about being on a busy street in New York in 1776.

I glanced up at the sun, wondering how long I had been sitting outside the millinery waiting for the girls. I pulled up my sleeve to glance at my WristCom, wondering if it would still function on solar power or if it had been damaged in the portal.

It was dead. I'd have to tinker with it when I had some time.

I heard the door open behind me. Before I had the chance to turn around and see what Roxy looked like in her dress, I heard her thought.

That coat you're wearing is one part of 1776 I could get used to.

Her face turned red as she realized I had heard her. I felt a silly grin spread over my face as I glanced down at my long navy tailcoat with brass buttons and my white cravat peeking out from the waistcoat. And I only noticed the details because she thought about them.

"So you like it?" I made a show of posing for her. She tried not to smile. That's when I noticed her dress. I was used to seeing Roxy in historical dress, but something about her was especially lovely. She wore a bonnet that made her look downright adorable.

So feminine and sweet.

"Looks can be deceiving," she said wryly.

I took a step toward her, remembering just before I reached for her that we were on a public street in a time where rules of propriety were strictly followed. I folded my hands behind my back to keep me out of trouble.

She scowled, but in a way that told me she was embarrassed, not disgusted. Staring at her reminded me of what had happened in the snowstorm.

"Your hair isn't quite long enough to be fashionable," she said, feeling the ends of my shoulder length hair. "Maybe you should run back inside and buy a wig."

I saw her smirk and made a face at her. "I'll grow it out. There's no way I'm wearing a wig."

"Such a rebel," she said with a tsk. "I have to do the corset, but you won't put on a silly wig."

"We all have our lines we won't cross. And rebels are in high demand these days."

She raised an eyebrow. "I guess you're right. In fact, George Washington didn't have a wig, either."

Madeline stepped out of the shop and we both turned. I caught myself before I audibly gasped.

"You look nice." Roxy didn't seem very happy about her understatement. She frowned at Madeline's blue silk gown. I had the feeling Roxy had complimented Madeline so she wouldn't have to hear me say it. I was sorry for my first thought, but there was no way to look at Madeline without being at least a little awed.

"Thank you. You both look like you belong here." Madeline smoothed her skirt. "I don't know why I got such an extravagant dress. You seem to have gotten by with outfits a little more comfortable-looking."

I knew what Madeline meant by her words. She thought her own dress was too conspicuous. But Roxy took it the wrong way. She didn't say anything, but I felt the emotion she tried very hard to hide. It was almost like a physical heat radiating from her mind.

"I think you're both pretty," I said. I was instantly sorry. Madeline's expression was a desperate plea for me to take back the words, and Roxy glared as if she was waiting for me to give her one more reason to punch me.

I cleared my throat. "Let's find Washington's men and get back to camp."

Most of the soldiers had returned to camp, but a few remained around the tavern, stocking up on ale and secrets. We were obviously out of place, but to my surprise, they seemed to accept us. They allowed us to follow them back to Richmond Hill, a half-hour walk from Pearl Street.

I figured the home was set on what one day would be Greenwich Village. In this time, it was about a mile outside of the city, set in a reaching estate with flower gardens and ancient oak trees, with the Hudson flowing behind the house.

The soldiers headed to the back field where tents were set up, but Washington invited us inside the house. We stepped up on the porch as a cheerful woman opened the door.

"Welcome home, General. Your wife is waiting in the drawing room. Supper will be prompt tonight."

"Thank you, Mrs. Thompson. We will have four extra guests tonight."

She glanced at us. Was she surprised? Did I read distrust in her expression?

She's just wondering where she's going to put us all, Roxy assured me.

"What accommodations shall I ready, sir?" Mrs. Thompson asked General Washington. He frowned at me. He must have decided I was the spokesman.

"Will you introduce your party, Mr. Koenig?"

For the first time in my life, I was glad for the etiquette tutoring my mother had insisted on while I was growing up. I had the sense that George Washington associated manners with character. "I'm Levi Koenig. This is my wife, Roxanne, and my friend, Mr. Greer. Miss Madeline Koenig is my sister."

It occurred to me I should have said Roxy was my sister and Madeline was my wife, since Roxy and I both had dark hair and eyes and Madeline was as blond and fair as the sun.

Roxy covertly jabbed me in the ribs.

"Prepare a guest chamber for the Koenigs and an adjoining room for Miss Koenig. Greer, I assume you will be fine in the tents with the other soldiers?"

Greer nodded. "It would be an honor, sir."

"Excellent," Washington said, distracted. Even though he was polite, I could tell he was getting tired of dealing with us. I was sure he had plenty of things demanding his attention. "My man, Joseph Reed, will get you signed on as soldiers. Where did you say you were from?"

"We come from Ohio," I used the same ruse we had used in 1874.

Washington had started to walk away, but he turned back at my words. "Ohio? Do you mean the Ohio Valley? Do you have news from Fort Necessity or Fort Pitt?"

I had no idea what he was saying, but I nodded.

Roxy came to my rescue. *He's curious if we know about the Indian raids on the settlers in the Ohio Valley. He hopes we have news from the forts.*

"No news about the Indian raids, but I know your men are working to establish a peaceful environment for settlers coming into the area."

Washington nodded. He still frowned, but he seemed relieved. I hoped I was right.

Greer and I signed contracts pledging our loyalty to the American colonies, an almost anti-climactic moment considering how invested we were in seeing them succeed. Mrs. Thompson showed us to our rooms and told us to dress for dinner. Since we only had the clothes on our backs, I hoped what we were wearing would suffice. After the woman left, I closed the door and turned around to see Roxy sitting on the bed, her arms wrapped tightly around her chest and her eyes shut. I crossed the room and crouched in front of her.

"What is it?"

She frowned when I spoke.

"Please tell me you're okay," I said quietly. I reached for her arms and let the energy flow from my fingers. Finally she pushed me away and rubbed her temples.

"My head hurts."

"Why?"

She opened her eyes slightly, as if the light in the room was overwhelming, and watched me for a moment before she answered. "It started when I read his mind."

"So you've been reading everyone's thoughts."

She shrugged. "Like I said, I've learned to control it."

"Does it always hurt?" My fingers traced her jaw.

"I've had headaches before. But this is the worst it's been."

I was frustrated at my inability to fix her. She leaned back and put her head on the pillow, so I pulled the thick quilt over her. I leaned beside her and pushed the stray hair from her eyes.

"We're going to figure this out," I said, wanting to believe I was right.

"Is Roxy okay?" Madeline stood in the doorway, watching us.

"I don't know," I said. "She has a bad headache."

Roxy groaned.

"I think you should stay in bed. I'll check on you when I can and see if Mrs. Thompson has any remedies."

"Why can't you heal her?" Madeline stepped forward, bringing with her a sweet, flowery smell.

I shook my head. "I don't know."

"I'll be fine," Roxy muttered. I wasn't sure she believed it.

FIFTEEN

"I'll be back as soon as I can," I whispered to dawn's light, in case she listened. I kissed Roxy on the cheek because she was sleeping and I could get away with it.

Fighting the Revolutionary War had its boring aspects. I woke up at dawn every day when the housekeeper tapped on the door. I stood and stretched my aching muscles, cramped from the night folded up in an awkward pose on the small settee in front of the fireplace.

Roxy had been clear our first night together in the room. She did not wish to reenact the snowstorm.

After a hasty breakfast, I joined the other troops in the field for morning exercises. It bothered me how green the soldiers were. Greer and I had worried we would stand out as the inexperienced, but instead, we were promoted to Sergeants the first day. And by the end of the week, George Washington had approved my promotion to Sergeant Major.

Greer, Madeline, Roxy and I met away from the house behind a sand hill the night after I was promoted. I felt like we needed to come up with some boundaries.

"We need to promise right here and now that we will do whatever it takes to preserve history," I said, staring out over the water as a humid summer breeze blew against my face, bringing with it a fine mist of sea water.

"You're the one getting promoted twice in the first week," Roxy said, watching me pace. "You'd think you were some kind of born leader."

"Or the son of a tyrant." I shook my head. "I don't know why people keep trying to put me in charge. You'd think I would have lost that right by default."

"You're good at it," Madeline insisted.

Greer nodded as well. "You gotta own up to the fact that you have leadership skills, Gov. No matter where you go, people are going to notice it. These troops are about as green as they come. Most of them are just boys, but you know how to motivate them to learn fast. It makes sense you would stick out."

"Except that we're trying to blend in," I reminded him.

Roxy sat on a fallen tree trunk, her arms crossing her chest. "History says these colonies won in spite of themselves. They weren't as experienced or organized as the British army. They just had the heart and vision to give it everything they had. You play on that strength as their leader, so you will only help."

I considered her words. She was quiet for a moment before she continued. "We need to worry about Leona and Joe. I'm pretty sure they aren't committed to saving history."

"We should write down our goals," I lifted the sleeve of my shirt to uncover my WristCom, which I had finally got working again. I powered it and projected a small notepad function onto the night air.

"How are you charging it?" Roxy let her fingers fall under the light.

"Levi invented solar tech that is built into devices like our WristComs," Greer said, tapping his own com. "These babies power themselves no matter where we go."

"Sounds like a smart thing to invent." Roxy said, and for a moment it almost felt like she was proud of me.

I speed-texted two entries.

1. DO NOT CHANGE HISTORY.
2. FIND LEONA AND JOE.

"We need a power source to get us back, unless we want to become permanent residents of 1776," Greer said.

I was overwhelmed at the thought. We had barely made it out of 1874 with a portal and a primitive solar-powered machine to generate power. We had nothing here. The area of the portal was a swampy marshland surrounded by sand hills and vegetation.

But then my eyes fell on Roxy. Roxy, who had held the portal open by the force of her will.

I dismissed the idea as quickly as it came to me, even though she was willing to try.

You're not strong enough to even consider it.

"We'll think of something," Madeline said as I wrote the next entry.

3. FIND A POWER SOURCE TO GET HOME.

"Why do you think the portal sent us here?" Roxy asked, her brows drawn together thoughtfully.

I considered her question. "You're asking if it was really just a malfunction?"

She shrugged, waiting for my answer. I shook my head.

"I don't know. But remember how we got home from 1874? How I said quantum entanglement would make the future want us back, and grab us from the wormhole if we went back through?"

"Seems you were right," Greer said. Roxy nodded and Madeline watched me with interest.

"Well, I think it's the same principle, but reversed. I think the portal sent us where we needed to go."

"So you believe we're supposed to be here?" Madeline asked.

I took my time answering, because there was a part of me that wasn't sure. "I think we are. But I couldn't guess why."

Not long after I was promoted, we changed locations. The men told me that Washington moved around quite a bit. From a military perspective, it made sense. We'd be easier to pin down if we had one set location of operation, especially since our company and larger regiment had the Commander-In-Chief in attendance.

We moved from the Richmond Hill location to Battery Park, the heart of the oldest part of town. A man named Archibald Kennedy had a large home in the fashionable, high society area on the corner of Reade Street. The river flowed close to the narrow, cobblestone street, and every window of the large townhouse had a view of the landscapes.

If I thought the outside of the house was impressive, the inside was more so. I listened to Roxy's mind. It was one cool thing about having an in to a girl's mind. Roxy thought about the details I never noticed.

The palatial doorway opens into a long hall with a regal stairway, and marble tiled floors gleam from the entry back to the kitchens, where servants are making dinner. A large dining hall takes up the entire right wing of the house. It has several tables joined together that could easily seat fifty people or more. Rich green draperies and patterned wallpaper blend well with walnut furnishings. There's a parlor and ball room on the other side of the hall with many chairs and settees, tables and an ornate harpsichord.

Leona would love this, I thought. I felt Roxy's eyes on me but I didn't look at her.

We followed the housekeeper up the steps where a drawing room covered the length of the home. A group of bedrooms adjoined either side. I noticed that General Washington went to the right. Roxy and I were shown a small bedroom in the front left portion of the house, and Madeline was again given the room next to ours.

"Home sweet home." Roxy trailed a finger along the edge of the dresser and sat down on the bed, thinking something about the red brocade fabric.

I closed the door and jumped onto the bed, kicking off my boots and throwing my hat across the room where it landed on a stiff chair. I put my hands behind my head and sighed, closing my eyes. "This place is too formal."

"And your home isn't?" Roxy scoffed.

"I didn't decorate the citadel."

Roxy didn't answer. She went to the open window and looked out. A warm breeze blew stray tendrils of her hair across her shoulder, making me wish I was kissing it.

She frowned.

"If you don't like my thoughts, don't listen," I retorted. I wished I could pretend I was asleep while I watched her. "Are you mad that we're sharing a room again?"

She shrugged.

"They'd think it was strange if a husband and wife didn't want to stay together, wouldn't they? And if I had told them we weren't married there would be no reason for you to stay here at all. You'd probably get sent to a farm in Ohio."

She sighed. "I don't care that you told them we were married."

I waited for her to continue, but she went quiet again.

At dinner, Madeline was seated across from Roxy and me, near the end where George Washington sat, with his wife on his right. Other top officials were scattered around him. As I scanned the group of officers, suddenly Roxy grabbed my arm and squeezed, making me wince in pain.

Ouch! Why can't you just talk to me like a normal person? What?

She shot a directive look toward the arched doorway of the dining room. *Do you realize who just walked in?*

I eyed the tall, arguably good-looking soldier who had entered. *I'm guessing he's someone you recognize?*

I took another look at the guy. He was dressed in a crisp new uniform, and couldn't be more than twenty years old. I noticed that everyone covertly stared at him. I wasn't sure I wanted to know why Roxy thought he was so special. I narrowed my eyes and gave her a mock pout.

Don't flatter yourself, she thought. *That's Nathan Hale, you idiot!*

I looked back at him and tried to remember why his name sounded familiar. "Old boyfriend?" I whispered, and then tried to escape her fingers when she reached over to pinch me.

"Remember the book I was reading? About Nathan Hale during the Revolutionary War?" She gave up her attempted assault.

Then I remembered. She had told me the story of her hero who was executed as a spy. She'd told me the night in the snowstorm. The night we …

She poked me in the ribs with her elbow. *Do I need to remind you that your brain is an open book? I'm going to talk to him.*

I was going to let her go, but as soon as she stood, heading in his direction, we started getting looks of disapproval. I caught her hand. *I don't think you're supposed to just get up and go talk to some guy, Roxy. There are rules.*

She shot me a doubtful look. *Why in the world would anyone have a problem with me talking to him in a roomful of people?*

Because you're my wife. Everyone here would think you were being disrespectful.

Disrespectful to whom?

I shrugged. *To your husband.*

She rolled her eyes and shook off my hand. *Then it's a good thing I don't have a husband.*

I grabbed her hand and pulled her back down. *Come on, Roxy. We both know better than that.*

It definitely wasn't what I meant to think. I was going to tell her we had to be low-profile, so she had to pretend to have the same ideals as the people we were living with. But instead, all I could do is claim her like a piece of land.

A few hours in a tent together doesn't mean you own me, Levi.

I never said I owned you. How about I just introduce us to Hale?

Don't do me any favors, mudsill.

She stared at me for a long moment before she sat back down and went completely silent for the rest of the meal.

I noticed she didn't eat, either. I hadn't seen her eat more than a few bites at a time since we'd arrived in 1776. I looked at my plate of overcooked, gamey turkey and limp brown vegetables in a sauce so rich it felt like swallowing a stick of butter. I figured I couldn't really blame her for her lack of appetite. But I also couldn't ignore the clawing suspicion on the inside of my brain that something was wrong with her.

George Washington carried on a lively conversation with the lieutenant and captain of the company, but I noticed he also watched us. Was he suspicious? Did he wonder why we pushed the food around on our plates? Did he know we were not who we said we were—that we were not from Ohio and we weren't married, but we were time travelers from a New York so far in the distant future few traces of this time remained?

He couldn't know. He couldn't know he was risking everything for a city that would fall. If he knew, he might lose the will to pursue it, and everything would be much, much worse.

In the time it took me to make a pact with myself to protect the general from all knowledge of the future, I realized Roxy had slipped out of her chair. She stood near the doorway. Carrying on a conversation with the soldier, Hale.

The really good-looking soldier, Hale.

If Roxy ever listened to a word I said it would be a miracle and I'd probably die of shock.

I moved to join their conversation as everyone in the room probably expected me to do. But as I approached, Roxy suddenly covered her mouth and ran to the door.

I was left alone with the man I was presently convinced was trying to steal the love of my life. We both listened in awkward silence to said love of my life puking over the side of the front porch.

"Excuse me," I managed before I left Nathan Hale without

introducing myself.

Roxy was turning around to come back inside by the time I reached her. I started to follow, but I caught sight of a group of formally dressed men marching around the curve of the street corner. They were headed our way.

"Sir," a man in British uniform spoke to me without sparing Roxy a glance. "Colonel Patterson. We are on the errand of the King. Is a Mr. George Washington available, please?"

It sounded more like a demand than a question. I put an arm around Roxy's shoulders and pulled her inside. I didn't want us getting in the way if this was an important meeting. I went to summon General Washington.

In the dining room, Washington eyed the men waiting in the doorway while I explained. Without a word, he stood up and straightened his uniform. He walked toward the group with our company looking on.

"You are George Washington, I presume? I am Colonel Patterson of the British, Adjutant-General to Lord Howe." He cleared his throat and presented the letter. "Lord Howe wishes to reach an understanding between the crown and the colonies."

General Washington stared uneasily at the outstretched letter. Everything in me said he shouldn't accept it. I wouldn't. I wouldn't even touch it. I'd think up any excuse. They were clearly trying to undermine him.

Apparently Washington agreed with my silent advice. He smiled politely as he glanced at the letter but did not reach for it. I saw the flourish of calligraphy across the front.

George Washington, Esquire, etc., etc., etc.

Patterson smiled uneasily, still holding out the unclaimed letter. "The three et ceteras might mean everything," he said.

"Surely." Washington folded his arms across his chest. "Unfortunately, I am in my official capacity. My men have joined me for dinner and we have many a fair lady among us. You understand I can only receive letters officially addressed."

Patterson's hand fell back to his side, and he barely kept the icy smile on his face. "Lord and General Howe request that you relinquish your command."

"I don't suppose a red-headed woman had anything to do with that request," I muttered. Patterson glanced at me like I was an annoying mosquito buzzing around his head.

Washington folded his hands behind his back. "My compliments to both."

After another awkward silence, Patterson motioned to the soldiers behind him. "I will give your compliments to their rightful recipients."

"Give them to Leona, too," I said. As the men filed out, Washington gave me a curious expression.

"That was ... polite," I said.

"More polite than interesting," he replied with a frown, but I saw a flash of humor behind the expression. I chuckled.

"Mrs. Thompson," Washington called the housekeeper. "I do believe the young people are in need of an evening of dancing. Have the servants clear away the furniture and send someone for musicians immediately."

A flurry of activity followed his words.

SIXTEEN

The servants didn't seem surprised by the order. They moved all the furniture out of the ballroom. Soldiers with musical instruments crowded into a corner and began to practice as the few women excused themselves to change into more formal attire.

"Go put on your ball gowns, girls. There are extras in the closet in my bedroom if you are lacking." Martha Washington put an arm around Roxy and Madeline and gave their shoulders a friendly squeeze.

"Thank you, Mrs. Washington," Madeline said politely.

Roxy frowned. "What's wrong with the dress I'm wearing?"

I shrugged. When she looked at me, I smiled and gave her a thumbs up.

I took my cue from the other men by putting on my tailcoat and tricorn hat. Most of them put on white wigs. I declined when one was offered to me, poor unfortunate soul that I was not to own one.

When the women returned, the higher ranking officers and their wives began to dance. While I waited for Roxy and Madeline, I finally introduced myself to Nathan Hale.

"Sergeant Koenig," he said as he firmly shook my hand. "I've heard good things about you. Barely enlisted, yet already promoted. You are a rising star, it seems. Captain Nathan Hale."

I nodded. "Pleasure."

His voice went quiet. Confidential. "I spoke to your … to Miss Eisen briefly at dinner. She explained how the two of you were posing as a married couple so she would not be sent back to Ohio by herself."

"She said that?" I sighed. Apparently it was important for Hale to know Roxy was single. Important enough to risk our cover.

"These are times when not everything can be as it seems. I will keep your secret," Hale promised.

"Thank you."

"She is beautiful," he said, then coughed like he wished he could take it back. He hurried on. "And so committed to her beliefs. A champion of freedom. She is different than other girls I have known."

"There's nobody quite like Roxy," I said, trying not to sound morose. I didn't add that Nathan and Roxy were very much alike.

"You love her, then."

"I do." I stood up taller and made sure he knew I meant he should stay away from her. Besides, how could I let Roxy get close to another guy? I knew from personal experience she was hard to lose. Hadn't Joe tried to kill her because he couldn't have her?

Nathan and I chatted about the war effort for a few minutes before he went to speak to General Washington. I watched them with curiosity. Were they discussing the spy mission? I didn't know my history well enough to be sure of the timing. I wondered how Roxy would handle it when it happened. Would she stand by and let it happen?

We have to stand by and let it happen.

It was a good enough reason for all of us to keep our distance from Nathan. But even I had to admit, he was easy to like.

When Roxy and Madeline came into the room, I noticed Madeline first. In fact, every male in the room noticed Madeline. Several guys started toward her, but Nathan got to her first. He held out his hand and bowed, inviting her to dance. As she moved out of the way, led by Nathan to the dance floor, I saw Roxy.

She had allowed someone, perhaps Madeline, to pull her hair

up in curls, decorated with a jeweled headband. It got my attention because she obsessed about it and tried to adjust it. It was a conservative hairstyle compared to the other women in the room, who seemed determined to outdo one another with powdered wigs heaped a few inches tall on top of their heads.

I didn't notice any other details other than she looked amazing. Her uncertainty and pink cheeks only made her more attractive. I crossed to her, held out my hand and bowed like I'd seen Nathan do.

"Do we know this dance?" She stared at the dance floor full of swishing skirts and buckled shoes. It reminded me of the first time we had danced, at Leona's ball. The night she had seen the portal chamber for the first time. It seemed a lifetime ago. She'd looked amazing that night, too.

I caught her attention with my thoughts, and I saw a flash of vulnerability as she took my offered hand.

"I can pull it off," I assured her. "I'm not going to get to touch you any other way."

She rolled her eyes so she wouldn't smile.

I grabbed her waist and pulled her out into the dancers. "They aren't going to kick us out of 1776 for improper dance etiquette."

"You never know."

She tripped over her shoes but I held her steady. We twirled around the room while she fretted.

"I hate these dumb slippers we have to wear. How in the world did they expect women to move around in these things? I need my boots."

"You can't wear boots with that dress." I earned a smile for my appreciate glance.

"I bet Nathan wouldn't mind." She watched him across the room as he laughed at something Madeline said.

"Are you trying to make me jealous?"

She shrugged in what seemed an awful lot like a flirty glance.

"Careful, Eisen. You smile too much and I'm going to have to kiss you."

"Careful, Koenig. You don't control yourself and I'm going to have to punch you."

I laughed and she sighed, but her thoughts didn't seem so against the idea. Maybe I could sneak her outside. Or in a closet. It made me grin like an idiot when she raised an eyebrow in response.

I managed to keep us both upright and follow the other dancers. I considered it one small advantage to being Leona's son. I knew how to fake regality.

Nathan asked me if he could dance with Roxy, so she left me standing next to Madeline. I wondered if I was supposed to dance with her. I went to the refreshment table and grabbed two glasses of wine. Was Madeline disappointed I didn't ask? I didn't know for sure because I couldn't read her mind.

I *could* read Roxy's, and her thoughts were decidedly *not* in favor of me dancing with Madeline.

"So are you having a good time?" I took a chug of my wine.

She sipped from her own glass and nodded.

"You look really nice." I choked over the words while I tried to avoid Roxy's glare from across the room.

You are the one dancing with another guy. Am I supposed to stare at the wall? I have to say something.

Do whatever you want, mudsill. What do I care?

I sighed in frustration.

"What's wrong?" Madeline asked.

I took a longer gulp of the tart wine. "Nothing that would make sense if I tried to explain."

She followed my gaze out to the dance floor. "I think I can imagine."

Had I hurt her feelings? "I'm sorry, Madeline."

She shook her head. "Don't be sorry. You never made your feelings for Roxy a secret. I didn't mean to—" Her voice trailed off in embarrassment.

That was when it occurred to me. Did Madeline … like me?

"Sometimes I wish it were different," I said and looked at her. I couldn't say more. I was surprised I had admitted that much.

Madeline nodded and forced a smile. "Do you think it would be a problem if we danced? She's dancing with Captain Hale, after all."

I had a feeling it would be a problem, but she had a point and suddenly, I felt like a fool. I was free to dance with a pretty girl. I set my wine on the table.

"Would you like to dance?" I bowed and held out my hand. She smiled and set down her glass, taking my hand and following me to the dance floor.

I may have overdone the cheerfulness a little. I wanted to prove to Madeline and the whole room that I was a man and I could make up my own mind about dance partners. I ignored Roxy as if I didn't care that she danced with Nathan a total of three dances. In turn, she refused to talk to me either audibly or with our minds. So I shrugged and held Madeline a little closer.

I let my reservations go and lived it up for two more dances, until Nathan suddenly returned Roxy and swept Madeline away once again.

My confidence disappeared.

"Hey, beautiful. How's it going?" I tried to break the ice. And it was definitely icy. Downright polar.

"Did you enjoy your little dance?" she said sarcastically, as if she was asking if I enjoyed my life because now I was going to die.

"I suppose. Did you enjoy yours?" I braced for whatever she had planned for my sorry soul. To my surprised, she let it go.

"These clothes are making me sweaty," she said with a huff. "And they obviously don't have deodorant here."

I tried to cover a laugh with a cough. She narrowed her eyes at me. "You asked."

"All aces, Roxy."

"Why do we always have to time travel in the summer? We could at least go somewhere with climate controlled houses." She covertly lifted her arm and sniffed. "Do I smell?"

I snaked my arm around her waist and pulled her close to me, leaning in and taking a lingering deep breath near her neck.

"You smell pretty good to me," I said, knowing very well I was pushing my luck. "Do you really think you're going to smell worse than all the hot, sweaty guys in the room?"

She wrinkled her nose and didn't move away from me. In fact, she leaned into me a little. "You do kind of smell."

"So you're saying I'm hot, then?"

She scoffed.

"You know, Roxy, some girls do think I'm hot."

I expected her to play along, but she stopped smiling and looked away. I searched for her thoughts but she had closed them off. It wasn't fair. She knew everything I thought, but I wasn't allowed to see what she didn't want me to know.

She shook her head and looked at me, miserable. And I had that bad feeling again.

The dancing and socializing went on into the early hours of the morning. I began to wonder if we were still going to have to be present for military drills. In fact, it seemed odd to be part of the animated and cheerful setting, knowing we were all fighting such a dangerous battle.

Maybe it was how they coped.

SEVENTEEN

"Sergeant Koenig, please have a seat."

George Washington was offering me a seat in his private room. George Washington—the guy on the front of the quarter in my antique coin collection—wanted to talk to *me*.

I'd been nervous since breakfast at dawn, when the general had politely informed me he wanted to speak to me after morning exercises. I was sure I was going to screw everything up. What if I tripped over a piece of furniture and accidentally kicked a log by the fireplace that hit him in the head and killed him and thereby broke America before it ever got started?

I sat down on the chair opposite him and tried not to make any sudden moves.

"Sergeant, I am most appreciative of your assistance the past few weeks."

"It's my honor."

He nodded, looking up from his desk where he was drawing a map. "Forgive me my curiosity, son, but tell me how you and your wife came to be in New York."

I knew instantly he was on to me. He might not realize I was the leader of New York three hundred years in the future, but he knew my story was a cover. I stared at my feet while I came up with something to say.

"I … we …" I tried to remember what I had told him before.

"Are you a spy, Mr. Koenig?" He turned away from his desk and frowned at me.

"Absolutely not, sir," I said as I looked him in the eye. "I did not mean to come here. It was an accident."

He sat back, confusion clouding his features. "Then why are you still here?"

"Because there was a complication, and I can't leave until I know it's been dealt with." I sighed, thinking of my mother standing at the bow of that ship the day we came through the portal.

"You have a strange way of speaking that I'm having difficulty placing." Washington tapped his fingers on the table, as if counting down the moments until he turned me over to the firing squad. Or however they dealt with traitors in eighteenth century America.

"I suppose you wouldn't believe me if I said I really am from New York City," I said.

He shook his head, crossing his arms. I searched for the right words. Was there a way to avoid saying too much?

"I suggest honesty, lad. It may seem better to concoct a story, but in the end it only causes more trouble."

I nodded, agreeing with him. I took a deep breath and stared at my folded hands in my lap. "Well, sir," I began. "I'm not sure you're going to accept the truth, because it's really weird."

"Weird?"

"Strange."

"I am your captive audience." He gestured for me to go on.

I hoped he was as progressive a man as history made him out to be. Because I decided there was no way to keep him safe except to reveal everything.

"Sir, it is a great honor for me to meet you. I know who you are, because I have heard about you from books, monuments, and art that my mother hid in the archives below the streets of her palace in midtown Manhattan."

He stared at me as if I had suddenly grown an extra head and started juggling it in the air. He gave a short laugh of disbelief. "I beg your pardon …"

I shrugged. "I'm the son of Regal Manager Leona, who took over New York City during dark days in your future when the country had started to come apart. I came here from the year 2076."

His face, the original to all the depictions I'd seen in my life, went pale. He was more to me than an image on canvas now—he was a living human being. A man who spoke solemn-faced jokes. Who argued with his wife behind closed doors and stole pastries from the kitchen between meals. He was just a guy, like me, trying to lead people through a difficult transition.

To his credit, Washington hadn't thrown me out of the house yet. So I decided to explain. "My friends Madeline, Greer and Roxy—"

He frowned. "Not your wife?"

I searched for the right words. "I love her, sir, but she is not legally my wife in any time."

He sighed and signaled me to continue.

"Roxy dethroned my mother, and the city made me the governor in her place. But she got away. You see, we have a portal, and the portal has a wormhole to the past, and—"

"Man, what are you saying?" Washington stood up and stumbled backward, holding the back of his chair. "Speak the king's English, son."

I nodded, swallowing hard. "A star was dying, and it started to pull the earth … too far away from the sun. We would have all died. Roxy's mom and mine found a way to fix it, but at the same time, it gave us the power to travel through a hole in reality. It brought us back in time to you. My mother came here to escape her trial, and I had to stop her before she destroyed your destiny. Our past."

Silence was his only response for a long moment. I was sure he would put me in custody, maybe on the grounds of lunacy. But finally he spoke, and his words were even and quiet. "Do you know where your mother is?"

I nodded. "I saw her on the ship with General Howe."

"My enemy," he said in a thoughtful, quiet tone.

"So you see my problem," I said. "I can't let her interfere here, or our country will never have a chance at freedom. There won't be anything for us to save."

He stared long at me as if he was summoning his nerve. "Is there a chance at freedom, son of the future?"

I quickly answered. "More than a chance, sir. Freedom will happen."

He seemed lighter, as if I'd given him hope he wasn't sure existed. Maybe it was the only reason he chose to believe my story—because he needed a reason to keep fighting.

He sat back down. "We do not bear this sword in vain."

"You don't, General," I assured him. "But you might if I can't stop Leona."

He tapped his fingers absently on the desk.

I had to ask the question. "Do you really believe me?"

His expression remained even. "I am acting upon the knowledge that you must be one of two things. You are mad, and I am humoring you as a gentleman, or you are right, and I have impossible insight into a war that otherwise will be a dismal failure."

Late that night, a storm hit with a vengeance. Thunder crashed, rattling the window pane and waking me up. I sat up, my eyes falling on Roxy's form in the bed. She stirred, but she didn't open her eyes.

I looked out the window just as the wind started to pick up. Leaves beginning to show signs of autumn's approach flew madly in circles. A steady spray of rain began to hit the window.

"What's happening?" Roxy sat up, staring at me with groggy eyes. I heard her mind wonder if the crashes had been cannon fire.

"It's okay. Just a storm."

She came to my couch and sat beside me. We watched as nature took command, unleashing its fury on the sleeping city.

"I talked to Washington last night. I told him the truth."

She didn't speak or react in her thoughts, but I felt her look at me.

"I didn't know what else to do. I'm losing control of everything, Roxy."

Neither of us said it aloud, but we thought of the storm as an omen. Tension hung heavy in the city, and the storm communicated it well. It warned of the final result of the strain created by opposing viewpoints. At some point, all the pieces would be in play, and there would be bloodshed.

It was an inevitable truth, and it would happen soon.

Roxy suddenly slid her arms around me and leaned against my chest. I wrapped my arms around her. Neither of us said a word. We fell asleep listening to the anger of the storm as we took solace in each other.

Maybe that was the only way to face a war.

The next morning dawned wet with an ominous kind of silence. We went through the motions of chores and breakfast and exercises, playing blind to reality. I felt it more than most, because I had a limited ability to see into the future.

I knew the day would be full of meetings. Washington had asked me to sit in on them. I didn't exactly like the idea. I didn't want to be responsible for history. I was determined not to react or speak. I thought it would be better for me if I could read the minds of the men around me, but I hated asking Roxy to use her ability to help me.

"I'm coming with you," she made the decision easy by answering my thoughts. She had been in the army camp collecting bedding at the request of Mrs. Thompson. I had, of course, been following her around as I ate my lunch, enjoying the envious expressions of the other soldiers.

She stopped by a cot to pick up a musket and examine it. "But don't let me say anything stupid, either. You know how well I fit in."

I smiled. "You fit here." I pulled her hand to my chest, over my heart. I thought it was a beautiful sentiment and I expected her lip to quiver or a tear to shine in the corner of her eye.

Instead, she scoffed. Loudly. And made a gagging sound as she dropped my hand and walked away.

Nothing like a little rejection to get the afternoon off to a fine start.

I gulped the rest of my coffee and followed her to the house. We dropped off the laundry in the back yard and went inside. The parlor table was covered with maps and documents. Uniformed men gathered around, some sitting, some standing or pacing. They looked down their nose at Roxy, obviously miffed Washington had allowed her in. Roxy ignored them and plopped down in her chair.

There was one pair of eyes that showed no disapproval. Captain Hale gathered up his pile of papers and moved to Roxy's other side.

I had a lowly position in the army compared to the men around me, but General Washington seemed to fixate on me. He asked me several times for my opinion. I didn't have to read Roxy's mind to know the other men in the room wondered why he cared so much what I thought.

I tried my best to be vague and cliché. I hadn't considered the problem of anyone believing the truth about us and where we were from. But I understood. If our roles were reversed, with so much riding on my actions and decisions, wouldn't I do the same?

After a few hours of listening through Roxy's mind, I noticed she was having trouble. She held her fingers to her temple and squeezed her eyes shut, leaning forward over the table. I leaned forward with her.

Are you okay?

EIGHTEEN

"What's wrong?" I whispered, causing several of the men to look our way.

She shrugged and tried to sit back and act like she was fine. I felt the veil go down around her thoughts, too.

You can tell me.

I caught her hand and squeezed it under the table.

Aren't you worried about impropriety?

I'm more worried about being too involved in this fight.

Things had to go the way history had already dictated. Even if it meant losing Manhattan to the British. Even if it meant they would be in danger, and many of them would die.

I held her hand more tightly. It would be handy if there was a rule book on time travel.

Roxy watched me. *What makes you think it would go any better for them if they listened to your ideas?* She gave me a tired smile. I stared at her, really wishing I could kiss her.

Her eyes left my face and wandered around the room. Everyone had gone silent.

"Sergeant Koenig, would you like us to leave the room so you might have a moment alone with your *wife*?" He frowned, but I saw humor in his eyes.

"I'm sorry, General. I got distracted by how pretty she is."

Roxy made a face as titters of laughter went around the room.

General Washington leaned over a map he was holding open and sighed heavily. "Carry on, Mr. Koenig. Heaven knows I would be doing the same if Mrs. Washington were here."

Everyone laughed and I raised an eyebrow at Roxy.

Mudsill.

The men around us returned to the zone with battle planning while I watched Roxy. *Look who's talking to me again.*

I never said I wasn't talking to you.

You haven't been as free with your thought-sharing since you learned how to put up your mind wall.

My mind wall? She smiled. I went back to pretending to write out letters like I was supposed to be doing. But I kept glancing at her. When she thought I wasn't looking, she winced and pressed a finger to her temple.

Does your head hurt? Please tell me, Roxy.

She wanted to let go. Her resolve faltered and I felt the veil between our minds fall. Her emotions flooded into my mind. Trying to be strong. Taking it without complaining. Not wanting to bother me because she knew how important it was that history be intact and we get back to our own battles.

It's not complaining to tell me what's wrong. Maybe I can help.

She had another long moment of indecision before she gave up. *It hurts. Being in the same room as people. I guess learning to control my power comes at a cost.*

How does it hurt?

Headaches, mostly.

She wasn't going to give me information easily. I pressed. *How bad?*

She tried to reinstate the veil between our minds, but it was too painful. She sighed. *Bad. They keep me awake. They make me sick to my stomach.*

It troubled me. And it made sense in a way, as well. When I used my healing powers without thinking about the consequences, I could get so weak I almost passed out. Theoretically, though we couldn't know for sure unless it happened, our powers could kill us if we weren't careful.

Maybe you should see a doctor. Just to make sure it isn't something easy to treat.

So they can bleed me? She shook her head. *No modern medicine here.*

She had a point. A doctor might insist upon a bloodletting. I shrugged. *Who knows, maybe you'd get the leeches.*

She tried to pinch me but I moved out of her reach.

It frustrated me that our time had modern remedies for headaches that cured them almost immediately.

Just stop worrying about me, okay?

I don't know how to do that.

The news that the British had attacked came early the morning of August 27. I didn't wake Roxy. She would be mad at me for going with the army. But what else could I do? To not fight by their side was treason. For better or worse, I was part of the colonial army and I had a job to do. I kissed her forehead and left the room before dawn fully broke over the eastern horizon.

The soldiers made a somber group, even if pride ran as a current beneath everything the army did. These men would follow Washington wherever he led, and they'd consider it an honor to die under his command.

I couldn't blame them, because I would, as well.

He rode his horse a short way up the hill so we could see him. His long legs extended regally into the stirrups; his arms held the reigns at an angle mid-air. His mouth was set firmly in a line indicating his wish that his men would be okay.

But we all knew better. Today we would put it all on the line. We had to be willing to sacrifice everything.

"The fate of unborn millions," he said, looking directly at me for a moment, "will now depend, under God, on the courage of this army. Our enemy leaves us only the choices of resistance or submission. We have to resolve to conquer ... or die."

There was silence following his statement. I looked around and saw brave young men given one life in a time that demanded their willingness to lose it. I saw their chins in the air and their eyes alive with burning desire for their country to be free.

They reminded me of Roxy. She was one of them. She would give anything she had, including her own life, without a second thought, if it meant setting someone free.

NINETEEN

I leaned on my gun, staring at the back of the soldier in front of me, eyeing the position of the sun as it shone over the East River and Flatbush where we were engaged in battle.

At least we were supposed to be.

My idea of war was automatic laser weapons, heat sensors and gamma ray rifles, all firing at once. In army camp, as an 11-year-old, and in my special training with a military strategist, I'd been taught to avoid the attack of at least three combatants the same time I hit three more.

In comparison, the fighting style of the past seemed leisurely. For reasons I couldn't figure out, it was downright polite. We made formation, marched and unloaded weapons row by row. As a sergeant, I stood to the right of my row and made sure they stayed in line. I followed the orders of the company captain in front of me. And it was this duty alone that kept me from falling asleep.

If I couldn't look across the field and see plenty of bloody corpses minus body parts, I'd expect us all to take a break together for tea and biscuits.

When it was finally my turn to fire my weapon, I felt dissatisfied with the gun. It felt inconsistent. Finicky. Sometimes it did what I wanted it to do, sometimes it didn't. I had my laser pistol on my belt, hidden under my coat. If I had to, I would use it to save

Greer or Washington.

When the captain called the order, I repeated it loudly, and we fired. I shot the musket, sending a lead ball straight into the heart of a British soldier who was still lifting his weapon to his shoulder.

"Do you ever miss?" the boy to my left, a youngster named David, said under his breath.

I shrugged. "When my gun decides not to fire."

We moved on, stepping over dead or dying bodies to pursue the enemy. I watched for signs of my mother when we passed the British camp.

I also watched for Greer. I hadn't seen him that day. I searched the faces of the wounded and the dead, hoping I wouldn't see his.

Even at the slow pace, or maybe because of it, it was easy to feel exhausted at the end of a long day. But it wasn't just physical. I had a hard time fighting battles I was pretty sure we were destined to lose.

By the end of the day they had us cornered by the river. I wished we would just surrender and go home. It seemed inevitable. But General Washington stayed till the end. He came up with spur of the moment strategies to keep the battle going. Only at the last possible moment did he direct the remainder of the men to get in the boats and head back to Manhattan.

Two days later, as we retreated across Manhattan on foot, I happened to look down and notice my hands were glowing.

I quickly hid them under my sleeves, but I could still see the bluish light, so I told the company captain I was taking a break. I stepped out of formation and let the rest of the lines pass as I tried to get my bearings and figure out where we were in the city.

"It's the portal. It knows we're here."

I whirled around at the familiar voice. "What do you think you're doing, Leona?" I stared into my mother's intelligent, lovely, but icy cold eyes. She leaned against a tree at the edge of the forest.

"Don't you feel it?" She folded her hands in front of her and approached me. "The portal is waking up. It knows I'm here and wants me back."

I stared at her, unable to speak. How could this woman be a mother? It was against the nature of motherhood—to be completely self-absorbed.

She smiled and grabbed my arm.

"What do you think you're doing?" I jerked away from her touch. "What kind of sick satisfaction can you possibly get by ruining history?"

"I only went through the portal in the first place because *your* Roxy tried to kill me," she said in a huff. "And I'm not ruining anything. I call it an adjustment."

"I think most would disagree." I turned away from her in disgust.

"Why are you hiding your hands?" She followed me. I could guess she already knew why. She reached for my hand and examined it, smiling. "I remember when you used to cure my headaches.

I pulled my hand away. "I should never have helped you."

She pouted, her eyes still on my hands. "What a thing to say."

"I'm not healing you now. Forget it."

"Did I ask you to heal me?" She responded in a tone that told me it would have been her next question. She cleared her throat. "Where's Roxy? I'd expect her to be out here fighting beside you. Maybe she's not as tough as she wants everyone to think."

"She's safe. You will *never* hurt her again."

She stared at me in disbelief. "As if I would ever hurt the child of my best friend and the one my son loves. I said it before, *she* was after *me*."

She was offended. She was actually offended.

"You *have* hurt her, plenty of times," I said with a loud sigh. "Just tell me what you are doing. With the British. And just because I'm not pointing this gun at you doesn't mean I won't."

She scowled. "The Howe brothers are dears. Really—dears. Both of them. They have been kind to me, taking me in after I told them I was their lost sister. They listen to me, Levi. It's validating."

I scoffed. "You've been forcing people to listen to you your entire life. People are tired of listening to you. You have to know tyrants get what they deserve eventually."

"Is that a threat?" She tilted her head to the side, her voice unnaturally calm. "Remember, I have allies in high places. Your George Washington and his band of ragged children and farmers may have won this war in the history you think you know, but now that the Howes have me, the rebels don't stand a chance. *You* don't stand a chance. And don't think I won't run you over, you and Roxy both, to get what I *deserve*."

I gave a harsh laugh. "There's no doubt in my mind you would. And it's really, really sad for you."

Her sweetest smile returned to her face, lighting up her features in a way that would make her beautiful if it weren't for the darkness that oozed out of every pore. "Just stay out of my way and you'll be fine. I have plans, Levi, and they're already in motion."

She started to leave, but she hesitated. "If you try to interfere, I won't go after you. I will head straight for Roxy."

She gave a final, wistful glance to the spot that would one day become her citadel and portal. Then she abruptly left.

The weapon burned as I gripped it. Why didn't I just raise it to my shoulder and end the threat? I could almost hear Roxy's voice, asking me why in all the worlds I hadn't already done it.

When I found the courage to point the gun at her back, she turned around. She folded her hands in front of her and stared at me. She didn't say a word.

Blinding pain filled my head and knocked me to my knees.

"Stay out of it. Consider this your final warning."

She disappeared into the brush.

The battle finally ended. Too many American men lay dead or dying, and too many more were British prisoners. I was dragging when I turned the corner on Reade Street. But it called to me as if it was home. Roxy was there.

The house was quiet. I searched for her downstairs, but found

Madeline instead. She sat in the parlor, drinking tea with Nathan Hale, who apparently had time to bathe and change into clean clothes.

"Levi!" Madeline's relieved tone surprised me. Up to that point, she had been mostly reserved around me, except when she was around electricity. "We were worried! Especially after Nathan told us about the battle."

It was nice to have someone worry about me. I took in the sight of her, a pleasant contrast to muddy, bleeding soldiers. Before I realized it, I was reaching for her hand and squeezing it.

Madeline squeezed back instead of pulling her hand away and calling me a mudsill. She smelled like flowers, a welcome change from the smell of gunpowder and death. I let her hand linger in mine and smiled into her pretty eyes.

Nathan cleared his throat loudly. I had to give him credit for trying to warn me. But I missed it, so when I felt the push from behind, I wasn't prepared for it and went careening into the staircase, trying not to crush Madeline at the same time.

"You *mudsill!*"

I honestly believed Roxy was attacking me for holding Madeline's hand and gawking at her. Madeline probably thought the same. We were wrong.

"What were you thinking? You don't walk off into battle without telling someone where you're going! How was I supposed to know what happened to you? As far as I have known, you've been dead for days!"

I stared at her as if she was a creature from another planet. That was how well I seemed to understand her, even having had the ongoing invitation to live in her mind. She loomed over me as I was sprawled on the floor, wrath oozing from her mind like lava flowing down the side of a mountain and destroying everything in its path.

Would it have made me less of a man to admit I was a little scared of her?

"Roxy, if I'd told you, you would have insisted on going with me." I stood up and brushed off my jacket, until I remembered I'd been in battle for three days and I was already a mess.

Nathan and Madeline both shifted uncomfortably, like they thought we should take our problems somewhere private. I tried to direct Roxy to the stairs, but she jerked away from me.

"Don't ever touch me again!"

Then something happened I didn't expect to ever see. Roxy Eisen started crying.

She turned and ran before any of us could respond. I glanced at Nathan and Madeline.

"Did something happen while I was gone?" There had to be an explanation. Because all the reasons my brain could fathom for Roxy crying were bad scenarios.

Madeline glanced up the stairs after Roxy. "I haven't even seen her apart from mealtime. She's been either in her room or out in the back working with the servants making bandages for the wounded."

"Forgive my intrusion, but I must say that emotional reactions are not unheard of in the fairer sex," Nathan said, giving Madeline an apologetic smile. "In my own experience, that is."

"You don't know Roxy," I said, trying not to take satisfaction in that fact.

"You are correct," he agreed. "I have talked to her, though, and found her highly intelligent, with an undeniable strength of character."

"That's putting it lightly," I said, my voice softer.

"Yet life can become too much, even for the strongest people." Nathan lifted his shoulders in a slight shrug.

"You should talk to her," Madeline said, looking down at the floor. Her tone sounded sad. "Maybe she'll tell you what it is so you can stop worrying."

I went upstairs.

"Roxy?" I opened the door and peeked inside. She was on the bed, facing the window. Her eyes had been wiped dry and her mouth was set in a line that told me she was done crying. And talking.

"I'm sorry." I sat beside her, looking at her long, graceful arms and bare feet sticking out under her dress. Being close to her always brought back to mind what had happened in the spring. She wore her strength without sacrificing her femininity, a talent that captivated me. In a way, it was harder now than before the blizzard, because I knew exactly what I was missing in not being allowed to hold her. I ached to touch her.

"Don't ever touch me again," she whispered the words again with less conviction.

"I'm sorry I didn't tell you, but I didn't want you to follow me. I just wanted you to be safe. I have to fight, but you don't."

She looked at me. Her brown eyes rimmed in red caught me in the stomach like a sucker punch. "You mean like I wanted you safe?"

I nodded, swallowing my pride. "You're right. I'm sorry."

She didn't respond. Her gaze went back to the swaying tops of the trees that rose from the shore of the Hudson.

"I saw Leona," I told her.

She gave the smallest sigh. "Did she say anything?"

"Only that she's planning on messing with history and defeating George Washington, and if I try to stop her she's coming for you."

"Let her come. I'm not afraid of Leona."

"I'm not going to let her hurt you," I promised.

She scoffed, and then we were quiet again. I felt the silence as an obstacle. With Roxy, there were so many impasses. So many walls. She was a locked door, and it felt like there were so many keys to open her up that it was overwhelming to try.

"I didn't ask you to try."

The mind reading thing didn't help.

"I'm sorry it's so hard to be around me, Levi. You could always go live with the army."

I decided to go for the forbidden territory instead. I went to her and kissed her jaw below her ear. She didn't immediately push me away, and I saw her features soften. She wanted me close. She wanted to be held. I could almost read the thoughts she hid from me. I leaned in closer, kissing along her jawline and across her cheek, heading for her lips. But just as I got there, she moved out of reach.

"I mean it, Levi. I don't want to do that anymore. It just makes everything harder."

Her words weren't harsh. They were desperate, and it looked like it had taken effort to stop me. I could see it in her mind. A wall as high as my ability to see, and something behind it she refused to let me know.

TWENTY

For the next week, most of my time was spent with the general and his army. I wanted to see Roxy, but she avoided me.

I was responsible for preserving the entire history of the country. And when I stopped to consider that, I knew I couldn't obsess over Roxy. No moment in the country's history was more pivotal, and since Leona had kept me from knowing the details about America, I was sketchy on what battles we should be winning. It worried me that so far, we were losing. New York was falling to British control.

The colonies were the underdogs. I knew that much. But I wished I had a way to gauge what was history and what had been changed.

I stewed about it for days. Then one night when I dragged my exhausted body upstairs to sleep for a few hours before we did it all again, I saw that Roxy had left something on the end of the bed before she went to sleep. I picked it up.

"You brought it." I smiled. I held up the book about Nathan Hale Roxy had been reading the night of the snowstorm.

The night of the snowstorm ...

I opened the book and started reading. I read the entire book in one night, and when it was over, I saw Captain Nathan Hale in a new light. He really was a hero. He was polite, kind and popular with the ladies, but he was deeper than I'd given him credit for. He was real.

He was dangerous.

He didn't know what he would do. He didn't realize the extreme measures he would take to give the country a chance at a beginning. And my eyes kept straying to the date that loomed on the page.

September 22, 1776.

We were only a week away.

I didn't see my mother again. I looked for her whenever we were fighting, but she stayed out of sight. That worried me more than if I'd seen her every day.

One evening, General Washington called me to his room. He wanted to discuss a battle strategy he was thinking of trying. As I sat there a second time, I decided I wanted his opinion about Leona.

"What is it, son?" he asked. I must have been frowning.

I shrugged. "What do you do when your own mother forces you to take sides against her?"

He set down his map and folded his arms across his chest. "You are not the only one who has a difficult mother."

"Are you saying you have one, too?"

He nodded slowly.

"Did she take over New York City and punish people by hurling them into the past?"

He raised an eyebrow. "Nothing like that. But she did desperately attempt to take over *my* life. She desired to make my decisions long after I had become a man. I often wondered whether I should be obedient to her even though she humiliated me, or if I should find a way to respectfully go against her wishes."

"What did you decide?" I asked.

"I learned to take each decision as it came. I went along with her when I could, and when my conscience would not allow, I went against her in the most respectful way I could. All the time I wished my father would return from the grave and proclaim me a man who knew his own mind."

"I never knew my father," I said, staring at the burning embers of the log in the fireplace. Sparks crackled up to the chimney. I hadn't allowed myself to think about my father much since I was a young child. When I was little, he was all I thought about. But the disappointment of his absence was too much.

"I believe the measure of a man is in his ability to think as his father would lead him, were he there to do so," Washington said, thoughtful. "Assuming he was a worthy man."

I nodded. "Sometimes I imagine him. I ask him what to do."

"And what does your father say in response?" Washington asked.

I thought about my answer. "I shouldn't say I'll do things just because people want me to do them. I should help people learn to take care of themselves and think for themselves. I should teach them how to make wise decisions by my example instead of trying to control everything they do and say. And I should make people responsible for their actions."

"All excellent points. Your father is a wise man." He clapped his hands together in approval.

"I guess he is," I said with a short laugh.

Washington watched the fire thoughtfully. "*My* father also reminds *me* to remember the value of humility, even as a leader. To be mindful of my imperfection and take refuge from my tyrannical nature in the stability of advisors."

His answer was way better than mine, of course. I started getting the feeling *he* was the father I was getting my advice from.

"Great leaders are also great followers." His words resounded in the room and spoke to the inner part of me where I stored my insecurity. That place started to feel a little smaller. Maybe a little bit healed by the devastation of my father's nonexistence and my mother's craziness. I didn't feel so alone. Washington had lost his father, and his mother was a challenge, and he still managed to become the greatest president of a nation of freedom unlike any the world had ever known. Maybe I could be that sort of leader, too. *Be humble. Listen. Follow.*

George Washington failed to mention how to stay humble when someone was moving in on your woman.

To be fair, Captain Hale was always a gentleman. And even though he knew Roxy and I weren't married, he still kept his distance out of respect. But one evening, while I was in another strategy meeting, staring out the window and trying not to pay attention, I noticed Nathan and Roxy leave the house together.

I was irritated. But big things were coming, and I needed to stay focused. Being mad at Roxy for dishonoring a bond she hadn't asked for probably wasn't the best use of my time. I forced them out of mind until I was headed to bed. When I heard muffled voices on the porch, I had to see.

I knew I should have told Roxy I was there. But Roxy probably knew. Maybe she didn't care. Maybe she wanted to make me jealous. It was hard to tell these days. One minute we were … together, the next we were strangers.

Nathan's words caught my attention. "I know this may sound a fair bit like I am flattering you to win your affection, but I would be dishonest not to tell you I find you most lovely tonight."

I stared into the large mirror on the opposite wall where I could just barely see their backs and wished I could punch him in the nose.

"Yeah, you're right; you totally sound like a player," Roxy said.

"If a player is someone who finds women most alluring, I confess I am guilty," Nathan said with a small sigh.

Roxy looked at him. "Just so you know—I'm not the kind of girl that will be impressed by flattery."

"I know," he said. "I suppose that is what makes it so tempting."

She chuckled. Even if her laugh was for another guy, I liked hearing it.

"You don't have to try," she said. "I think you're great. I've heard about you and I've always wanted to meet you. I think we have some things in common."

He seemed surprised. "I am intrigued. Do go on."

She hesitated, so Nathan gave her a surmising glance and continued. "You wish for me to find the likenesses myself? Well, then, I suspect you approve of my argument that women should be allowed an education. Since you are so educated yourself."

"How do you know that?"

"You read. You are in the library nearly every day. And you have well-formed opinions about topics most women would not consider."

"If I went into detail, you'd be shocked," Roxy said.

"Whatever the truth, I suspect it would make sense."

Roxy went quiet and Nathan spoke again, his voice quieter. "You have told me you are not married to Sergeant Koenig, but I would have to be blind not to notice your attachment. So I hope it is not too forward of me to say I enjoyed our walk this evening."

"I don't need Sergeant Koenig's blessing to be your friend, Nathan. As for Levi and me, it's complicated."

"What could make love so complicated?" he asked. "I can see the obstacle of a marriage being forbidden by a parent or a promise to another, but as far as I can tell, the only one who holds your relationship back is *you*."

I smirked.

"I don't hold it back," Roxy argued. Her voice was so quiet I had to strain to hear.

"I cannot claim to know the truth about something so personal, Miss Eisen. But I know the look he gives you. It is one I long to give a woman. Someone I would do anything for, someone with whom I could share everything. But it has been withheld from me. And I think I know why."

Roxy didn't respond, but her mind felt agony.

"I think perhaps God has prevented my entanglement with anyone. And though I am at peace with his decisions, I envy those who find love." He smiled. "I wish for them to do well."

He was quiet for a time. Pensive. Roxy shifted like she was uncomfortable.

"I only wish to keep you from making a mistake where Sergeant Koenig is concerned. He holds you in the highest regard."

"I know," she answered.

"May I ask why you are not married?" Nathan Hale was pushing his luck. I wanted to warn him he might get punched if he kept pressing.

Her tone bordered on angry. "With everything happening, it would be selfish."

"It is not selfish to accept such a gift from the Creator. Love at its very heart is the opposite of selfish."

"You sound like Levi. 'Love is power, Roxy,'" she said in a mocking voice that I didn't think sounded at all like me.

"You would do well to listen to him."

She was quiet for a long time. "There are things I can't tell you. I don't even know how to tell him. If he knew, he wouldn't feel the same way about me."

Her words gave me a jolt. What was she talking about?

"I think you underestimate him," Nathan said.

She played with her fingers in her lap. I couldn't see it, but I knew. She kept pushing the hair behind her ear, too, which she only did when she was nervous. I wanted to walk out onto the porch, push Nathan the Player out of the way and tell her there was nothing she could do or say that would make me stop loving her.

"What about you?" Roxy's voice took on a new tone. I could tell she was trying to take the focus off herself. Maybe she didn't want to hear my cheesy thoughts on the subject. "Why don't you think God wants you to have love, Nathan?"

"I have given it much thought. I fear my answer might cause you distress."

She shrugged. "I don't *distress* easily. Try me."

Nathan took a deep breath. "I think he wishes to spare me the anguish of leaving her."

"What are you talking about?" I heard the tremor in her voice. She knew exactly what he was talking about.

"I have always had this feeling, in the farthest corner of my mind where I try to ignore it most days. But it never really leaves me. I think I shall die young." He stared at her with wide eyes. "It seems more real when I speak of it aloud."

"Oh, come on," Roxy said, her voice high and tight. "You can't know that."

"I know it sounds absurd. I would not mind being proven wrong," he said with an anxious chuckle. "But I believe my entire purpose is to be hung. I hope it would be in pursuit of our freedom and not as a traitor to the cause."

Roxy gulped hard.

"See, I have upset you," he said with regret. "Please give it no further thought. It is only my morbid imagination."

"What would make you think it?" Roxy's voice was breathless.

He stared out into the night. "It will sound ridiculous, but when I was young I was teased about this mole on my neck." He showed her. "My schoolmates said it meant I would one day be hung."

"What a horrible thing to say!" Roxy whirled to look at him, which meant I had to dive into the parlor so she didn't see me. Which was stupid, since she had to know I was there. "Those kids are the ones who should be hung."

Nathan smiled in a sad way. "If they are proven right, I suppose I should be grateful for the time I was given to be prepared for my fate."

"May it never be," she said in a softer tone, shaking her head.

She thought of her words as hollow. Trite. Both of us knew better. His sacrifice, that would ignite the future with freedom's fire, would not happen in years, or months … but in days.

TWENTY-ONE

Roxy's mood was understandably bad later when we were alone in our room. After collapsing in the chair by the fire, she started complaining. She complained about the soupy mess of overcooked meat and vegetables we'd been served for dinner. She complained about the inefficient way the servants failed to keep fires going enough to keep us warm at night.

"I could keep you reasonably warm without too much effort," I said as I flipped through the Nathan Hale book.

She glared at me.

"Roxy, you're complaining about everything except the thing you're really upset about."

"Look who suddenly became a psychotherapist," she mumbled, staring into the fire. I noticed the blaze burn more brightly for a few moments.

"Did you do that?" I sat up in the bed, intrigued.

"Do what?"

I shook my head and leaned back against the pillow again. "Roxy, do you think you should be talking to Nathan Hale so much?" I went back to my flipping and braced for her response.

"Jealous?"

"Yes. But besides that, what if you did something to change his story? Generations could be affected."

She frowned. I sat up again and turned, dangling my legs over the side of the tall bed.

"I hate it that he has to die," she said. "He should have a long life ahead. He should have a ton of kids just like him."

"You're right. But even if you warned him, I have a feeling he'd still walk right into his destiny." I stood and pushed the book under the mattress so no one would find it. Then I pulled it out. A maid could come across it. And what if we found a way back home? We couldn't just leave the book here.

"Burn it," Roxy said, as if the solution was obvious.

I stared at it for a few moments. Then I walked to the fire and tossed it in. Flames leaped around it, hungrily eating away the dry pages. I considered that the book had been decaying with age three hundred years before it was printed.

"A waste, like his death," Roxy said.

Sickness hit the camp hard. Influenza in 1776 could be fatal, so I became obsessed, again, with trying to keep Roxy safe. I asked Madeline to keep her at the house when I was with the army.

"I will keep an eye on her, but Roxy is her own person. If you try to make her do something, she might do the opposite just to spite you."

I saw the glimmer of disappointment in her eyes and felt like a jerk.

"I'm sorry, Madeline. I wish we'd met in a different time and place," I said.

She met my eyes with a somber expression. Maybe she was surprised I was hinting at the thing we never mentioned. "We are in a different time and place."

I reached for her hands and she let me hold them for a moment.

"Levi, you don't have anything to be sorry for." She eased away from me. "Your love for her is what makes you special. Maybe my feelings for you come from watching your loyalty to her. Don't prove me wrong."

She left me there after we both realized I had nothing to say in response.

When I got to camp, I found Nathan in his tent, so sick he could barely move.

"Was the doctor here?" I asked.

"I shall be right again," he said in a weak voice. "I have endured worse and recovered."

I got a bowl of water, a rag and a cup. He drank as I rinsed out the rag for him to put on his head. I thought about holding the rag there and healing him, but I was afraid he would notice the blue light. Finding out his new friend was a time-traveling healer had more potential to ruin everything than a bout of sickness. I figured the best thing was just to stay with him and talk. Several military endeavors were going on, but Washington hadn't asked anything of me in several days. So I stayed with Nathan and we talked guy stuff. We bragged about our military accomplishments. We argued about what the policies should be for the new government. We discussed a few "fair maidens."

After sitting there for a few hours, I could see why Roxy liked him. His perspective was uniquely selfless and forward-thinking; it was hard to believe he had no idea what was going to happen.

"We all die, Levi," he said, lying on his cot with his arm behind his head. "But would you not choose, if you could, to make your death mean something for the future?"

"I would." I meant it.

"Sometimes a man has to consider the greater good. All of these young men and boys, dying of this or that—why have I been spared affliction? Perhaps because there is a plan for my life to be given for this cause."

"Be sure, Nathan. Be sure what you're doing is what you think is right."

He smiled wearily. "I always do."

When I left Nathan's tent, he slept, unaware of fate looming like a dark cloud.

It was well past midnight, and I only had one thing on my

mind.

Roxy.

I had come to appreciate the night when she slept. I could watch her uninterrupted. I could try to heal her.

When I opened the door, something felt off. It was hard to see in the dim light, but I felt better when my eyes adjusted enough to see her form on the bed. I went to her and touched her cheek. The glowing from my fingers lit her face.

"I like watching her sleep, too. It's almost like she's dead."

I saw a form by the edge of the bed, leaning against the wall. It wasn't a solid form. Something about it was false. And it was larger than any man I'd ever seen.

I remembered the shrouded figure in the hall of the citadel.

"Joe?"

It was quiet for a long moment. "Hey, Little Brother."

"Are you really here?"

He laughed at me. "You can see me, can't you?"

"You look like a projection. How'd you learn how to do that?"

"Smarts run in the family. You should know that. I seem to have Leona's aptitude for science and technology. This hologram projector is my own creation."

"You should have stayed in 1874. People like you shouldn't have access to tech."

"People like me?" Joe smirked at me. "I'm just a guy trying to get by like anyone else. Like you."

"You're in the past trying to kill the most important person in my life. That's the kind of person you are, Joe."

I saw him shrug in the ambient light of my hands.

"So Joe Brant got some upgrades." I tried to make my tone indifferent, even though I wanted to shoot him in his holographic head. "Doesn't make you any better of a man."

"Oh, I disagree," he said, stepping closer. "It makes me more of a threat, so it makes me better."

"What do you want, Brant? Did you come here with Leona? Are you helping her ruin history?"

He sighed. "I came with Leona. And I'm helping her with her plan. But I think you can guess why I'm here."

I wanted to punch his ugly face until it was silent. But it would only make me look weak to lose my temper on a hologram.

"She'll be dead by the time I leave. And I might leave you alive just so you can enjoy it. So just know that while you're fighting your little freedom war, I might be strangling the life out of her that very moment."

"You stay away from Roxy," I said, barely controlling my rage. "Or I will kill you. That's a promise."

Joe didn't seem very worried. "You can't protect them. They're gonna die."

"You're going to die." As I spoke, I wondered who "they" was. Madeline? Greer? I couldn't remember seeing Greer that day. I needed to find him, make sure he was okay.

"We'll see," he said before he abruptly turned to static and faded out.

I was aware of my powerlessness. Our not knowing where Joe was or what he was planning made Roxy incredibly vulnerable.

Nathan was still knocked out with influenza on September 11. I knew from Roxy's book this would be an eventful month for the battle-weary rebel soldiers. General Washington was advised at one of our never ending strategy meetings to burn New York City. The British soldiers had claimed it and were acting like playground bullies. They burned people's hay and killed anyone even suspected of being sympathetic to the rebels. Just like it would be one day under the thumb of my mother, tyranny reigned free on the island of Manhattan.

I wondered if Washington would give the order to burn it if Congress hadn't shot it down. He didn't seem opposed to the idea, though he was hesitant. Maybe he didn't want to resort to being just like the bullies. Maybe he wanted to leave New York as undamaged as possible.

I hadn't been called into any more private meetings, but

Washington kept me close. Lately, he hadn't been anywhere without a lieutenant colonel named Knowlton. I felt a twinge of regret being replaced, but I was glad for the sake of history. Besides, it was hard not to like Knowlton. At the battle of Long Island, instead of staying behind his men, he led them into battle. Being in the first line in an eighteenth century battle wasn't for cowards. It didn't seem to bother Knowlton as he marched with his rifle in one hand, the other beckoning the troops.

"Come on boys!" he always shouted, and they always cheered.

Washington and Knowlton decided they needed a man in New York to spy for them. I knew it was coming, but it still caught me off guard. It was proof that Nathan's story was about to unfold.

I couldn't blame the general for wanting to know the plans. Finding out what the Howes were thinking would give us hope, and that was critical in a war that wasn't going well at all.

And that's what Washington said after he gathered all the troops in front of the army camp. Even Knowlton's group of reconnaissance men, the Rangers, stayed silent. I waited for Nathan to speak.

And he did, finally. As everyone stared at the ground, Nathan stepped forward, still pale-faced and shaky from his bout of sickness.

"I will undertake it, sir."

The response started with whispering. Soon, men were gathered around him, urging him to reconsider.

"Think of your family," someone said.

"It's a death sentence," another argued..

"What about your future, Nathan?" One of his closest friends spoke. "You could accomplish so much. Don't throw it all away on one mission."

Nathan took a step back from the men and looked at me. I didn't want to have to tell him to do it. After all, his friends were right. But Nathan had already made up his mind. He only needed confidence. I gave him a small nod.

He stood a little taller. "I owe it to my country. I know of no other way to obtain the information than by assuming a disguise and passing into the enemy camp."

He took a deep breath and continued. "For a year I have attached myself to the army and have not made a return on the compensation I have been given."

His friend Hull pulled on his arm. "They cannot make you compensate with your character! You would not succeed in an occupation of lies, Nathan. You are honest and open." The man held up his hands in frustration as Nathan shook his head. "Who respects a spy? As soldiers, we do our duty in the field. Don't strain the honor by sacrificing your integrity."

Nathan paused for a long while. "But what if I was successful?"

"At what price?" Hull asked in a softer tone. "Does your country demand moral degradation to advance the cause?"

Nathan sighed and shook his head. He knew what he would do. But unlike his fellow soldiers, he didn't believe it was wrong.

I wondered if the true measure of a man was in what he was willing to do that everyone judged him for. How far was Nathan willing to go against the grain of society's rules to accomplish the goal? He would stand on his integrity even when everyone else thought he was sacrificing it.

"You will die," Hull said bluntly.

Nathan gave a humorless laugh. "I wish to be useful. If a service is necessary to the public good, it becomes honorable."

Hull started to argue, but Nathan stopped him by putting a hand on his shoulder. "I will reflect, and do nothing but what duty demands."

Unfortunately for me, I already knew what duty's harsh demand would be, and it took everything in me not to sit him down and talk him out of it.

TWENTY-TWO

"We have to leave."

George Washington was as agitated as I'd ever seen him, and he wasn't the sort of man that got rattled easily.

His wife went a little pale. "What do you mean?"

He put a hand on hers and relaxed his worried features with effort. "There is talk of our position being compromised. It is just the way of war, my dear. We cannot stay in one place too long or we become vulnerable."

The situation must have been bad, because by nightfall we were as far north. We marched into Harlem Heights, which was largely forest and swamp. A plantation-style mansion stood at the top of a hill. Welcoming light shone from front windows, framed by columns and a large porch.

General Washington led us through the front doors into a quaint hallway. "It is known as Morris Hill for the family that owns it," he announced to the group of women, servants and officials who would be staying there.

I looked at Roxy and we both smiled at the familiar name.

Interesting. She raised her eyebrow.

I wouldn't be surprised if Morris showed up. Would you?

The general disappeared into an oval shaped room where drawings and maps had already been spread across the long oak table. Martha Washington approached us.

"This house is a bit smaller," she said with apology in her tone, directing her words to me. "There is only one extra room. I assume that you will share it with your wife?"

I glanced at Roxy, who had turned red.

You know we've been sharing a room for almost a month, right? I reminded her.

Mrs. Washington seemed uncomfortable. "Forgive me. I only assumed ... I know some couples prefer to keep to their separate areas."

I touched her shoulder in reassurance. "Thank you so much for the offer, Mrs. Washington. I believe it would be more gentlemanly of me to offer the room to the women. I can stay in the tents with the soldiers."

I smiled at Roxy, thinking I had made a great personal sacrifice for their good, but she frowned at me.

Mudsill.

I seriously can't do anything right by you.

Humor didn't last long in a house tuned to war. In fact, war was all we thought about. It was the conversation at breakfast and the subject of evening prayers. How much human history had been wasted by war? Days that could have been spent creating art, furthering our knowledge or bettering the lives of others—we spent fighting with each other. Even those determined not to get pulled in were inevitably pinned in the corner of conflict.

Being in favor of peace didn't mean a leader could avoid war. The privilege of being free came at a hefty price, because as soon as someone found it, someone else waited in the shadows to steal it. Someone like my mother. Nothing about freedom was easy or lasting. For one to exercise his freedom, another often forfeited theirs. For my mother to have unlimited power, the people of New York had to be either afraid or desperate enough for leadership to allow her rule.

It made me wonder. Did the fact that the United States would eventually lose their freedom mean this war was a waste? Were all the people dying worth what the country would get in exchange? And how much should I ask of my own soldiers in the future in order to regain the status of "free"?

My eyes fell on Roxy's form across the room. Did the limitations apply to my relationship with her? Did I have any right to call her mine or bond with her if she wasn't willing or able to relinquish her independence? Did anyone have the right to connection without giving up an aspect of being free?

Maybe being connected to others meant that sometimes, freedom wasn't possible.

The next battle came as a messenger boy presented a sealed letter to the general while he ate his breakfast. Washington left the paper beside his plate until he had finished every last crumb of biscuits and ham and every last drop of tea from his cup. We all watched as he sighed and wiped his mouth, throwing down the napkin with resignation.

"Permission to take the Rangers and find out the British position and strength," Knowlton said to Washington as he read. He nodded. Knowlton left, jamming his tricorn on his head with ferocity as the front door slammed behind him.

I cleared my throat as I braced myself for the mind protest I was about to get. I stood up, and Washington looked at me expectantly.

"Permission to join the Rangers, sir." I saluted him. He eyed me for a long moment while Roxy fumed next to me.

"Are you sure, Koenig?"

"I am."

"Then go."

I didn't look at Roxy. I knew what she would say and I didn't have time for arguments. I was responsible for this fight and I refused to fail.

I caught up to Knowlton and we went together to inform the other Rangers of our mission. Even before the fighting started, we were all expecting to lose. It seemed like all we ever did was retreat. That battle started out no different than the others. We fought until reinforcements arrived, but we were outnumbered, big time. As we retreated, the British started taunting us.

What were we to do? We turned around and fought. We fought for Washington. We fought for freedom. We fought without thinking about how many of them there were. I left at noon to find reinforcements, and by the time we came back, tension was thick in the air.

"We held them back!" Knowlton grinned. "These boys are going to have their victory tonight! Nothing will hold them back!"

Nothing did, to all of our surprise. Washington had told us to create a "feint." With 150 volunteers engaging the British to pursue them, the rest would wait to ambush.

It worked. The British were cornered in a buckwheat field by nightfall, and when they ran out of ammunition, they ran.

But the victory didn't come without loss. Knowlton fell in that field, and he never got up again.

I stood over his body as the men around me shouted "Huzzah!" and ran after the British soldiers. Knowlton had given everything to his mission. He had led with his whole heart. And now his blood that had given him life and vigor drained out onto the battlefield, a waste.

Was it my fate as well? Did a good leader have to die for his people? If so, I would do it. But it scared me—the unknown on the other side of death and the thought of leaving Roxy unprotected. I couldn't do everything. I couldn't be everywhere. I was just one man.

When the high from our win wore off, things got really quiet. We carried the dead and wounded on stretchers, hearing nothing but our feet crunching the gravel and seeing nothing but the evidence of death. I looked back and saw a trail of blood as far back as I could see. I smelled it. My vision blurred red. All I could think was how fragile people were.

What if I was one of the corpses being brought back to camp? What if Roxy found my dead body? Had I accomplished anything with the one short life I had been given? Was the world any different because of me?

"Why does it matter?" I said to Greer under my breath. Greer, who had reappeared that day with a vague explanation about where he'd been that didn't quite satisfy me.

"Why does what matter?" He walked next to me, also carrying the end of a stretcher.

"My life. Other than help Roxy, what have I accomplished?"

Greer shrugged. "Isn't that enough?"

I shook my head. "No. It's not enough. I have a debt to my society."

Greer didn't give me his usual wise answer. Actually, he seemed kind of spaced out.

I was tired of sleeping in the tent with unwashed, snoring soldiers. I missed Roxy. I wished we could go back to the Kennedy House.

Or Hudson Bay during the snowstorm.

Just thinking about that night was enough to get me out of my tent and into the house.

"Just saying goodnight to my wife," I told the housekeeper, who let me by with a nod.

I slipped up the stairs and opened the door to the girls' room after knocking softly. Roxy was asleep on the comfortable-looking bed. I saw Madeline sitting in front of the fire in a wingback chair, knitting something. My eyes returned to the bed. I watched the gentle rising of Roxy's chest, at the hollow of her collarbone peeking out from the nightgown she wore. I ached to take off my boots and jacket and crawl under that quilt, next to her warmth. She sighed and turned her face so a strip of moonlight from the window fell across her features.

"Do you regret your decision to let Roxy and I share this room?" Madeline smiled at me, though I heard sadness in her tone.

"I don't think you'd like sleeping with the army. They smell."

She chuckled. I pulled a stool next to the fire.

"Your Roxy is a sound sleeper," Madeline said.

"She must be tired."

"It's no wonder. She's a hard worker."

I was curious. "What does she do?"

I watched Madeline's fingers fly in and out of the stitching. It reminded me of the way she had worked with the wires of the maglev van. I started to ask her what she was making, but she spoke first.

"Roxy writes letters for General Washington. She hauls army guns to the kitchen by the dozen and cleans them so they don't misfire. I'm not sure, but I think she makes adjustments to the design as well so they are more consistent than the average eighteenth century musket."

I smiled.

"We both try to help the cook in the kitchen as well, and we encourage her to make healthier dinners for the men. Roxy was up to her elbows in flour this morning when I came to cut vegetables. She thinks the extra nutrition we are sneaking into their food will give them an edge."

"I didn't know," I said. I looked back at Roxy's sleeping form and loved her so much my chest ached. When I finally looked at Madeline, her eyes were shining with tears.

"What's wrong?"

"Nothing. Your love for Roxy—it's just beautiful, that's all."

"It's not something I do on purpose." I didn't know what else to say.

"I think it *is* something you do on purpose. Isn't love mostly a choice? Something you decide to do and then you do it, every day?"

I didn't think the statement needed a response.

"Tell me how you and Roxy happened," she asked quietly.

"My mother tried to kill her," I said. "I was five and she was a toddler. I got her out of the palace."

"You hadn't told me that before," she said with interest.

"I didn't see her again until she was sixteen. I had been looking for her from the time I entered the citadel army and had access to the city scanners. I found their hidden bunker and made sure no one else could find them. I watched them for a few weeks, until I realized their protector was gone and there were about two hundred teenagers and babies." I smiled. "I brought Roxy a cow I'd stolen from the park. That was the night I introduced myself, and she almost killed me for it."

Madeline nodded. "That I can believe."

I smiled. "I knew I would do anything for her. I knew I'd betray my mother. What started when we were kids had only grown while we were apart. She's the stars in my sky."

Madeline was quiet when she finally spoke. "I can see why you love her."

I caught the wistful edge in her tone. I made myself look at her. There had to be some way to tell her I wasn't an idiot—that it was only because of Roxy I hadn't fallen head over heels for her.

"You're amazing, Madeline. I don't know how we could have managed without you." I reached a tentative hand to brush back a strand of hair that had fallen forward on her shoulder.

"Please don't patronize me, Levi. I don't think I can handle that. I haven't done anything here. I'm useless."

"That's not true. You've done so much to help, and you haven't expected any thanks in return."

"I know what you're doing, Levi," she stopped her work and looked at me with dark eyes reflecting the firelight. "You're trying to apologize for not being interested in me."

I shook my head. "I don't want you to think I'm rejecting you."

She shrugged. "I never offered myself."

I nodded. "You're right. I just sensed ..." I dropped my hand and my voice trailed off. She caught my fingers.

"You weren't wrong." She studied my hand as if it were a rare artifact. "Levi's hands. Hands that heal. I'd be dead if it weren't for these hands."

I didn't respond. But staring at her, I almost forgot I wasn't interested. In that split second of time, I was tempted to trade everything.

She met my eyes. "I can guess what you're thinking. But I wouldn't let you betray her even if you worked up the nerve. I came to your story too late. I know my fate."

I squeezed her hand. "What do you mean by that?"

"Some things are best left unsaid." She let go of my hand, but raised her fingers to my cheek. "It will be okay."

I didn't like what I saw in her eyes, and I couldn't define it. Something told me it wouldn't be okay. Not at all.

She took the item she had been making and wrapped it in paper. She put it in a drawstring canvas bag and held it out toward me.

"These are for Roxy. Keep them with you until she's ready for them."

"How will I know?" I took the bag, wanting to open it, wanting to ask what it was.

"You'll know when the time comes," she said in vague assurance. "Goodnight, Levi."

TWENTY-THREE

New York was on fire.

I heard it murmured among the troops during morning exercises. Roxy met me at the door when I came in for breakfast. I heard her thoughts racing before she spoke. She pushed me into the foyer and leaned close to my ear.

"Nathan's in trouble," she said, her eyes brimming with tears. My hands went to her arms. How could I have forgotten? It was September 21. Today was the day.

"He's been taken?"

She nodded. "It happened just like my book said. He got information on the British but on his way out of town he found out it was irrelevant. So he went back to get more. He got desperate, and then he got sloppy. He let a man in a tavern fool him into exchanging too many beers for too much information. He was taken before Howe, who offered him a way out."

"He had to sign the agreement to be loyal to the crown," I said dully.

She nodded. "And in true Nathan fashion, he refused."

"Where is he?"

"A mansion on the other side of Manhattan. Beekman, I think."

I squeezed her shoulders. "There's nothing we can do, Roxy."

She pulled away. "I'm going to see him. He needs friends."

"You're not going," I said, trying to sound authoritative but, judging by her scowl, I probably sounded more desperate. "Washington wouldn't approve it, anyway."

"He didn't," she said, her chin rising rebelliously. "He said the city was on fire and it was too dangerous for a *lady* to travel south. It's a good thing I'm not a lady, I guess, because I'm going. You don't have to come."

I knew she had already made up her mind. "There's no way I'm letting you go alone."

We packed provisions and waited until night. We crept out of the house when the crescent of the moon was the only light.

When we reached the road we would follow to the British camp around Mount Pleasant, a cloaked figure waited. Roxy brandished her knife and I put my hand on my sword.

"I'm coming with you." I heard Madeline's voice.

"This is dangerous, Madeline. General Washington has forbidden it, in fact." I gave Roxy a pointed expression.

"I'm coming," Madeline said again, standing and swinging her bag around her shoulder. "I have something I have to do."

I wanted her tell me what it was, but she wouldn't look at me. She started walking down the path.

"We're right behind you," I said in a louder voice. "As soon as Roxy takes her knife back inside."

Roxy glared. "I'm not leaving my knife, idiot!"

"I'm not an idiot, which is why I know we'd be asking for major trouble when the soldiers find your knife with the solar heat function that belongs 300 years in the future."

"Who's going to save your butt when the soldiers try to run you through with their bayonets?"

"Put it back, Roxy." I leaned against the tree and folded my arms across my chest.

She scoffed, but after a few seconds she trudged back up the hill, fuming, to stow her beloved knife under the porch.

"Morris gave me that knife," she said as we set off down the road after Madeline.

"I know."

"He gave it to me to *use*. Not to keep under a colonial porch where some pimply-faced soldier will probably steal it."

"I'm sure it will still be there when you get back. And if it's not, I'll buy you a new model. I did the upgrades myself. You wouldn't believe how fast the new one gets hot."

She sneered.

We saw the devastation in the city long before we reached the streets. It was a seven-mile hike from upper Manhattan to the Beekman mansion by the East River. Though we were on the fringe of the city, smoke hung thick in the air. There were more people on the streets than I would expect for the early hours of the morning. Everyone was being questioned.

We were stopped not long after we came down the road into the city.

I nodded at the soldier who forced us to stop walking. "What's going on here?"

He didn't answer. He grabbed Roxy's bag and mine and emptied them on the ground, kicking his feet through the contents. I clenched my fists, wanting to grab him by the collar and teach him a few things about respect.

The soldier found an apple with our things and took a large bite as he motioned for Madeline to put down her bag. He made me take off my shoes and coat.

"What are you doing out this late?" He eyed me suspiciously as he pulled a book from Madeline's bag and flipped through it. I shot her a look, hoping she hadn't brought something that would get us in trouble.

It's a Bible, Levi. I saw the front. You should answer his question. It might irritate him if one of the "ladies" speaks. Roxy poked me in the ribs.

The soldier tossed Madeline's bag and its contents at her feet. He frowned, waiting for my answer.

"We live further up in the countryside and saw the smoke. My wife and sister and I came to check on our parents who live near the river, to make sure the fire did not reach them."

The soldier leered at Roxy and Madeline. "Who is the wife and who is the sister?"

I laughed. "I would think it obvious." I braced for Roxy's bulldozer mind reaction. "The dark one is my sister and the fair one my bride."

You are the worst kind of mudsill slime.

Sorry, Rox. But you look more like my sister and you know it.

I'm disgusted that I ever let your filthy hands touch me.

I know.

The soldier seemed doubtful. I figured I didn't have anything else to lose, so I put my arm around Madeline. I smiled at the soldier and turned my face, intending to kiss her cheek, but she looked at me in surprise in the same moment and I had no choice. I kissed her on the lips. And if I were going for full disclosure, they were the most insane brand of sweet.

The soldier grunted his approval and motioned for us to move on. I had to wait for the blinding pain in my toes to stop, when Roxy finally removed her boot heel.

Madeline quickly moved ahead of us.

We had to be careful to stay hidden when we reached the camp. I walked along behind Roxy. She was the expert on staying in the shadows. She'd been doing it her whole life.

We had to peek into a few tents before we heard someone say Nathan was being kept in one of the rooms in the mansion. We sneaked in through the lowest level. Madeline pulled the Bible from her bag and thrust it toward Roxy, who frowned at it.

"Take this," Madeline whispered. Roxy didn't take it. "Just do it, Roxy! For Nathan."

Madeline pushed the book into Roxy's hands and went up to a guard.

"Oh, I do hope you can help me!" she gushed, very un-Madeline like. "My brother is missing. He was stationed here, and I was to meet him in the city, but he never came. You have to help me find him!"

While the guard was distracted by Madeline's sad tale, or more likely, Madeline's pretty face, Roxy and I slipped inside and tried to act like we belonged there.

It didn't take long to find the room where Nathan was being held. I could hear him pacing, whispering to himself in an anxious voice.

"Though I walk through the valley of the shadow of death, I will fear no evil …"

Madeline found us and used the same story on the soldiers outside Nathan's room. While they were distracted, Roxy and I found an empty room used for storage with an adjoining door allowing us access to Nathan's room.

We didn't have time to greet him, because as soon as we got into the room, we heard heavy footsteps in the hallway and someone demanding the door be opened. We hid behind storage barrels in the corner as a large man with an intimidating sneer stomped into the servant's chamber where Nathan was held, bringing with him an aura of unease.

"What do you want?" He spat on the floor in front of Nathan. "Do you know you are disturbing my sleep, filthy spy? No one cares about you. Not them, and not us."

"Please, sir, I would like a copy of the Scriptures. And I would be grateful to speak to a minister," Nathan asked.

I was very curious how Madeline had known he would ask for a Bible. And it wasn't a comfortable kind of curiosity.

"A lying spy who threatens the crown and you think religion will do you any good now?" His voice was cruel, and was followed by a harsh laugh. "You made a deal with the devil, and in the morning you will face your master for eternity. Because no one of sound mind believes a spy will ever be forgiven."

You pompous, ugly windbag! He is a thousand times the man you are! How'd you like to spout your garbage to my knife, you creepy mudsill!

I had to hold Roxy back from jumping the guy.

We saw the shadow of the soldier as he exited the room. He

spoke to the guards as he went. "See that no one goes in or out. He gets nothing until morning."

TWENTY-FOUR

I stood up and watched as Roxy crept across the boards of the floor and held her hand out to Nathan, warning him not to react. The look on his face made my throat feel tight.

"Roxy! Levi! What are you doing here?"

She held a finger to her lips and sat next to him on the cot. She placed the Bible in his lap.

His voice broke as he chuckled. "You must be an angel."

"Don't listen to that mudsill," Roxy said softly. "He's just trying to break you. You did well, Nathan. You're a hero."

He shook his head and ran his fingers across his hair. "I am a terrible liar, and a worthless spy."

"That's not true," she insisted.

"What happened?" I asked.

"I didn't want to go back to the general with nothing," Nathan said as he looked out the window. I saw Madeline's shadow as she came to distract away the soldier who guarded the window. "While I wrote my new notes, the city started burning. The British army started questioning everyone in the streets to find those responsible for the fire. Did General Washington give the order?"

"No," Roxy said. "But I don't think he's too torn up over it."

Nathan sighed. "They caught me. I gave them my diploma and my story about being a schoolteacher looking for a job. I said I was

158

a Tory. The guard almost let me go, but he decided to check my shoes, and found my notes."

"You did the best you could." Roxy slid her fingers between his and held his hand fiercely. "It was a dangerous mission."

He stared at the floor. "I was a fool to trust the man in the tavern. He said he would help me; said he was a spy, too. I let down my guard. He confirmed my guilt." He shook his head.

We were quiet for a moment, then Nathan spoke again, as if an afterthought. "There was a woman here, in the mansion. She acted like she was on my side. She said she was going to get me freed."

"Did she have red hair?" Roxy said dully, meeting my gaze briefly.

He nodded. "She was a compassionate sort. She said she hated to see a young life wasted."

"Sure she did. Wouldn't fit her plan, after all," Roxy said with sarcasm.

I agreed. "My mother is a stone-cold killer."

"She told General Howe to let me go. She said I was a confused boy. But he demanded my confession. So I told him the truth. I said we had the right to liberty and the right to fight for it. To create a government to serve our needs, and not be focused on the whims of one spoiled man on the other side of the ocean," Nathan said. "He seemed rather impressed by my words, but I've been sentenced to hang in the morning if I do not sign the document stating my loyalty to the king."

Roxy put her other hand on top of their joined hands. "It was brave to refuse. I want to tell you that you should sign it and save your life. But if I'm being honest, I wouldn't."

He nodded sadly. "How could I live with myself if I turned my back on this pursuit of freedom to save my insignificant little life?"

Roxy's voice faltered. "You're not insignificant. Believe me."

He shrugged. "I am rather afraid it will not mean a thing, Miss Eisen. It will be for nothing. I failed the mission, and my death will be of no use."

"No!" Roxy let go of his hand and grabbed him by both

shoulders. "It means *everything*. You'll be an inspiration to every soldier on the other side of Manhattan who secretly thinks we'll never win this fight. You'll show every colonist what great big courage can do. This country will be *free*, Nathan! And for almost three hundred years it will stay that way, and everyone will know your name! Nathan Hale will be synonymous with the guts to fight for something that sets people free."

He breathed a short laugh. "You speak as if you have been to a future time and seen things on the other side of tomorrow."

"Maybe I have. Maybe time sent me back to this night, to tell you to have faith in your beliefs."

"I would like to believe it is true." He watched her for a moment, and then glanced at me. "You should go. I don't want them to find you here. You would be hanged by my side."

Roxy looked my way. I tried to speak in a normal voice. "Are you sure? You can still come back with us. We'll make it happen."

He shook his head. "They would discover me, and you would be in danger. I will not allow it. I can at least protect your lives by my sacrifice."

"You'll do a whole lot more than that, Nathan," I said quietly.

Roxy's voice was thick. "I will never, ever forget you."

"And I will carry your words and your beauty with me, and think only of them until it is over."

He touched her cheek with a trembling finger. She slid her arms around his waist and hugged him tightly. He didn't hold her long. He stood and saluted me.

"Sergeant Koenig."

"May I shake the hand of a hero?" I extended my hand and he took it, taking a deep breath and letting it out as a shudder.

"Be safe, my friends," he said, motioning us out. "And take this; I wouldn't want to try to explain where it came from." He handed Roxy the Bible, smiling fondly as he put his hand on the black leather cover. "It is enough to hold it and remember the words I have known since I was a child. They give me strength.

"I know I have made mistakes, but God knows my faith in his

plan. He is wiser and more loving than I can comprehend." Nathan sat back down on the bed and folded his hands in his lap. "I will go to him."

Roxy was sniffling as I helped her climb up to the window. The lower level of the mansion was sheltered in the shadows of a portico. The plan was to sneak around the guards by the front steps and meet Madeline in the bushes by the pond.

"Roxy," Nathan whispered after we had crawled out. She turned back.

"Don't be afraid to trust him. He loves you."

She watched him for a long moment, as if they had some silent connection like the one she had with me. Finally, she gave him a quick nod and turned so we could make our escape. I looked back at him, and he gave me a sad smile.

TWENTY-FIVE

Roxy and I sat in a dark corner of Dove Tavern until dawn. We didn't speak much; we didn't sleep at all. We tried not to think about what was going to happen.

Madeline hadn't shown up at the meeting place. We waited as long as we could before we'd be spotted. I was worried that something had happened to her, but Roxy reminded me she had been fine the last time we saw her. She must have had someone escort her back to the house when she missed the meeting.

At first light, a crowd gathered. The town crier announced the public execution.

"They want to make an example of him," I said quietly. Roxy didn't answer.

We pushed our way through the crowd and waited for Nathan. I looked around the grassy knoll where an old oak rustled its fall-tinged leaves as if it did not realize the atrocity it would commit. It wouldn't forget, though. This place, this earth would not forget the crime, even as a metropolis.

When Nathan was led down the gravel lane, no one spoke, save the occasional sob of compassionate witnesses. The hush was eerie.

Roxy's mind was loud with protest. I slipped my hand into hers. She held on tightly with all her unexpressed frustration.

The executioner put the noose around Nathan's neck and threw the end over the limb. Nathan held his head high, though I saw the frantic rise and fall of his chest.

"Say your last words," the British soldier said as he held the rope.

Nathan's voice was small and shaky. "It is the duty of every good officer to obey any orders from his Commander-in-Chief ..." His voice trailed off, but after a moment he continued in a stronger tone. "I desire that you all might be prepared to meet death it whatever shape it might appear, so I offer you a goodly example today."

He looked into the face of the soldier who had come into his room the night before. "You are shedding the blood of the innocent."

His eyes sought the hushed onlookers and soldiers standing around. He met my gaze.

"If I had ten thousand lives, I would lay them all down, if called to it, in defense of my injured, bleeding country," Nathan said, his voice faltering. "I am so satisfied with this cause, my only regret is that I have not more lives to offer in its service. There is no death which could not be rendered noble in such a glorious cause."

As the executioner prepared to pull the rope taut, Roxy pulled her hand out of mine and fumbled with the Bible.

"I wish I knew where they were." She flipped through the pages.

"What?"

"The words he was saying last night."

I took the Bible and opened it to a page marked by a small piece of paper. I read Madeline's artistic script.

Psalm 23—when the time comes.

My voice broke through the quiet. "*Though I walk through the valley of the shadow of death, I will fear no evil; for thou art with me: thy rod and thy staff, they comfort me. Thou dost prepare a table before me in the sight of mine adversaries: thou dost anoint mine head with oil, and my cup runneth over. Doubtless kindness and mercy shall follow me all the days of my life, and I shall remain a long season in the house of the Lord."*

As I read, the rope was drawn tight and Nathan was lifted into the air. He struggled for a minute as Roxy made a sound of agony that ripped apart the silence. She held her neck, as if she was choking, too. I put my arm around her, but I knew I couldn't stop it. She was feeling his death on a level no one else could even imagine.

"You're going to be okay," I whispered in her ear as she tried to catch her breath and tears rolled down her cheeks. "It will pass. Just try to breathe."

When his body went limp, dangling in a circle and swaying gently in the morning breeze, a call suddenly rose up.

"For those who have gone before! For freedom!"

The first second after the words were spoken, I was inspired by the brave young woman who had risked being singled out to shout the words.

But in the next instant, panic moved through me like white hot electricity pouring from the portal.

The voice sounded like Madeline's.

A chant began as a few brave voices, hidden within the group of onlookers, but it grew stronger until it became a refrain, shouted long and hard from every direction. It was a cry of people tired of being controlled. A cry for the most basic need of the human soul.

"For freedom! For freedom! For freedom!"

I looked at the faces of the British soldiers and expected to see anger or annoyance. Instead, I saw fear. They watched the crowd uneasily for several moments before the soldier who appeared to be in charge grabbed someone from the crowd and hurled her forward. My heart pounded when I saw the long golden hair of the girl he had taken.

Madeline.

I shuddered, my breath catching in my throat, my mind

swarmed with frantic worry. Roxy started to move toward the front, but I grabbed her back. She would either be trampled or captured, and there was no way I would lose both of them.

You can't protect them. Either of them.

"They won't kill her. They're just trying to keep control of the crowd," I said, though I wasn't sure I was right. "I'll find a way to save her if it gets any worse." I held Roxy while she fought me and prayed for Madeline to be safe.

But without a second thought, the soldier took a noose and put it around her neck, motioning for the solider to hoist her up beside Nathan. It was done within seconds. There was no time to think, let alone respond in time to save her.

"No!" I said the word in disbelief, and it stuck in my throat like a rock. Roxy fell to the ground and coughed violently.

The quick execution did the trick. The people, now anguished at the sight of the two young freedom fighters, began to disperse. I pulled Roxy away from the scene, behind a tree, and we fell together, our bodies shaking as we held each other and grief mingled in our minds.

Why did she do it?

Roxy grabbed my face between her palms. "I'm sorry, Levi. I know you cared about her. I did, too."

I hadn't realized until that moment how much Madeline's friendship had come to mean to me. There was still so much about her I didn't know. And in that moment, I wanted to know. I really wanted to know everything.

I clung to Roxy. I felt broken in this war. In the struggle that seemed the story of my life. I would never be able to fix them all. Death was always ready to steal away the people I loved. I couldn't protect them all.

It seemed like a hundred years later when we got back to camp. When I pushed back the canvas, exhausted in every thinkable way, I saw the square package on my cot.

I picked up the note and recognized Madeline's script.

Dear Levi,

If you have found this letter, I assume I did not make it back, and I am dead. I knew it was a risk. I ask that you don't dwell on this. You couldn't have prevented my sacrifice. It was my choice.

I was approached last week by a man named Morris. He asked me questions about our friendship. He said he had a job for me if I was willing, but it was dangerous, and he would understand if I said no.

Morris told me Leona has been trying to halt Nathan's execution. She wants to put the attention on Roxy and have her hung instead. When I begin the freedom chant at the execution, it will be to keep Leona from being heard. Morris hopes they will take pity on me, but if you are reading this, it means they did not.

Since I am writing this letter with the assumption of my death, I might as well be honest with you. I love you, Levi.

You may think it's impossible for me to know this is true in so short a time, but I didn't fall in love with you when you saved my life in the kitchen. I loved you years ago, when I was in the archives undergoing the tests. You happened to come along when one of the doctors was about to inject me with a solution that would have killed me.

I don't know how much you knew about the tests

your mother was doing down there, but when you killed that doctor and had me moved to a different sector, you saved my life.

You may remember this, and argue that the young woman was not me, but it was. You moved me to a group that was selected to be spared and become servants at the citadel. When my wounds were healed, I was given beautification surgeries to alter my appearance. It was me that day in the archives. The real me.

But please don't have any regrets over this. I have watched you love Roxy, and as much as I wish it was me you love, she is your future.

You told me once that I should learn to paint. I took your advice when I met a painter in town the first day we were here. He has been giving me instruction. This is my first and final painting, and I want you to have it.

So take my love and my gift and never, ever leave her. Love her and all that she will bring to your life. Live for freedom.

"Sometimes the tree of liberty must be watered with the blood of patriots and tyrants." Thomas Jefferson said that, only recently. And we were here for it! We got to see it all.

Goodbye, Levi.

Madeline.

I pulled back the fabric covering the canvas. When I saw the picture, I could only stare in shock. It was the form of a girl, staring into a sky of a thousand stars. The frenzied but orderly beams of light traveled in circles almost as if they would sweep the girl off her feet and into the night sky that held the faintest tinge of dawn.

I knew the painting. It was in the archives with the other art hidden by my mother. I had never known the artist, but I loved the painting because it reminded me of Roxy.

It was the reason I had been in the archives, the day I saved the girl about to be put to death. The day I had saved Madeline. I had wanted to see the painting.

I stayed in the tent for the rest of the day. When I missed dinner, Roxy came to find me. I handed her the note and rested my elbows on my knees and my head in my hands, staring at the painting I had propped on the end of my cot against the canvas wall. After Roxy read the note, she gazed at the artwork for a long time.

"There's something I didn't tell you about Madeline," Roxy said, long after she had handed me back the note. She stood in front of me, crossing her arms over her chest.

I looked at her.

"A few mornings ago when she was washing at the water pitcher, I woke up. She tried to cover herself, but I saw what she tried to hide."

I frowned. "What?"

"Scars." Roxy's voice was no more than a whisper. "Terrible scars, all over her torso."

I shook my head. I didn't want to hear it, but I needed to hear it. Roxy had pity on me and continued silently.

I asked her if Leona had beaten her. She said that the scars were from tests. Before they became servants, they had to go through tests at Leona's archive "hospital." They were subjected to radiation, they were burned with acid, and they were given vaccines. They were exposed to horrible diseases to see if the vaccines worked, and if they were no longer useful, they were disposed of.

I felt the pressure in my head. I held it, as if it might explode if I didn't hold it together.

The strong ones were allowed to recover and become citadel slaves as a "reward." But before they were released, they had to have "contouring" surgery. Their bodies were altered to reflect perfect proportions and features—at least what Leona considered perfect.

I asked her why the scars weren't lasered off. She said the scars were left in areas that wouldn't show, as a reminder to the servant of who owned them.

My eyes burned. They ached to release the pain.

"Did you know what Leona was doing to them, Levi?" Roxy asked me quietly. I couldn't stand the sound of her voice. I didn't want to consider her insinuation. I'd considered it before, and the only answer I had put me in a very bad light.

"I knew, Roxy." I made myself look her in the eyes. "I knew she was doing it and I didn't stop it."

TWENTY-SIX

We kept moving from place to place. I wondered how Washington kept his polite manner and dry sense of humor. He and his wife acted like they were visiting at a garden party, even if Hessian troops were on the move and headed our way, which they usually were.

The worst thing was watching Roxy suffer. Every time we moved to a new place she seemed to sink deeper inside herself and her pain. The last time she had tried to read a mind for me, she had been so sick she couldn't get out of bed for a day. I didn't ask after that. I was tired of fighting and marching. My shoes were worn thin. I wanted to complain about it until I noticed that some soldiers weren't even wearing shoes. Things were different without Madeline, and without Greer, for that matter, as I rarely saw him and when I did, he seemed distracted. Roxy and I didn't talk about them. We didn't talk about any of it, but we both carried around the weight of the memories and regrets like blocks of cement.

We had crossed the Delaware and were camping on the farm of Thomas Barclay, a revolution advocate devoted to the cause. Martha Washington made sure that Roxy and I were given a quiet room away from the others, knowing we had suffered a loss and were grieving. I spent many hours of those few days helping her sip water and holding back her hair while she gagged it back up. Her throat was raw and she had faint red marks on the skin, as if someone had tried to strangle her. I knew it was her empathetic sharing of Nathan and Madeline's executions. Nothing I did seemed to heal it. Gradually it began to heal on its own, and I supposed it was because her devastation had begun to heal.

I wondered—not for the first time—if her unexplained sickness since we had arrived in 1776 was because of her empathetic gift. It would explain why I hadn't been able to heal her. I got why she had tried to live away from people. I completely understood it. It made me sorry I'd dragged her back into the world.

The December weather was cold and gray. No one felt like fighting, except the German Hessians who were stationed in every town, waiting for us. We had to fight to hold our ground. I went out in the morning with my bayonet rifle on my shoulder, and came back with dirt on my clothes, leaves caught in my hair, and the deaths of men on my conscience.

Roxy gradually began to do better. She eventually started helping Mrs. Washington again. One early December morning as I dressed, she got out of bed and started pulling on the uniform of a colonial soldier.

"What do you think you are doing?" I stared at her in disbelief. "Where did you even get that?"

"Who do you think does the laundry? I stole it." She proceeded to pull a pair of men's boots over the socks that were too big for her.

I pulled the boot away from her. "You can't go."

"I can," she said as if my opinion wasn't worth her getting angry. "I'm going with the army. I feel fine and I want to help."

"You've been helping here, Roxy," I said, knowing I was fighting a losing battle. But I couldn't let her fight. I couldn't risk her. "You help the injured. You listen to them and help them eat and encourage them to keep fighting. You let them know what they are doing matters. Do you realize how important that is?"

"Spoken by someone who could just heal them and get them

back on the field," she said, yanking the boot back. "I need to go with you. It's pointless to argue with me."

I sat on the bed for a long time before I got up and met her at our bedroom door. I opened it, gesturing for her to go first. She snuck down the hall and out through the kitchen. When I got to the bottom of the stairs, I saw her running across the field toward the army camp.

A bad feeling settled in the pit of my stomach. But she was right. I couldn't hold her back. I couldn't ask her to be less than she was or less than she was capable of.

If I just stay close to her, she'll be fine.

"Sergeant Koenig, my husband asked me to send you into the parlor," Mrs. Washington squeezed my arm as I entered the dining room for breakfast.

I nodded and stepped across the hall. General Washington poured over maps and notes. I didn't envy his job, but I remembered the same job awaited me in 2076. The work he was doing to stitch together the union, as tedious as it was, wouldn't last. I'd have to fix it when I got home. And keep my mother from ripping the seam wide open.

"These are hard times, Koenig," he said with a sigh. He rubbed his eyes and squinted at the small printing on the paper.

"They are, General," I agreed. I came to stand next to him.

"How is your wife this morning? I trust her illness is subsiding?"

I swallowed back my worry and tried to sell the lie for her sake. "I think she is better. She talked of getting some fresh air today."

"Just warn her to stay clear of the fighting," Washington said absently.

I tried.

"I shall require most of my men to head toward Newark," he said, pushing back against the table. "I should like you to command a small force to infiltrate the Hessian outpost at New Brunswick. They are few in number, and it would secure our passage toward Trenton."

"Of course," I said. "Shall I choose the men?"

He nodded and dismissed me with a wave.

"Bring them all home, Sergeant," he said when I got to the doorway. "We can't spare a single man."

"I will, sir."

The march into New Brunswick was a morning's walk. Roxy stayed at the end of the line of ten boys and men I had chosen that morning. We traveled mostly in silence, but the men seemed calm and determined.

We surprised the small Hessian fort. Only a handful of soldiers had stayed behind—most were fighting the battle that raged down the hill. The remaining soldiers weren't prepared for trouble.

We exchanged fire for a few minutes and their number dwindled. I expected it to be an easy win. I still had all my men (and also my woman) and I guess it made me cocky. Sloppy.

Their reinforcements arrived over the hill, and we were ambushed.

"Go!" I yelled to the men. "I'll buy you time, just run!"

I hoped "buy you time" was a phrase, or maybe I had just invented the saying, but they seemed to understand and retreated back down the other side of the hill. I turned my attention to the Hessian that was coming for me. Our swords clanged together as I looked around for Roxy. Had she retreated? A part of me knew she wouldn't have listened to my order.

As I blocked an attempt by the Hessian to run me through, I caught sight of her. She was across from me, fighting off another Hessian twice her size. His maniacal smile faded when she pushed him back against bushes. I saw her plunge her sword into the brush and assumed her fight was over. I looked back at the brute I was battling and threw all my strength behind a jab to his stomach. He countered it. I lost my grasp of the handle of the sword and it fell.

The Hessian wasted no time in pushing me to the ground. I heard Roxy scream as the sword came down on me. I managed to move but not far enough to avoid the blade. My side erupted in burning pain.

I figured he would finish me in the next breath, and I knew there was nothing I could do to stop him. A series of flashes went across my brain. My mother in her throne room at the citadel. Roxy, the first time I saw her when we were grown. Madeline, sounding the freedom call.

I haven't done enough. The voice came from deep within my spirit, maybe even an echo of my soul. *I wasted my life.*

I heard a loud thud. The soldier disappeared from view.

With difficulty I managed to sit up and saw Roxy on top of the soldier, pounding away at his face and yelling. He was dazed by the beating, and she would have knocked him unconscious, but in her wild rage she didn't notice his sword was near enough to his hand for him to grab it.

My whole world crumbled when I watched him effortlessly slide the sword into her abdomen.

Blood oozed freely from my own wound when I stopped pushing on it, but nothing could have stopped me from trying to get to my sword. It was just out of my grasp. The Hessian stood and laughed at my attempt like I was a simple child.

I braced for death once again, but suddenly the soldier stopped and his smile faded into a disturbed frown. I followed his gaze and saw Roxy, lying still on the ground, staring intently at his face. I realized what she was doing.

I can read your thoughts, you disgusting pig. She poured her words into his mind. His eyes widened and his face went pale.

You think I'm a witch. You're afraid I'm going to curse your soul. I don't blame you. I'd be afraid if I were you. You have no idea the powers I have to control your life from this moment on. I will haunt you when the blood has drained the life from me. I will be even more powerful as a spirit, and I won't rest until I see your rotting corpse. You will die the death of a coward ...

Roxy, I think you can stop.

The soldier was running back over the crest of the hill as fast as he could go. It would have been funny if I didn't see the crimson spreading across the middle of Roxy's white linen shirt.

I dragged myself to her side.

"You're hurt," she snapped, like I'd gotten injured on purpose to annoy her.

I calculated how much strength it would take to heal her without killing myself in the process. I wasn't opposed to losing my life to save hers, but if I could control it, I would.

Her eyes suddenly got big, like she'd just remembered something important.

Very important.

"I'm pregnant!" She cried, grasping my arm so hard it hurt. "Levi, I'm pregnant!"

Nothing in the world could have prepared me for those words to come out of Roxy Eisen's mouth. A million questions flooded my mind. Pointless questions of processing such as *Am I the father?* and *Is it a boy or girl?* and *Why in all the worlds would you not tell me something like this?*

"Of course you're the father, you mudsill! Do something!"

I shook the confusion from my brain and forgot to be careful with the energy that quickly flowed from my hands to her abdomen. I imagined my power transforming her body, her organs … and the baby's ... to their uninjured forms.

"Stop!" She kicked me back and broke the connection as things were starting to go black. I came back to her side and pulled up her shirt, searching for the wound. I sighed with relief when I saw the faint scar just to the right of her navel.

My attention was drawn to her swollen abdomen.

"Is this why you were sick?" I ran my fingers through my hair, feeling an enormous weight of responsibility. How in the world had I missed it? "How long have you been this way?"

She rolled her eyes. "Levi, use your brain. I've been pregnant since it happened. In the snowstorm."

I calculated the months. "You're like six months? Seven months? Why didn't you say something?" She'd let me believe the whole time that there was something wrong with her. Something I couldn't fix. "Not cool, Roxy."

We were quiet as she pulled her shirt over her stomach and sat up, a little sulky.

"How did you hide it for so long?" I finally asked.

"I didn't show much, and eighteenth century fashion helped." She stared down at her stomach and put her hands on either side. "Do you think the baby is okay?"

I put my hand over the bump. She was right, it was small, but now that I saw it, it was unmistakable. After a moment I felt faint movement underneath my hand. I looked at Roxy, speechless.

She pushed me back to the ground and ripped open my shirt to look for my wound. It hurt like hell when she touched it, but her mind assured me it wasn't life-threatening.

"We'll clean it when we get back," she said, standing and reaching to help me up.

I stood in front of her, shocked completely senseless.

I was going to be a father.

Roxy and I were having a baby.

Roxy and I were having a baby in 1776. *In the middle of the freaking Revolutionary War.*

We started back down the path through the woods.

I glanced at her. "You realize we are both lucky that German spoke English, right?"

TWENTY-SEVEN

We went back to the tents. Roxy found water and bandages to clean my wound while I took my shirt off and sat on a free cot. She rinsed a cloth in water from a bowl and pitcher and rang out the excess water. I must have been frowning at her as she worked, because she sighed.

"I know I should have told you, Levi. But every time I tried, I didn't know what to say. I shouldn't have let it happen."

Any remaining irritation I had about her silence disappeared. I reached a hand to her cheek as she leaned over me to dab the cloth against my side. "It was a mutual decision, Roxy. And it was bad timing. But it wasn't a mistake." I put my other hand on her stomach. "*This* isn't a mistake."

She stopped what she was doing and stared at my hand. I thought she would argue, but she nodded slowly. "You're right. I don't know why, but I know it was meant to be this way."

I sat up. "But fighting in a bloody war in 1776 *pregnant* was a BIG lapse in judgment."

She frowned and sat on the cot across from mine. "That's why I stayed close. In case something happened. But when I woke up, I was dreaming that you were hurt in the battle and left alone. I couldn't let that happen." She opened her mouth as if she would say more, stopped.

Finally, she spoke. "Levi, part of me *wanted* something to happen." She looked at me desperately, like she was afraid of my reaction. "I wanted the pregnancy to end, so I wouldn't have to tell you and I wouldn't have to think about it anymore. I was scared. But when I was lying there, bleeding, all I could think about was the ... person inside me. The one I was responsible to protect."

I nodded, reaching for her hands. "I know what you mean."

She shrugged and kept her eyes fixed on mine. "You really never suspected?"

I shrugged. "I was clueless. It's not like you ever let me get close to you."

She surprised me by moving next to me and putting her arms around me. She leaned against my chest. "I wanted to. I was just afraid you'd find out before I figured out what I was going to do."

I couldn't hold back my smile. "You wanted to what?"

She hesitated. "I wanted to be close."

I held her as close as I could and took full advantage of the moment by kissing her.

When we stopped for breath, I shook my head to clear it. I was suddenly having visions of another encounter in a tent, and this time we weren't alone in a snowstorm. "We need to get home. It's too risky for you to have a baby here."

"How?" She stared outside the tent into the camp, inhabited by wounded soldiers and those tending them. I wasn't sure how many men were dead or captured, but I could tell by the feeling that hung heavy in the air it had been a massive loss. Again.

"We're stuck in limbo in this unending war," Roxy said.

"There's got to be a way at the portal site. I felt it, when I went across it. It activated my power."

She looked up in interest. "But we need Leona and Joe first. We can't leave them here."

"And the portal site is occupied by the British," I added.

She rinsed the cloth, staining the water pink with my blood. "There's something else, Levi."

I knew from her tone I wasn't going to like the *something else.*

"I saw Joe. In the battle. He was standing on the edge of the field. He smiled at me, like he knew something I didn't."

"Are you sure it was Joe?" I cringed as she poured alcohol over my wound.

"You don't forget a mind like that."

I felt exhaustion set in. I was going to get up and try to make it into the house and up to our room, but Roxy told me to stay and rest first. She left to change and clean up. Because of the healing, it took no time for me to fall into a deep sleep.

I knew I lived in my nightmare. I felt the chill of the autumn night, heard the rustle of brittle leaves. I smelled blood, but I knew I dreamed it.

I was almost sure.

I ran through the woods, tearing my coat on a limb and tripping over my boots when they hit a tree root. I called for Roxy. I knew she was close. I could sense her mind, and it screamed.

"Where are you?" I yelled as the wind began to blow harder and the dark clouds pressed in, so close overhead I thought I would be able to touch them if I raised my hand.

A bolt shot out from the cloud and sent me sprawling as electricity charged my body and singed my clothes. I tried to control the spasms and force my feet to stand. To run. I had to find her.

Bolts continued to blast onto the path around me, taunting me. "Roxy!"

I fell into a clearing. Everything around me was overgrown with vegetation and something else, like electrical wire. I crawled through it, feeling pain as I dragged my hands and knees against the wire that seemed to have sprouted a million tiny barbs.

A tapping noise echoed through the meadow already impossibly loud with wind and thunder. I looked everywhere, but I couldn't find the source of the tapping. It was a quiet, insistent sound.

"Where are you?" I cried. The raging wind swallowed my

voice. She wouldn't be able to hear me.

"I told you I would find her."

Suddenly he stood over me, tapping his boot against something metal in the ground. He was eight feet tall, and his features were exaggerated within the shroud of his cloak, but I knew it was Joe.

"Don't touch her!" I yelled, trying to lift powerless hands toward his neck that stretched out a mile away from my hands.

His laugh sounded like the thunder. "You're not going to save her. See? She's already mine."

I looked, and in the center of the meadow, over a cement block, she was there. She stood in front of the portal, holding her arms across her middle, staring at me with wide, sunken eyes. She wasted away as I watched. Her skin shown white as snow against the blood red dress she wore.

"It's not red." Joe sneered at me. "That's her blood. Their blood."

I shook my head, unwilling to believe he had done it. She couldn't die. I wouldn't let it happen.

"Roxy, I'm coming!" I stood up, racing toward the cement platform, my hands glowing hot with blue light as I made the mad dash to heal her.

"Oh, no, Little Brother. Not this time."

I heard the clash of steel and a blinding glint hit my eyes as he brandished a sword that must have been six feet long. With a stomach-turning sucking sound and pain like I couldn't have even imagined, my hands were both severed, falling into the tall grass, staining everything with blood. The grass went dead and brown around it. My hands turned black and shriveled to nothing.

Roxy fell to the cement, her gray eyes empty and cold as they stared in my direction.

"I told you this would happen," Joe said. "Why didn't you believe me? You can't protect her. You can't protect either of them."

He turned away from me, leaving me there in the grass as blood poured from the stumps of my arms.

"You shouldn't have even tried."

I sat up, grunting at the crack of thunder. I looked at my hands and felt a rush of relief when I saw they were still there. I was in a tent, and I heard nothing but a hundred snores. I tried to breathe as my heartrate started to come down.

But as the dream wore off and reality set in, I panicked big time. I was absolutely convinced that Joe or Leona had just stolen Roxy away from me. I knew he had tech that could pull it off. I was sure of it. She'd been taken.

I took off for the house where the army officials were still returning from the battle. After a search of our room and the house, I was sure my dream had come true. I found General Washington.

"Roxy has been taken. I need to find her. She might be somewhere in the area."

Washington frowned, but I sensed he was willing to help. "Taken by your mother?"

"Or her other son. Maybe both of them."

"Son of the future, your troubles worry me more than mine at times."

"Me too, General."

"Take a few of the men and search the woods as far as the river."

I thanked him quickly and ran. I made sure my laser pistol was working and gathered the men and took off. "Make sure you don't try to engage him," I warned the men, who only slightly veiled their annoyance at receiving another mission while they were trying to recover from the last one. "He's dangerous. Just find me and tell me where he is."

We searched for an hour, and I got more panicked and desperate as it became obvious there was nothing in the woods around us except a few drunk German soldiers. I sent the soldiers home and pulled out my WristCom.

"Greer? Greer, please come in. Roxy's missing."

There was no answer. The com was dead, silent, as if it had no power, even though I knew it did. I was starting to wonder if Greer had betrayed us. I couldn't even imagine it, but I didn't know what else to think. I pressed on, running through the woods toward something I only felt, but couldn't see.

A sudden electric surge caused my body to go rigid. It felt like I had walked into a wall of static. A moment later it stopped. I opened my eyes and looked around.

I was in a white, sterile-looking room. The sides of the small area were stocked with futuristic meds and tools. Data centers with med tech floated in the air above a plain steel table.

Roxy was lying on the table, unconscious. She was dressed in a thin white robe, and her abdomen was exposed.

"Levi," I heard a voice, and Arabella Eisen stepped into the room.

I stared at her in disbelief. "How …?"

She smiled and came to me, putting her hands on my shoulders. "It's so good to see you, Levi."

I accepted her hug, still in shock. "It's good to see you, too. I can't describe how much. I left you in 1874 with a bullet through your head."

She nodded and smiled again, as if I had brought up a happy old memory we shared.

"I'm fine," she said as she turned back to the table where Roxy slept. I was not done with my questions, but I decided to put them on hold when I saw her.

"Why is she unconscious?" I went to the table and reached for Roxy's hand. It was cold. I felt panic, but I told myself Arabella would be upset if there was something wrong.

"Don't worry, she's fine," Arabella said, reaching for Roxy's arm and pressing an injector to her skin. "She'll wake up in a few minutes. I put her in a deep stasis coma while I did the surgery."

"Surgery?" I almost didn't want to hear her answer. "What's wrong with her? Is it the baby?"

Arabella took my arm and led me to two plain chairs side by side at the wall. We sat down and she took my hands in hers. "Levi,

I'm so happy for you and Roxy. I'm so glad you are going to have this child."

"I am, too," I said, and I meant it. I hadn't realized it until I saw Roxy on the table. "But is something wrong with the baby?"

"No. The baby is fine. I just needed to fix something that happened when Roxy was stabbed with the sword."

"Something I couldn't fix?"

She shook her head. "Don't worry. Nothing is wrong with your gift. But the baby had an extensive injury. You saved your little one's life, but you didn't have enough strength to overcome the problem that developed in the heart. I was sent back to correct the issue and guarantee your child's good health."

"Thank you."

She shrugged. "As I remember, you saved my baby once upon a time. I owed you."

I looked at Roxy. "I'd do it again in a heartbeat."

"You have," she reminded me.

We were quiet for a moment before she spoke. "Levi, when you left me in 1874, I was dead. You weren't mistaken and you didn't leave me without doing everything you could to save me. Don't misunderstand."

"Then how are you here?"

"One of the members of our village council decided to go against the decision to bring my body back to the village and revive me. She thought it was better to alter the timeline and prevent my death."

I heard sadness in her voice, though I didn't understand why. "What village? What council?"

She watched me, as if she was wondering if I would make sense of it on my own.

"You have heard of it. When you met Sophie." She continued to watch me with interest.

Again, the name was familiar, but I couldn't remember why.

"Sometimes I have trouble remembering where we are. What you already know," she said with an apologetic smile. "Sophie came to live at the bunker with Roxy for a short time before she was taken into custody at the citadel."

I remembered then. I felt a rush of emotion when I remembered the young girl who had died in the chair. One of the many I hadn't been able to save. And she'd reminded me of Roxy. "I remember Sophie."

Arabella nodded. "Anyway, I was glad for my friend's decision to save me in 1874, but there were repercussions."

She didn't elaborate. "Levi, I need to know if you've seen or talked to Joe or Leona."

I nodded. "Both. They're here. They want to kill Roxy and change history so that the United States never happens."

"I know they went into the portal with homemade tech, but I haven't been able to see what they are doing. I need you to tell me everything you know."

"Wait, what do you mean you haven't been able to see them? Didn't you come here from 1874? How have you been watching them?"

She hesitated. "I didn't come here from 1874. I came here from a time beyond yours. From the Transient village."

"I know that name." I frowned in thought. "Sophie. She said it all the time. It was the only thing she said. 'I am Sephora of the Transient.'"

"She was. Born to save the past."

"So you're older than the Arabella we saw in 1874?" I asked, still somewhat confused.

She smiled. "A few years older."

I shook my head. "I think I need a spreadsheet to get this all straight."

She nodded. "That's why we keep them in the village. It gets quite complicated."

"Something tells me that's an understatement. So you came from the Transient village to fix a heart problem in our baby. And because you need to know what Joe is doing."

"Basically," she said. "Have you seen him?"

"Not technically. He always appears as a hologram. He invented some kind of tech that allows him to interact—quite dramatically—with us. I'm almost sure he can also influence our dreams. But Roxy saw him yesterday. And we both think he's here to kill her."

I didn't like to even say the words. I looked at Roxy, who was starting to breathe more normally and regain color in her cheeks.

"I know you'll do what you have to do to protect them," Arabella patted my hand. "I believe in you, Levi. You have what it takes to be a great leader."

I was doubtful, but encouraged by the words. "I want to be. I want to save my city."

"You will. Just be the kind of man I know you can be and you will inspire the kind of changes you're hoping to make."

Roxy began to stir. Arabella got up and went to her side, smoothing back her hair and smiling in a motherly way. I watched in fascination and envy. What would it be to have a mother like Arabella Eisen?

"It's amazing," Roxy answered me in a croaky voice.

"What's amazing?" Arabella put her palm on Roxy's cheek.

"Having you for a mom. Levi asked."

She nodded and glanced at me. "I'm proud of you two."

Roxy gave her a miserable frown. "Why? I was weak, Mom. I made mistakes."

Arabella chuckled. "Yes, my precious girl, you have. So have we all. Your character is found in what you do with those mistakes."

"I don't know why you're still alive, and I'm sure there's an explanation, but right now, I don't care." Roxy reached out to hug her mother. "I love you, Mom."

"I love you too, baby girl. And Levi will fill you in. But my time is up. I have to get you both back to where you belong."

"To 2076?" I asked, hopeful. She shook her head.

"Not just yet, Levi. But soon. Right now I need you to stop Joe and Leona."

"I had a feeling you'd say that," Roxy said with a sigh. She reached down and felt the faint scar on her stomach. "Is the baby okay?"

"Yes. Your baby is just fine," Arabella said quietly and kissed her daughter's forehead.

"Mom, I don't think I'm ready for this."

"You're never ready. It's something that is created in you when your child is born. You'll know what to do and you'll know how to take care of this little one. I promise." Arabella looked at me. "You both will."

I nodded at Roxy. "I guess we better go find Joe and Leona."

"I'll send you back." Before Arabella touched the controller on her arm, she went to the supply shelf and handed me another injector gun. "This is good for one reviving. You'll know when to use it."

I nodded, gulping at the responsibility. She grabbed my arm and waited until I met her focused gaze.

"The injector is for *you*, Levi. Don't use it on anyone else."

TWENTY-EIGHT

I knew she was in the tent. During the battle, my eyes kept wandering to it. She was watching. She was calculating. I was sure my mother was waiting for the right moment to interfere.

I crept away from my line and approached the back of the tent. I lifted the coarse fabric enough so I could slip underneath. I stood up inside, surprised to see a large china cabinet on one wall of the tent and iron bedposts on the other. Wasn't this a war? Why were they carrying all that crap with them wherever they went?

"I've told the Howes that they should leave the furniture and china behind. It's slowing them down. But the English have their traditions," Leona said.

I came prepared to confront her. I was determined to end the threat so I could find a way to get Roxy home. But when Leona faced me, I hesitated. I could see hints of the young woman in the video file. She was in there somewhere. She was a part of the woman my mother had become.

I knew Roxy didn't get it. She was black and white. Right or wrong. My conflicted feelings about my mother had driven a wedge between Roxy and me since the day we met and I was wearing the uniform of a citadel officer. And I didn't blame Roxy.

But Roxy hadn't known my mom before she went crazy with power. I wished somehow I could show Roxy who Leona was when she was just a young mom trying to save the world with her genius. When she was the forgotten teenager who had lost her parents and everything else, and had to teach herself and make her own way. There was a part of me that stubbornly refused to believe her past didn't count for something.

"Leona," I spoke, leaning on my bayonet rifle.

"Levi." She nodded with a regal air.

I had to do something about her. It wouldn't be easy, but it had to happen. If history was going to be set right, and if my bond with Roxy was ever going to work, I had to deal with this person in front of me.

"I didn't expect to see you," she said, her voice soft and melodic. It matched the rest of her appearance, refined and pleasant. It was hard to imagine she was ruthless.

"We're not going to let you go." I shook my head, trying not to let the torn, sad feeling get in the way of my sense of justice. "What you're doing is wrong, and I'm going to stop you. Now."

Her expression remained even. "I simply ended up here and I'm making the best of it. I haven't done anything to change the course of this war."

"You're trying to give the British the advantage to win. You're trying to keep America from existing."

She laughed in disbelief. "Levi, I don't know where you get these ideas. I'm only trying to stay alive. If I'm going to remain in 1776, the safest place is in the British camp."

"You told me you were influencing General Howe, Mother. You can't change your story now." I felt my jaw clench.

"I'm not changing anything," she said. "What makes you so sure the colonies are meant to win this war?"

I made the mistake of looking into her eyes. Everything I wanted to be in her expression was there. Care, compassion, affection, concern.

"Don't." I took a step back, trying to remember my resolve, reminding myself of everything at stake.

"Levi, listen to me," she said, taking a step in my direction. "I know that you think I have harmed our relationship. I'm sorry you were wounded by my aspirations. If I could go back and mend it, I would. I'd do anything for you. Don't you know that? You're my son."

Underneath my disappointment, realization came to life, awkward and unsure and ugly. I wanted her love. I craved her approval.

She's lying! She's manipulating you! I heard Roxy's voice in my head. I looked around, afraid she had joined the battle again, but the words had come from my own consciousness. From the place in my brain where Roxy would always live.

This woman wanted to destroy what I hoped would be a long life of never being separated from Roxy Eisen again. I was an idiot to crave love from someone who manipulated instead of treasured, and schemed to get what she wanted.

But it was like a drug—the hunger.

She crossed to me. The dramatic swishing of her skirts was the only sound in the room. She reached a tiny, delicate hand to my shoulder. "I saw her."

"Who?" I fidgeted with the buttons on my coat.

"Roxanne, of course. I know she is expecting, Levi."

I didn't answer. Was she giving me a veiled threat? I remembered Roxy, starved and tortured in the archives, and gripped my weapon tighter.

"I'm not upset," she said with a prim smile. "How could I be angry about becoming a grandmother?"

I met her eyes, anger pulsing. "Let's get one thing straight. Roxy and I don't know anything about being parents, but we're doing it *on our own.* You will not be involved."

She kept her even expression, as if I had not spoken. "I remember when I was expecting you. I was so scared and so alone. I didn't know how I would handle raising you by myself."

"Yeah, about that," I said. "You mind telling me who my father is?"

"It's not important now." She gave me another infuriating smile. It wasn't important to *her,* she meant. "You will be a good father."

"I'll do my best, no thanks to you." I watched her face transform into a pout.

"Why do you hate me? Haven't I always tried to do what was best for you? I gave you everything you could have wanted."

"All at the expense others," I snapped back at her. "You pushed your best friend into the portal. You tortured Roxy. She would have died if I hadn't healed her. You sent us through the portal to be hunted down by your mongrel son in 1874. You escaped the justice you had coming, and you are trying to destroy the history of America. Don't forget any of these things, because I haven't forgotten. None of us have. You're going to answer for them. You're going back to 2076."

She narrowed her eyes.

"I'm not letting it happen again. It's better for everyone if your story ends here," I continued.

I felt the intense pain in my head, and radiating through the rest of my body. I knew what she was doing—she'd done it to me every time I crossed her as a child. I tried in vain to escape her gaze, feeling exhausted with the mental effort.

"Are you here to kill me, Levi?"

I groaned at the physical pain she inflicted. It felt like I was going to self-destruct.

"If you make me," I managed.

"Why?" She let go of me and I fell back, released from the painful possession.

"Because I love Roxy. I choose her. I choose the principles of the founders of America. They have a right to be free. We all do." I paused, stepping backward when I heard voices outside the tent. "I don't get you and your British friends. Don't you realize martyrs only strengthen causes? When you kill someone for standing up for what's right, you make your enemy stronger."

"No mother should be hated by her own child," she said in a wounded tone. She hadn't heard a word I said. "Everyone makes mistakes. Why do you cling to bitterness, Levi?"

I hesitated. Was she admitting, on some level, that she was wrong?

British soldiers were returning to camp. I shouldn't have left her there, but I knew she would make a scene if I tried to take her with me, and I'd be outnumbered. It would have to wait until another day.

"Soon, mother. Count on it."

We were staying at the Keith House in Bucks County, Eastern Pennsylvania. Washington gathered the residents to the drawing room the following evening to tell us what he had not told the soldiers yet. We were facing another battle. He had labored over the decision, but he had decided to have the entire army sneak across the Delaware River and attack unprepared Hessian troops in Trenton on Christmas Day.

His gaze caught mine as the room went silent with surprise. Washington watched me as if gauging my reaction. He thought I had some insight into whether he was making a mistake or not.

I remembered a painting in the archives. George Washington and his men, crossing a river. It was so big that as I stood in front of it, I felt like I was with them in the boats, crossing the Delaware in the cold, icy night. After I'd become governor of New York I'd had it brought up and hung in the throne room of the citadel.

He had the same look on his face in the painting that he had in the drawing room as he watched me. Determination, but mingled with guilt.

I gave him a small nod. He seemed relieved.

"My courageous friends," the general said in a quiet voice. "I have invited our comrade, Captain Thomas Paine, to read you a portion of his writing to aid your commitment to our cause on this holiest of nights."

At first I didn't know what he meant. But I'd noticed the festive dinner and decorations in the windows. Leona had banned Christmas celebrations, so I had no personal association with the holiday, but I could guess it had been an important day before the country fell.

"Tomorrow is Christmas Eve," Roxy whispered. Her hand absently held the growing bump on her abdomen. She couldn't hide it anymore, so she'd endured a few comments from the women in the house.

Actually, Mrs. Washington claims they already knew. They were just waiting for me to say something. Roxy rolled her eyes.

The women had ambushed her with advice. Some of it was shocking. It was no wonder so many mothers and babies died in 1776.

I took her hand and kissed it. "Happy Christmas."

"I think it's *Merry Christmas*," she corrected.

"I wouldn't know. Leona didn't even let us discuss it." I shrugged.

"Morris made sure we celebrated it in the bunker. He always had a small gift for everyone, and we sang songs and had a special meal."

I was glad. I wished I had been a bunker kid as well. "I think this guy should know about Christmas." I patted her stomach.

"I agree this *gal* should know," she said, raising an eyebrow. I grinned. Then I imagined having a daughter who looked just like Roxy, and it was hard to breathe.

Paine stood up. He wasn't a big guy. I heard his fear through Roxy's mind. He didn't even want to stand up in front of us to read his writing, let alone go out and fight the battle.

"He's sad," Roxy whispered thoughtfully. "He thinks he's got everything figured out, but he doesn't like his conclusions."

"No one likes ideas when they are first spoken or considered," I said.

"But it's more than that." She shook her head and sat up a little straighter, watching Paine. "It's like he's determined to believe the worst, because it is too much to hope for the best."

Paine began to read. "These are the times that try men's souls. The summer soldier and the sunshine patriot will, in this crisis, shrink from the service of his country, but he that stands it now deserves the love and thanks of man and woman. Tyranny, like hell, is not easily conquered. Yet we have this consolation with us, that the harder the conflict, the more glorious the triumph."

Roxy met my eyes. Neither of us thought specific ideas, but our feelings matched.

His words were timeless.

TWENTY-NINE

"I think I want you to go with us," I said to Roxy. I saw her frown and decided to phrase it differently. "Will you come tonight?"

She was pale. I had intended to make sure she was asleep in bed before heading out to the nighttime ambush, but I felt conflicted as I stood in the doorway of our room. I wasn't sure I should leave her. Not with her pregnancy coming to an end, and Leona and Joe so close. So dangerous.

She was surprised, but she didn't say it. "As a soldier?"

I debated. It would be easier to explain her presence if she went as a soldier. But I didn't want her to be a target.

"Take my civilian clothes. Plenty of the soldiers don't even have uniforms," I said, going to the dresser and taking out the clothes I had bought when we first arrived.

She didn't argue, which bugged me. Was she trying to stay close to me because she knew there was something wrong?

She changed in the shadows and came forward in my trousers and linen shirt as she pulled the jacket and boots on. She turned so I could tie her hair back at the nape of her neck, and then I set my tricorn hat on her head with a smile.

"Smokin'."

She scoffed, but she didn't complain when I chanced a quick

kiss.

"What is the plan, specifically?" She asked after we crept down the stairs and headed outside to the camp.

"Washington assigned regiments to different points at the Delaware River. We're going to cross, and march down to Trenton and surround them. We'll target the Hessian outposts and take Trenton for the colonies."

"Sounds simple when you say it like that." Roxy pulled her coat around her and shivered. "But did he take into account the weather?"

I hadn't missed the freezing rain that was quickly turning to snow. The river would be a mess.

"You almost have to wonder if Leona's doing something to the weather. It hasn't been this bad all December," Roxy mused.

I grimaced. If my mother could inflict pain on a person using her mind, it wasn't much of a leap to think she could cause a freeze-out.

As if on cue, the wind picked up. By the time we reached the regiment heading out toward the river, my fingers and toes felt numb, and Roxy's face was stained an icy pink.

The men stood in huddled packs, trying to stay warm. The ferries were loaded, for the most part. Washington paced in front of them.

He addressed a messenger boy with a sharp tone. "They were to be ready two hours ago, and they are still an hour out?" He held a hand to his head. "Start sending over the weapons and supplies."

It was going to be a late night.

As I stood behind Roxy—trying to block the wind from reaching her without letting her know I was doing it—I watched Washington pace in agitation. Finally, he grabbed his tricorn and shoved it on his head. He marched through the thin layer of snow accumulating on top of the ice to the edge of the woods nearby. He fell to his knees.

I watched in curiosity as he knelt in the snow, gesturing with his hands. His lips moved in silent entreaty.

He seemed to find peace. It occurred to me the guy knew how to come down from that panic, that responsibility for everyone else. I knew from experience it could be overwhelming. Curiosity got the best of me.

"I'll be right back," I said to Roxy. I was tempted to take off my coat and put it around her shoulders, but it would seem odd to everyone around us.

Back off. I'm fine.

I won't be long.

Washington saw me coming and stood before I got to him, reaching down to wipe the snow from his knees.

"What can I do for you this bitter night, Mr. Koenig?"

I realized I wasn't sure how to ask my question.

"You are the leader of your people in the future?" he asked tentatively. I wasn't sure what he was uneasy about—the time travel thing, or me being unable to carry on a conversation. We walked toward the river where men were trudging around, trying to stay warm.

"By default only. I was elected when my mother was dethroned."

"It saddens me to think of New York being taken once more by tyranny. May I ask the state of the rest of the colonies?"

I sighed. "As hard as it is to say this to you—I'm afraid to tell you too much. You are so important to our history. I don't want to mess anything up."

He nodded, showing no sign of being offended.

"I need to ask you something as one leader to another," I finally said. "What were you doing in the snow? Why do you seem so calm about the position you are in? Doesn't it make you crazy?"

Washington regarded me evenly. "You have no belief in God, I take it?"

I wasn't sure how to answer. "I don't know. It's complicated." He watched me expectantly, so I continued. "You have to consider where I've come from. My mother only taught me what she wanted me to know so I would be her unquestioning little soldier. I have no background of faith. I have no knowledge of anything beyond what I've been able to dig up on my own, and I don't understand why there is evil. But when I look at the massiveness of time and space, and the complexity of the sciences, it seems ridiculous to say there isn't some sort of intelligence—extreme intelligence—behind it all." I hesitated. "I guess I'm saying I'm not sure about religion."

He watched me thoughtfully as I spoke. "You know, many of the people here in the colonies were trying to escape religion in coming here."

I shrugged. "I thought they wanted to be free to be religious."

"Some. But there were some who were tired of the way the church manipulated people and sought its own gain in the name of God. They came here to figure out what it means to really seek and know the Creator."

"Are you saying *you've* found him?"

Washington looked out over the dark river, swarming with chunks of ice covered with a dusting of snow. The wind blew them haphazardly downstream, and they collided with each other, breaking and forming new chunks until the water was completely covered by them.

"He is hard to see," Washington said softly. "Until a man realizes he has no other option but to look up and beg for mercy. When I am confident in myself and sure of my path, I have no need of God. But when I am aware of my fragile condition as a man, and when I see how everyone hopes in me to lead them to freedom, I become desperate for a being more capable than me. And then I find his strength."

I nodded. "I can see you have peace. You've found a power source I haven't."

Washington stared out at the churning water. "There are still moments when I am unsure of anything. But in the end, I believe the point of it all is for me to understand it is not about me." He clamped a big hand on my shoulder. His eyes caught sight of Roxy.

"You and the young lady, things have seemed strained."

I looked at him in surprise, my eyes following his gaze to

Roxy, standing in the cold, looking pale and as uncomfortable as I'd ever seen her. When I looked back at Washington, he raised an eyebrow in silent challenge. I couldn't fool George Washington so easily.

I shrugged. "That's the understatement of the century. Or of three centuries."

He waited for me to continue.

"I know it must seem weird to you, since she's pregnant, and we haven't worked out our relationship yet."

"And by that you mean you have not married? I confess, I wonder as to the state of the future if such is commonplace." He didn't sound judgmental. Only concerned.

"My mother decimated the idea of marriage by forcing her wishes on everyone. But even before that, people weren't getting married as much."

"Why is that?" He folded his arms across his chest, moving back and forth in the snow to stay warm.

"I don't know. I guess it was because marriage doesn't seem to make people happy."

He shook his head. "I have never thought of marriage as a means to make one happy. Any time two people decide to live closely with one another there will be a conflict of interests. Do you and Miss Eisen believe you would be unhappy if you made a commitment to each other?"

"I don't care," I said immediately. "I've always known, as crazy as she makes me, I never want to be apart."

"Although I question your decision to bring her along this particular night, I do believe you have stumbled on the nature of lasting affection," he said with a faint smile.

"If only I could convince her."

"Well, she clearly holds affection for you," Washington said, nodding toward her.

"What makes you say that?" I was curious. Had Washington seen something I missed?

"I was referring to her delicate condition."

"Oh," I said with a chuckle. "I guess that part is easier. But she's scared."

"Does she not think she needs your assistance to raise the child?"

I shook my head. "I think she's afraid that if she gave in and committed to stay with me, it would make her weak. Dependent on someone who could let her down."

"A strand of two cords is stronger than one," Washington blew into his hands and surveyed his men with an eye of concern as they tried in vain to escape the driving wind and freezing rain.

"You don't have to tell me, President Washington."

After a moment, he seemed desperate to pick up the conversation again. To not think about what he was doing for as long as he could. "The young Miss Thomas held affection for you as well."

I looked down. I did not want to think about Madeline. I hadn't been able to protect her. She had died for me.

"She was a beautiful young lady." Washington mused.

You have no idea what that beauty cost her.

"I guess I like my woman rough around the edges," I said.

He chuckled. "Then you must persuade the one you love. Even the toughest shells need the same things. Unconditional love, respect, and loyalty. As far as I can see, these are the keys to a lasting union."

"I will remember your advice with great honor, sir."

"Governor Koenig, if there are men of your breed three hundred years in the future, I do not despair for our country."

I was going to leave the man in peace and go back to keeping Roxy warm, but he stopped me with a strange look.

"May I ask why you addressed me as *President* Washington?"

THIRTY

"I should have asked Washington for leave to stay back with you," I whispered, rubbing the back of her coat in an attempt to keep her warm. It was well past midnight and we were finally getting into the boats to cross.

"Levi, stop thinking," she said, rolling her eyes. "We're here. I'm a big girl. Don't be a mudsill."

We set off across the water. I helped push ice chunks away from the side of the boat with a long stick and looked at the other ferries on either side. How many times had I stared at that painting in the archives and never realized Roxy and I had been on these boats and part of this crossing?

I felt helpless to ease whatever bothered Roxy. As time went on, she seemed to forget she was supposed to be a soldier. She clutched both sides of her stomach, her face white and her lips blue. I was locked between two responsibilities—getting America off to the right start and taking care of my family. Could I do both? If I couldn't, which one did I sacrifice?

Had I influenced Washington too much? Had time accounted for my involvement, or was it readjusting? Could I only save history by knowing it? I wished I knew if I was doing the right thing.

Roxy didn't complain. She didn't make a sound. She would

push as long and far as I did, and then go an extra measure to stay ahead. But I could tell she was in pain.

The night possessed an eerie stillness, disrupted only by the sounds of disgruntled horses as they tried to keep balance on the ferries. Just as the bank of the other side came into view, a strangled cry suddenly tore through the silence.

Roxy.

I met her eyes, which were wide and afraid.

I shook my head. *Not now!*

I wasn't saying it to her, but I got a cold glare for my thought.

You can't protect them. They're going to die. Joe's words filled my head. I didn't want to think about the treasure I was dragging across the Delaware on an icy cold Christmas night so far in the past.

It's too early! Roxy gritted her teeth. *There's no way this baby's coming out right now.*

Babies don't follow orders. They don't wait. If your body wants to have a baby, you don't get a vote.

She seethed at me, but she'd seen enough of birth to know I was right. Then she gasped as if she'd had the breath knocked out of her.

The next moments felt like a full week of torture as I listened to her labored breathing echoing in my ears as loudly as the cries from her mind. Her fingers were latched on to my coat; her knuckles were white. She watched my boot and my stick push away the ice chunks with an intense stare. It made me dedicated to the task. Everything would get much worse if one of those shards ripped a hole in our boat and we sank into the nearly frozen water.

After our boat made contact with the other shore, I heaved her up the embankment with help from some of the soldiers. I noticed they were trying to pretend one of their fellow soldiers was not about to have a baby. The soldiers cleared their throats and moved away. Roxy fell back against a tree, clinging to her stomach. She was oblivious to everyone around her.

"The pains are close together," I noted, because it seemed

important. I didn't know anything about childbirth, but it was obvious things were getting real.

"That means it's almost here," she said between gasps, her voice breathless and panicked. She would know from her time in the bunker.

I desperately scanned the area, wondering where in the world I could take Roxy to have her baby. On this cold night, would the baby even survive? We needed shelter.

I saw Washington. I left Roxy by the tree and ran to his side.

"Sir, I need your leave from the battle. The baby is coming and there is no one else to take care of Roxy—"

"Say no more." He held up a hand to stop me. "You are excused. God be with you."

"And you," I said before I turned back to Roxy. I helped her up and put her arm around my neck. We headed in the direction of Trenton. It was the closest town, and if I could beat the army and get Roxy there before the battle began, we could take shelter.

I got halfway to Trenton on adrenaline. We kept having to stop while she got through contractions. Finally, I picked her up and carried her. The sounds that came from Roxy terrified me. Was it normal for her to be in so much pain? Without medical intervention, they could both die. I could fix some things, but I couldn't bring either of them back from the dead.

The injector gun.

As soon as I had the thought, Roxy opened her eyes and glared at me.

Mom said that was only for you. Don't you dare.

I saw an abandoned shed with no door ahead of us. I wasn't sure what lived in the shadows, but at least it would get us out of the snow and wind. Another contraction seized her, and her face turned purple as she fought it with hardly a sound. Something told me she should work with the contractions, not against them, but Roxy always fought. I remembered when she had fought the portal the first time we went through and she had nearly broken every bone in her body. Now she fought this the same way.

I set her on her feet in the shed. I took off my coat, laid it on the ground and helped her with the trousers.

"Don't attack it, Roxy. Go with it," I suggested as she laid back on the coat.

She turned fierce, wild eyes on me. "You idiot mudsill! This is YOUR fault! If I die it will be YOUR FAULT!"

Another contraction took her breath and she squeezed her eyes shut and tilted her face upward. When it passed, she kicked me so hard I fell back against the wall.

"I hate you! I hate you and I wish you were dead!"

Don't smile. Smile and she'll kill me.

But there was the mind-reading obstacle. "Give me my knife so I can slit your throat!" She added a few more colorful words. I gathered her face in my hands and put my forehead against hers, because suddenly the sight of her enduring such a huge act of love on behalf of both of us made me love her more than I ever had before.

"I'm so sorry, Rox. I wish I could fix this. I would do it for you if I could. You are so strong. So strong and beautiful, and you're doing great."

She cried out again and grabbed my knee so hard I had to bite my lip to keep back my own yell. She steeled herself and pushed with a power I'd never witnessed before. I was in awe, though I had the presence of mind to get in the catching position.

As she gasped for air, another cry joined hers. I stared in amazement when I realized what had happened. In that precious moment of time, even as we were lost in the past, our baby had entered the world, sputtering and gasping for air on my rebel uniform jacket.

I picked up the squirming, slippery mass in my arms. The little person reminded me of Roxy, fighting and protesting the state of things.

I realized it was a boy. I was holding my son in my arms.

I was a father.

THIRTY-ONE

The same moment I handed the baby to Roxy, canon fire erupted, shaking the ground.

The attack on Trenton had begun. I needed to get my family to safety.

At first I thought I was going to have to carry Roxy and the baby through the woods, in the dark, for the two-mile trek to Trenton. But as I scanned the dilapidated shed, something caught my eye.

It was a folded piece of paper, stuck between the rotting boards of the wall. I reached up and grabbed it.

It had my name on it.

I quickly unfolded it and read the message.

Dear Levi,

I had a feeling this might come in handy. Congratulations!

Arabella Eisen

I looked around to see what she meant. Beneath the space where the letter had been, there was a canvas bag tucked behind loose boards.

I pulled it open and laughed aloud.

"It's a jet pack," I said. "Your mom left us a jet pack."

What should have been a sleeping town was alive with frantic calls to take shelter. King Street glowed with the light of lanterns and torches. Before we entered the town, I stowed the pack in a hollow log, intending to return for it later. I heaved Roxy up in my arms, noticing her eyes had closed and her face was white as a ghost.

"We need a doctor! Is there a doctor in town?" I shouted as people hurried around me.

The door opened two houses down. A woman peeked out.

"Do you mean to call for a midwife?" She gestured to Roxy and the crying baby.

I nodded, and she motioned me in. The woman quickly shut the door behind me. She pushed a long board in place over the slats.

She wasted no time, motioning me to bring Roxy into the back of the house. She pulled a cot to the corner wall by the fire. I laid Roxy on it and stepped back as the woman sat down on the cot and took the baby.

"When was he born?" She took him from my coat and looked him over as he fussed and tried to get his fist in his mouth.

"Just a few minutes ago. Before the fighting started."

"He is small."

"I think he should have had another three weeks or so."

"His breathing and color are good. He should survive if we can keep him warm."

Her fingers fell to the faint, jagged scar across the baby's chest. "How strange," she murmured.

She began to wrap the baby tightly in blankets. "She gave birth by herself?"

"I was with her," I said, glancing out the window when I heard shouting and the whiz of musket balls.

"Men should nay be witness to a birth," she said.

205

I shrugged. "I wasn't going to leave her on her own."

"Has she delivered the afterbirth?"

I had no clue what she meant. I definitely didn't want to know, either.

"The baby was born about ten minutes ago. I haven't seen anything but a whole lot of blood."

She nodded and glanced at Roxy.

"Let me help," I said, reaching for the baby. "What can I do?"

She only hesitated a moment as she glanced at Roxy's pallid face. "Wash him and apply some of the oil in that decanter on the mantel. Rub him down and wrap him in the clean linens you will find in that top drawer. Keep him close to the fire. He will cry to eat, but I must see to your wife first. If he becomes inconsolable you can dip a clean rag in the milk bucket and drip it into his mouth."

I followed her instructions, and as I did I remembered the small pack Madeline had given me the night before she died.

I reached into my bag and found the parcel. Inside, hidden in the wrappings were a small wool cap, mittens and a warm blanket. I breathed my thanks around a lump in my throat as I dressed the tiny baby with awkward fingers that seemed too big for such a task, and wrapped him in the blanket.

I kept the baby close to me and near the fire as I watched Roxy. The woman examined her and frowned at the amount of blood. She told me to look away for a time and when I looked back she was at the fireplace grinding herbs to make a tea. She didn't tell me what she was doing, and she sent me several pointed glances as if I was invading her space. We listened in silence to the occasional booms and constant gunfire all around us. I determined to protect my son if any of that artillery hit the house.

The midwife helped Roxy sit up and drink the tea, and then exchanged the trousers and shirt for a clean nightgown. To her credit, she didn't ask why Roxy was wearing men's clothes. She helped Roxy move to the rocking chair so she could change the linens on the cot.

I came and put the baby in Roxy's arms and reached my hand under the sleeve of her gown to pass my healing energy to her body. The color returned to her face and she didn't seem so tired.

"Go in the front room, sir," the midwife said. "I must teach your wife to feed the baby."

Roxy's eyes got big and she looked at me. Silent name-calling ensued.

You'll be great, I promised her. I went to the front room and looked out the window, seeing the dim light of dawn on the eastern horizon. The cannon fire was more sporadic; I didn't see any soldiers. According to history, I was almost certain we were supposed to win this one. It didn't keep me from obsessing about whether I'd messed it up.

"I am Mrs. Cuthright," I heard the woman speak softly to Roxy. "I am the midwife here in Trenton. Your bleeding has slowed, and it is important for your wee one to eat. I will help you. Is this your first child?"

"Uh, yeah," Roxy answered, sounding not a little bit uncomfortable with her circumstances.

"What is your name?"

"Roxy."

I turned and listened to Roxy's mind as Mrs. Cuthright patiently helped her. Using her thoughts, I could picture Roxy's face, and I was fascinated by the mental image of her looking on in awe and a sweet kind of anxiety as the baby ate his first meal.

"It is my duty to ask you to name the father of the child," Mrs. Cuthright murmured, like she didn't want me to hear her. "Are you married to the gentleman who brought you here?"

Just agree with her. I said silently, but she hesitated too long.

"You could say that," she finally said.

The midwife was doubtful. "Have you had a ceremony and had your union blessed by a preacher?"

When's the last time you saw a preacher in our city, Levi?

I knew what she meant. *I saw them. But they didn't last long on their corners before they were dragged away.*

It was one of the worst aspects of Leona's regime. Taking the preachers to the citadel. Not the ones who spouted off hatred and bitterness, but the ones who were kind and respectful, even when the Peace Implementers pushed them around. Even when they were standing in front of the portal with their hands bound and their chests scarred by the brander. They were the ones who had spoken about the power of love.

That had stayed with me.

"It's complicated," Roxy said to the midwife.

"Then I am required by law to ask you the name of the father."

None of your freakin' business, lady.

Play nice, Roxy.

"He's the guy who caught him when he was born and hasn't left me yet. Levi Koenig is this baby's father."

Mrs. Cuthright didn't seem impressed. "If you have not been legally married, I must warn you that you will be expected to do so before you leave this town. Your husband could be imprisoned for refusing."

Roxy was irritated. "What if *I* refuse?"

"Why would ye refuse? Do you not want this little one cared for?"

"I can take care of him," Roxy said stubbornly. "But I know his father. I've known him my entire life. He'll be around."

I gave her my silent promise.

The midwife sighed like she was ready to be done with us. "What will his name be?" She said the words louder, as if she knew I was listening and addressed me.

Roxy and I had the same thought at the same time.

Morris.

"His name is Morris Koenig," Roxy said, and I heard the smile that played on her lips.

"A family name?" The midwife moved to stoke the fire.

Roxy paused before she answered. "He was my father. He died."

"He must have been a good father," Mrs. Cuthright replied as she began to prepare supper.

"The best."

I turned around and stared out at the street, stained with the blood of soldiers whose lives had ended the day Morris' began.

I prayed I could be half the man my son's namesake had been.

Roxy had been uncertain about motherhood the first night, but by the end of the first week she was an old pro.

I remembered the first time I visited the bunker. New mothers had been everywhere, and none of them were overly obsessed with their babies. They carried them around like baby monkeys, feeding them and changing them as they went about their other tasks, tying them on their chests with scarves as the babies slept.

Roxy carried on the traditions. She found a length of fabric and made a sling, and the third day after Morris' birth she started hauling water and washing vegetables for our simple meals with Mrs. Cuthright.

The midwife tried to make her stay in bed, but it was a lesson in futility.

"I've never seen Roxy sit and be still. You might as well just let her work," I told her as she complained about Roxy bringing potatoes up from the cellar.

Mrs. Cuthright only tossed her hands in the air, as if she was clearing herself of responsibility before she left the house to milk the goat.

"Girls in the bunker were required to be back to work two days after a normal birth," Roxy said as she unwrapped the baby to change him. "Why is this time obsessed with a girl lying around and hoping not to die?"

"Probably because it's common to die," I said, trying not to laugh. "Would it really kill you to rest for a few days?"

"Just because I gave birth to your child doesn't mean I'm going to be cooped up in a stuffy room for days and days. Besides, we have to get back to the portal site and find a way home. Every day we stay here is another day for Joe to find us. If he finds out about baby Morris …" Her voice trailed away. Neither of us wanted to consider that scenario.

I took her to the millinery after the army cleared out and we had cared for the dead. While Roxy picked up her new dress she'd been fitted for the day before, I listened to the reports on the battle from the old men who gathered in the street to discuss the war. The battle had lasted only an hour. The Continental army had suffered no losses. It had been a decisive victory. Spirits were high and the troops had found the courage to keep up the resistance when many of them could have gone home, released from their contracts.

When Roxy stepped out of the shop, she wore, most likely, the simplest dress in the plainest pattern available, but her cheeks were so rosy and her eyes so bright with love as she cooed to Morris that she could have been wearing an imported ball gown and not have been any more beautiful.

"I hate to waste the little money we have," she said in explanation to my thought as she smoothed the skirt. I caught her hand and squeezed it.

"You needed something. You look beautiful." *And your figure has ... changed.*

She hit me. It wasn't the first time I'd been hit for noticing her different profile, and you'd think I'd have learned to stop after the first hundred times or so, but I couldn't seem to help it.

I rubbed my sore arm. "I just meant to say you look nice."

I should have known I'd get hit again.

"Hold the baby," she said, pushing the small bundle into my arms. I took Morris while she adjusted her corset. She earned a few glances from the men standing around.

I tried to focus on Morris so I wouldn't get punched again. He stared at me with wide brown eyes, almost smiling, like he was making fun of me in my predicament. He waved his fist in the air, trying to catch it with his mouth and letting out a frustrated protest when he could not succeed.

"Mama will be right with you," I said. I could almost sense his thought, which was odd because I didn't think a baby had too many deep thoughts. It made me wonder—could Roxy and I pass on our abilities?

I listened, hearing Roxy's distant thoughts about the evil person who thought up corsets and why was she forced to wear it even with her bigger … ouch … but I could also hear different thoughts. Ones that went along the lines of being hungry and wondering where the other face went, but liking the sound of my voice and not being so tempted to cry when I spoke.

"You like it when I talk?" I bounced him a little as I held him up to look into his face. He smiled for a fraction of a second.

"He did not smile. He's too little. The bunker babies never smiled before they were a few weeks old," Roxy scoffed.

"He smiled. And not only that, I think he can do the mind voodoo thing you do."

She sneered like I was crazy, but then her eyes got wide and she stopped moving. She looked at the baby.

"I think you're right."

"He likes your figure as much as I do," I said, giving my interpretation of the baby's vague thought.

She hit me.

"Who knew we could pass on our gifts?" she said in wonder, as if she had not just assaulted me. There had to be a bruise. She always got me in the same exact spot.

"Our descendants could be born with variations of our abilities, Levi."

I had to admit, it was a pretty cool thought.

THIRTY-TWO

I opened my eyes, pulled from sleep by the baby's crying. Roxy stood by the fire, bouncing him and pacing. Her forehead creased with anxiety while she tried different things to make the crying baby more comfortable.

What's wrong? Why can't I make him stop? What if he's sick? What do I do?

Roxy had been a good leader in the bunker. I'd never seen anyone so determined to take care of others. But she had always held herself at a distance. She knew the pain of losing people. But now she couldn't seem to be aloof.

I stood up and went to her, easing the baby from her arms. "I'll hold him. Get some sleep."

She was going to argue, but the shift made the baby's cry soften to a whimper, and she was too relieved to be offended. She crawled onto the cot.

I looked down at my son, possessed by the kind of thoughts somebody thinks in the dead of night when all the other parts of life are silent. Thoughts I'd never had a reason to think in the previous twenty-two years of my life.

Being a parent had changed me. Suddenly, I didn't want to throw all caution to the wind and ride off in the battle for freedom. I would, if called to it, but I'd rather be with my family, living in peace.

Truthfully, I hadn't given any thought to consequences when Roxy and I did what we did in the snowstorm. I knew it could happen, but even afterward, I never suspected Roxy could be pregnant. I could see now why the idea of marriage and family had been invented.

Earlier in my life, I had thought of marriage as a means to control another, like my mother manipulating her people. I had never seen it as a good thing.

But now I could see how two people being committed made sense. George Washington was surprised anyone would associate marriage with a means to happiness. If anything, it was an invitation to be hurt. It was more cause to sacrifice self for the needs of others.

But now, standing in the middle of the danger of it, I didn't want to be anywhere else.

The next morning I cleaned my gun and packed provisions. I set off for Princeton to find the army. It was my duty. I'd made a promise, and I intended to keep my word.

When I got there, the battle had begun. Washington's army had moved on the British forces in Princeton.

I saw Greer standing in formation in front of me, and I called to him. He didn't turn around. Had he not heard me? Something seemed off every time I glanced at him.

When a bullet whizzed past Washington's irreplaceable head, I worried more than when one got close to me. The man seemed to think it was his duty to get himself killed. At one point, he rushed out to the front of the line on his horse, leading us down the hill in a surprise attack. He didn't give the order until the British moved toward us.

"Fire!" Washington yelled, but he didn't move.

"Get out of the way!" I called to him, and I wasn't the only one. General Washington turned and stared at us, as if daring us to disobey his direct order.

I held my breath while a hundred guns around me exploded. Smoke filled the ravine. Washington disappeared in the haze. I heard the whinny of his horse and saw the flash of uniform as we waited.

We were all pretty sure he was dead.

When the smoke cleared, his horse was there, terrified and jumpy, but not hurt. But Washington was nowhere to be seen.

I panicked. If I had lost George Washington ...

"The general has been kidnapped," a soldier came running out of the woods. "The dark man took him—I saw them disappear behind the bend, riding a horse. The general was unconscious."

I didn't waste a moment. I knew exactly who had taken him, but I had no idea why. It didn't make sense that Greer would turn on us. If there was anyone in the world I trusted, he would be at the top of the list. He and Roxy had grown up side by side. I couldn't comprehend his betrayal. But I couldn't argue with facts, either. He was the only dark-skinned man in our regiment.

"Organize a search party, and get the rest of the men focused on winning this battle," I yelled to the second-in-command.

General Mercer glared at me. It wasn't my place to pass out orders, but if he knew what I knew, he'd feel differently.

"General, we HAVE to win this battle. If we don't, we'll lose the war."

He frowned for another three seconds or so, but then he nodded. "Take the search party. I will see this battle is waged and won, by my very life."

The battle cry went up around me. I swung up onto Washington's horse. I kicked the sides of the horse and raced off into the woods after them.

It was dusk and hard to see where I was going. I pushed the horse forward, though the animal was jumpy and uninterested in my hunt.

That's when I heard it overhead. It was a nonsensical sound in an eighteenth century world—the deafening roar of an engine as large as the city. It ripped through the sky and set the ground trembling.

Between the trees I saw the lights of a ship. A space ship, unlike anything I'd ever seen. It was not tech from 2077.

That ship could only be from another dimension—or from the future. *My* future.

It raced toward the ground like it was heading straight toward me. I was convinced it was going to explode and kill everyone in the vicinity. But when it was a second away from impact, it stopped and hovered above the ground a half-mile up the path.

Who was on that ship? I couldn't fathom an answer. All I knew for sure was that I was about to find out.

THIRTY-THREE

When I was riding toward the ship, I came across the original reason for my search. Joe stood in the path like he was expecting me.

"Hey, Little Brother. Come to save your general?"

George Washington was bound to a tree, a cut on his forehead with a trail of blood coming down the side of his face. He wasn't upset. He looked more annoyed than anything, like he was disappointed in me for pulling him away from his freedom revolution because of my personal problems.

Greer pointed a Leona-branded laser rifle at the general's head.

"What's going on, Greer?" I took a cautious step toward him. He acted like he hadn't heard me. All his attention was focused on Washington.

"Put your gun down, Koenig," Joe said. "That old relic won't do much, anyway."

Greer rested the barrel on Washington's forehead.

"What did you do to Greer?"

Brant shrugged. "I convinced him to help me. He couldn't really say no."

It suddenly made sense. Why hadn't I thought of it? Joe had given up trying to control Roxy's mind, and had focused on Greer's instead. How long had he been influencing Greer?

"He's been handy. I didn't even have to walk into the battle to nab the most important guy there." Joe smirked.

"Let them go," I said as I tossed the musket at Joe's feet. "They don't mean anything to you."

"But they mean something to you," Joe said, picking up my weapon.

"You want me. And now you've got me. So let them go." I eyed the knot around Washington's arms and torso, wondering how quickly I could untie it if I got close enough.

"Wrong. I want Roxy. I want to make her pay for lying to me. I want to watch the life drain out of her body." Joe shrugged as if it was a commonplace desire. "But not before she watches me take her baby."

I was immediately possessed by the innate urge to leap on him and tear him to pieces with my bare hands. I didn't know how he knew about Morris. He must have been spying on us at some point and seen or heard something. Or Leona could have told him.

My voice shook with rage. "If you even LOOK at my son, I'll make you a permanent resident of the portal. I will cut you in pieces and send you there forever."

He chuckled. "Is that even possible?"

"Let's find out." I charged toward him, but Greer calmly turned his gun on me.

"I think I probably know the answer to this, but I'll give it a shot anyway. If you give me Roxy and your spawn, I give you your first American president and your preserved history."

"You are going to leave the general alone. You're going to leave Roxy and the baby alone. If you don't, you'll find out how much pain your body can take. I'll make it my own pet project."

He laughed. "Come on, Little Brother. You don't have it in you and we both know it."

I took a few steps forward. "You didn't watch me carry out the twisted commands of our mother for the past twenty years."

He hesitated. "It was her doing, not yours. Face it, you can't hurt anyone. You even tried to heal me once. I bet you wish you could undo that decision."

"I can, and I will."

"So I take it your answer is no?" Joe stood up straight and Greer immediately activated his weapon.

Washington didn't flinch as the gun hummed to life and flashed green ready lights. "Young man, if you think death frightens me, or that this honorable soldier will sacrifice his family even for the sake of this noble uprising, you are as deluded as you appear to be."

"You don't know the half of it, Georgie," Brant said with a drawl as Greer held the weapon, finger on the trigger. "What's it going to be, Levi? Where's Roxy?"

I didn't waste another second. I charged and managed to knock Greer over. His gun sent a laser blast into the air and hit a tree, causing sparks and a downpour of brittle winter branches. I grabbed it as another blast went off. I pushed the gun out of his hand as he snaked an arm around my neck and squeezed with power that seemed excessive, even for a solid man of twenty. I gasped for oxygen and struggled to stay conscious. With all my strength, I jammed my elbow into Greer's gut. He let go and fell back. I heaved a breath of air before I turned to Joe and took a hard swing. So many lives counted on it; I had no choice but to make it work.

I hit him as hard as I could several times in rapid succession, not satisfied until I saw his eyes dull and his face flow with blood. I sent one final blow to his jaw, and he was out.

I turned to free the general. To my horror, I saw Washington slumped against the tree. Blood seeped quickly across his uniform vest. The second blast from Greer's gun must have hit him. But now that Joe was unconscious, Greer seemed confused. He stared at the gun in his hand like he'd never seen it before.

Please don't let George Washington be dead!

I untied the rope as quickly as I could. With nothing to hold him up, he fell to the ground with a sickening thud. He seemed completely lifeless.

I didn't bother to check for a pulse or breathing. I just opened his shirt and put my hands on his heart and summoned every bit of strength I had in me to heal the most important man currently residing on planet Earth. I transferred energy until his entire chest radiated blue light. At first, it didn't seem like anything was happening. He stared with lifeless eyes, and made no response to my frantic actions. With one hand, I reached into my pocket for the revive injector.

As I did, I heard a tiny gasp. I searched his features and saw his eyes blink. He looked at me as he fumbled for words.

His voice was a strangled whisper. "I say, Koenig, you are certainly a man not lacking in secrets or talents." Washington sat up, touching the scar on his chest. "The wound is healed."

"Good." I sank to my knees and then my back crashed into the tree behind me as the extreme exhaustion hit me.

Washington stood up and pulled on the hem of his vest. "When this day is over and we are victors over our enemies, I intend to hear the story of how this came to be."

I would have responded but I knew I was going to pass out so I didn't waste words. "Go, sir. Before he wakes up."

Washington looked from the gun next to my hand to the unconscious body.

"Make sure you tie them up before you rest, Sergeant," Washington said before he mounted his horse and left at a gallop.

I reached for the rope, and tried to focus my mind on the task of getting Joe bound, but I could barely sit up. I managed a weak knot, and tried to pull it taut.

"Greer, help me," I said weakly. I couldn't finish it. Everything went black as I hoped Joe's unconsciousness would last longer than mine.

It felt like a longshot.

THIRTY-FOUR

I have to save them.

When I came to, I had no sense of how long I'd been out. I struggled for consciousness as if I was playing tug-of-war. I had to wake up, no matter how much my body wanted to sleep.

I pulled myself to my feet, which felt like boulders. I wasn't surprised that Greer, Joe and the laser rifle were gone, but I was intensely curious why he had left me alive. Maybe he had thought I was dead.

Whatever the reason, I wasn't going to question still having my life. I ran in the most logical direction—toward the still-smoking place where the spaceship had landed.

It was a hike to get there. Part of the immense vehicle lay in the middle of a swamp, far up into the wilderness north of Princeton. I heard the hum of high power tech before I saw the monstrosity. I got over the crest of the hill and saw the thing up close.

It wasn't fancy or flourished as Leona's tech usually was. I'd never seen anything like it, actually. It was practical and basic in appearance, as if the creators were far more concerned with function than style.

That wasn't Leona. But who else would bring a ship to 1777?

Whoever they were, they'd had a rough landing.

"Levi Koenig, it's good to see you."

When my gaze found the owner of the voice, the day got ten times weirder.

"Sophie?"

I was dreaming. That was the only explanation. Maybe I could imagine a spaceship showing up in 1777, but dead girls didn't come back to life and then travel to the eighteenth century.

She smiled sheepishly and stayed where she was next to the hangar door of the ship.

"That landing was a little more abrupt than I intended. Good thing I had the training program on," she said.

"Sophie, how can you be here? You were dead."

"You know that for sure?" Her eyebrow rose, and she seemed wiser than a young teenager should be. I thought back to that day in the citadel.

"I never confirmed it, but there was a report filed and a body. I figured Leona … but where did you go? How did you escape by yourself?"

I tried to remember Sophie. She had stayed in the bunker, following Roxy around for a few days, always murmuring something about the Transient. I had figured she was a street kid Roxy had saved. And Roxy and I had both assumed she was mentally challenged. But the way Arabella had spoken of her, she was not what we had thought.

She appeared to be quite right in the head now, as she stood in front of me, her hand on her hip and a smart-aleck smirk on her face.

"Who are you?" I asked in complete confusion.

"I am Sephora of the Transient," she began, and laughed at my expression. "Well, I really am."

"Who are these Transient?" I felt like it was time for an answer that made sense.

"I'd love to explain it right now, but we're standing next to a spaceship in a swamp in 1777 and history is about to be contaminated way above acceptable levels. Not to mention we must save Roxy and her baby."

Roxy. Baby Morris.

Another head appeared above the hangar door. "Hello, Levi."

Morris walked down the ramp, his strange copper-colored boots clinking against the steel.

"We had a feeling you'd eventually show up," I said, grinning in spite of everything.

He nodded, leaning his hand against the side of the ship as if it was completely normal to travel by spaceship. "We thought you could use some help. But I shouldn't have let her drive." He made a face at Sophie.

Had they come because I made a mess of things? "I'm sorry. I've been trying to get to Leona and Joe, but with Roxy and everything that happened with her … I shouldn't have let it all get so out of hand."

Morris came to me and put a strong hand on my shoulder. I saw in his expression years of experience and knowledge.

"It's okay, Levi. We came to help, not save the day."

I shook my head. "Joe's around here somewhere. I lost him. And he has control of Greer. I'm hoping he didn't make it back to the battle and that he and Leona haven't ruined everything—"

"Levi," Morris said gently. "It's not your fault. You can't fix everything."

I didn't want to hear it. I didn't want him to tell me I was absolved. It was *my* job to stop them.

"We need to find Leona and Joe," I said.

"Good news. You found Joe."

I heard the arrogant drawl from the trees. Joe stepped out, laser rifle pointed at me.

"Where's Greer?" I stepped toward him.

"He's on a little errand," Joe said with a vicious grin. He came closer to me, his finger flirting with the trigger.

"Not this time, Joe." Morris said calmly. I heard Morris speak again, but not out loud and not to me. *Sophie, activate the protection field remotely.*

Sophie nodded and closed her eyes while Morris took a few

steps toward Joe. I had the distinct impression she was communicating telepathically with the ship. But I didn't know why I could hear them. I had no personal power of telepathy. I could only hear Roxy because of her abilities. Which meant Morris and Sophie had the same powers as Roxy. Not only that, they were really good at it.

"Joe, I'm going to need you to put that rifle down and give yourself up. We can't allow you to impact this time any longer."

"If you think I'm going to let them get away with making a fool of me, you don't know me very well." Joe raised the rifle, but Morris took another step, apparently unconcerned with the weapon.

"I know you better than you know yourself, Joe. You were left without a mother and you were forced to clean up her messes from too young an age. Your father didn't pay much attention to you, and no one else would accept you because you were half American Indian. Even though you didn't favor your father, everyone knew.

"And I know Roxy hurt you. You think she tricked you and left you to be with Levi. You want revenge. You feel like you deserve it." Morris said the words calmly, almost compassionately, though there was a reserved tone on the edge of his voice that told me he was aware of the dangerous criminal in front of him.

"I do deserve it," Joe growled. "I deserve my revenge, and I'll have it." He raised the gun and shot it toward me. I braced for the impact, but it didn't come. The blast seemed to fizzle in the air in front of me.

Joe swore and shot several more times, but the same protective field took the impact of the blasts and left us unhurt.

Joe threw down the rifle and came at us with a frustrated yell, but it looked like he hit a transparent wall. He fell back on the ground. I heard a single word from Morris' thoughts, and the field was gone. He walked to Joe's rifle and picked it up.

"The game is over, Joe." Morris stepped across the line and reached for Joe's arm, but Joe held out a knife. He slashed Morris' arm and came running at me. Before I could react, he was on me, and we struggled. I almost got him pinned, but a strange feeling of powerlessness distracted me, and he got out of my hold. I felt searing pain in my abdomen. I looked down and saw the small spot of red surrounding the knife in my uniform. The spot quickly grew, and saturated all the fabric around it.

I'm going to die. In the first moments as I stared at the knife, it seemed like a dream, because after the initial stab, I didn't feel much pain. I felt fine. Normal. Dying was just a breath away from living.

I saw the span of my days flash in my mind like a banner. I had wasted so many of them doing what my mother wanted. I had compromised so many of my personal convictions in trying to keep the peace between us. I had eaten rich food and slept in complete comfort every night while Roxy and the bunker kids barely survived.

I couldn't die. Not knowing Joe would go straight to Roxy and the baby. And if I surrendered, I would have failed. If my son managed to survive, he wouldn't remember his father as a hero. I wouldn't be brave Nathan Hale who did what everyone thought was wrong because he believed it was right. I wouldn't be honorable George Washington who prayed on his knees in the snow for strength from a Power greater than himself.

It was time to answer the questions hiding in the back of my mind most of my life. Who was Levi Koenig? What would he be remembered for?

I began to feel the effects as the blood started pooling on the ground. I fell to my knees.

"No!" Sophie screamed as I fell. She ran to me. In the moment it took for them to react to what happened, Joe had the knife at Morris's throat.

"We're going inside your fancy ship now."

THIRTY-FIVE

Sophie had to drag me in. When we were inside the ship she propped me up by the wall and went to an enclosure, which she seemed to open with her mind. Before she could help me, Brant pushed her. A protective instinct overwhelmed me as she was knocked against the wall, but I couldn't do anything. I couldn't move my legs.

"Leave her alone!" I managed in a strangled voice.

"How does this machine fly?" Joe barked at Morris, who still seemed calm. Morris eyed Joe like a father might watch a child who was only digging his hole deeper.

"This isn't the answer, Joe. It won't make you stop hurting."

"Shut up!" Joe whirled around and brought the knife back to Morris's throat. "How does this thing WORK?"

"It recognizes our commands and does what we will it to do," Morris said, but he was guarded.

Joe leaned down and took a panel off the control board. He shook his head in confusion.

"Where are the wires? These things always have wires."

Morris didn't answer his question. "Have you wondered why your powers don't work in here, Joe? You can usually influence people. You've influenced the entire British army to do what you say, haven't you? You give out the commands while Leona doles out the punishment. She can inflict pain on people with her mind, can't she?"

She's the opposite of Roxy and me combined. I thought. *We're not like her. I'm not like her.*

"Leona is helping me get what I want. That's all."

"No, you're helping her get what she wants." I said in a weak voice.

Joe shook his head. His breathing revealed his agitation. "You don't know what you're talking about."

"She's my mother, too." I coughed, and felt the taste of blood in my throat.

"Shut up!" Joe yelled. "Someone tell me how the blazes this ship gets off the ground!"

Morris held his hands behind his back. "Your powers don't work on our ship, Joe. This ship is intended to transport timeline violators to their justice. Only those with connection to the mainframe can keep using their abilities."

We need to help Levi. Sophie's silent voice filled my mind.

Morris nodded. "Sophie is going to help your brother get more comfortable, Joe. You're going to allow it," Morris said firmly.

"You think you can do that to me?" Joe laughed harshly. "I know all about mind influence. I've been doing it my whole life. No one helps him! His job is to bleed out right there on your pretty white floor so Roxy can feel a good dose of miserable before she gets what's coming to her."

"Levi and Roxy are not going to die today. There's no need for you to forfeit your life, either." Morris eyed me with concern as he spoke.

"This is war," Brant said, pulling other console covers, looking for the missing wires he believed to be there somewhere. "Everyone dies. Nobody wins."

The room started spinning. Blackness loomed in my peripheral vision, and I wondered if he was right.

Joe continued his search, moving on to the few buttons on the console and pressing them. Banging on them in frustration. "Roxy reads minds and Little Brother heals. I influence and Leona inflicts pain. What do you do?" He turned around and held out the knife. "Just so all the cards are on the table."

"We can do everything you can do and more. You're not going to win this," Sophie said quietly.

"Don't listen to them," a familiar voice spoke from the hangar doorway. "We have all the power here."

Leona stood next to me. "Let the girl help him. Levi is not the enemy."

Joe eyed her with distrust. "Don't let the favorite son die, you mean?"

Leona laughed haughtily. "Please. I hardly know you. Levi has been by my side his entire life. He's taken care of me. Roxy is the enemy. Focus all your anger on the one who tricked you. Killing your brother only makes you appear weak."

Joe glared at her. After a long standoff, he finally waved his knife at Sophie. "Fine. Do it fast or I change my mind."

Sophie hurried to my side. She made a good show of using whatever was in the vials she had. She used a towel to press a strong-smelling liquid to my wound, and moved her body to block Joe and Leona's line of vision. I knew why when she moved the towel and her hand gave off a faint glow. I felt the unfamiliar buzz of someone else's healing energy flowing into me. She didn't flood her patient with power like I tended to do, not able to control the flow when I was worried. Sophie only gave me enough energy to stop the bleeding and stabilize my vitals.

"Thank you," I said. She gave me a small smile and winked before she stood up and went back to stand by Morris. Joe grabbed her arm and motioned to Morris to stand by the console. He tied them to it.

"Your errand boy came through. The army is waiting outside," Leona said. "We'll get them in the holding bay on the first floor. There's enough room if they stand shoulder to shoulder. We'll take the ship to 2077 and use the British army to take back the city." She smiled. "We'll be a real family. The three of us."

Joe lifted his chin and pushed her hand away, pointing at me. "*He* doesn't get to live. If she did a healing trick, I'll just stab him again. Through the head this time."

I saw Leona's eyes dart to mine, and I sensed hidden concern.

"Let's just get the army on the ship and get the girl to take us to 2077," Leona said. "The boy, Greer, will do whatever we tell him. He can find Roxy and we'll come back for her."

"That's the problem with you, *Mother-dear*." Brant opened a console that contained weapons, and pulled out a second laser rifle. "You're so unfocused. Not committed. It's going to get you killed."

She scoffed. "I know exactly what I want and I'm not going to let your petty little revenge efforts get in my way."

"I'm going for Roxy," he said. "I'll be back in an hour."

"No," I mumbled, though it reverberated loudly in my head. Sophie shook her head and signaled me to wait. Joe tried to walk past Leona, but she caught his arm. I saw her fingernails dig into his skin.

"Stay out of my way or I'll kill you, too," he growled at her.

"This is exactly why you'll never be the *favorite*," she said with spite. "You lack control. You're a child."

He roared. He threw back his fist and hit her in the face so hard she fell next to me. He turned to the weapons bin and pulled out a sword.

Before I could brace for it, he plunged the cold steel into my chest. Burning pain seized me, and a desperate panic assured me I would be dead in seconds.

"NO! Levi!" Leona fell next to me.

"Let's see you heal yourself out of this," Joe scoffed. He turned and, without hesitation, pushed the sword, dripping with my blood, into Leona's stomach.

Joe scoffed at us as if we were both pathetic for dying. He stalked away, out of my sight.

I can't die. I can't. Joe would kill my whole world if I let myself succumb to the forces quickly taking place in my body. I stared at Morris and Sophie, still bound, watching me. Sophie whimpered.

I tried to reach a hand to Leona's wound to heal her.

"No, Levi," she gasped, coughing blood. "You don't have enough strength. Just lie still, precious boy."

"I'm sorry," I said with great effort. I tried to force the healing power from my hands, but nothing happened.

She stared at me with glassy eyes. I barely heard her whisper the words. "I'm the one who should be sorry."

I gulped.

"I never thought about the end," she choked out. "I was only thinking about what I thought I deserved."

I squeezed her hand as tears burned my eyes. My wound had gone numb and my senses were dull.

"I forgive you," I whispered. The words took effort in so many ways. "I forgive you, Mom."

She gave my fingers a weak squeeze. Then her hand fell to my jacket, and she weakly pulled something out of my pocket.

The injector.

How had I forgotten it was there? Arabella had been specific about who it was for. She'd known I would need it.

"It's a revive injector," Sophie said in disbelief. "How …?"

I watched Leona process the information. She knew what the injector did. She had a choice. Save herself, or save her son.

My time was up. I braced for death, feeling my heart slow and my lungs give up their fight for breath.

The world faded away, and I was powerless to do anything except see what would happen to my soul.

But a moment later, my eyes opened as I felt a flood of adrenaline. I gasped and sat up, for a minute sure that I was dead and awakening on the other side.

But I saw my mother. Her hand had fallen limp. Her body was completely still and her eyes stared at nothing.

Sophie's voice filled my mind. *She didn't even hesitate, Levi. Leona used the injector on you with her last breath.*

THIRTY-SIX

For a long time, I stared at my mother's dead body. I didn't have a coherent thought. I just stared.

Finally, I looked for Morris and Sophie and found them right where they had been when I closed my eyes, tied up by the console of their spaceship. I pulled back my shirt. I touched the place where Joe had run me through. It was mostly healed.

"Revive injectors heal wounds?" It occurred to me I didn't even really know what "reviving" was.

"No," Sophie answered. "They only bring back someone who has just died. It has to be within thirty seconds or so."

"Then how …?"

"Morris did it." Sophie said. "He healed you."

"From over there?" I was amazed.

"We're lucky. It doesn't always work. I'd been trying since he stabbed you," Morris said quietly. "I'm sorry. I only had time to save one of you."

I realized Morris and Sophie were still bound, patiently watching me come to terms with my second chance. Or third chance. At least. I went to them and cut the ties.

Sophie rubbed her wrists and looked sadly at Leona. "I tried to heal her," she said sadly. "But I haven't had enough practice."

"You are both amazing," I said. "Where are you from?"

Morris shook his head. "That is a story for another day. Right now, Roxy and the baby need saving."

I remembered with a wave of terror. I went to the weapons bin and loaded up before I took off down the ramp and out into the wilderness where night was falling. I made an effort to push all thought of Leona from my mind.

"I'll meet you," I heard Morris call behind me. He gave further notification with his thoughts—that Sophie would have the ship ready when we returned. I still couldn't believe they'd come here in a time-traveling, mind-reading ship. But I couldn't ponder it long. There were two very important people who needed saving.

The truth was stranger than what I had gathered from Joe and Leona in the ship. The British army was standing outside, a collection of automatons. They had no expression, no emotion. They clutched their weapons with glazed over eyes and aimed their guns. They reminded me of the Domestic Service Robots in my time. No decision making of their own—they were at the command of others.

I saw pain in their expressions. It was the only human thing about them. They stared tragically from eyes dark with horrors. They'd been ripped from their own fight for their king and country. They'd been stolen out of their world and its troubles.

I had to escape their unfocused fire before I could get away. I shot at a couple and tried not to kill them, then made it through their line. I hopped to the other side of the brush and took off down the path.

I was able to trade my musket for a horse on a nearby farm, which I rode as quickly as possible back to Trenton. I went to the midwife's home, but Mrs. Cuthright shook her head when she opened the door and saw me standing there.

"She's not here. She said someone was coming for her and she had to leave."

I swore in frustration. "How long ago?"

"It was not long after you left to rejoin the army."

"Did she leave me any message?" I asked in desperation.

Mrs. Cuthright put a hand on my arm as if she was trying to help me hold it together. "She mentioned a place familiar to you both. She said it was your home at one time. She would go there and wait for you."

"Was she walking?"

"A neighbor was headed on a journey east. She asked if she could sit on the back of the wagon with the baby."

I grabbed her hands and thanked her before I jumped back on the horse.

And headed for Manhattan.

I had a few hours' journey ahead of me. My only consolation was that Joe didn't have a faster way, and he had no idea where Roxy was. I set out on the road to New Brunswick.

It became too dark to travel, and the horse needed rest after I got to New Brunswick. I made camp and managed a few hours' sleep before I left at first light. I reached the edge of New Jersey around noon and saw Manhattan resting in the mist of the river.

Thinking my best bet was to avoid the British-guarded bridges and Fort Lee, I traded the horse for a boat that had seen better days, and rowed as if my life depended on it down the river toward the tip of Manhattan.

As I climbed out of the boat at the Battery and walked through the Castle Garden, I could feel her presence. She was there on our island. And as I hiked through the city and north toward the portal site, the feeling grew stronger.

When the last of the sun disappeared on the horizon, I found her crouching behind a collection of black rock and oak trees, holding the baby and staring into the sky as if it held the answer to her dilemma.

Please show me the way. You're stars. It's what you do—lead the way home.

"Roxy?"

She looked up, her face a desperate mix of hope and despair.

"Levi." She looked at me with tears in her eyes. I kneeled

beside her; put my hand on the baby's soft brown hair. He grunted in contentment. He was glad I was there—glad our family was together.

She watched me for a moment. "What's wrong, Levi?"

It flooded back into my mind. "She's dead."

She didn't answer right away. "Leona?"

I nodded, feeling the sting of the tears that wanted to fall. My mother was dead.

"Did you …?"

I shook my head. "Joe killed her."

I braced for her initial reaction, expecting her to feel happiness, or triumph, or maybe just justification. But all I sensed from her mind was love.

"I'm sorry, Levi," she whispered.

"She died for me, Roxy," I said. "She could have saved herself, but she saved me instead."

I felt her surprise. She didn't answer. She just held my cheek with her palm and watched me.

"How did you know you should leave Trenton?" I asked.

"Joe's coming," she said dully. "I feel it as strong as I felt you getting close. He's nearby. He's taunting me. He's going to hurt the baby."

"Your feeling was right. He is coming after you." I lifted my shirt and showed her the scar and the blood stains. "But he tried to hurt me and failed, thanks to your mom."

She touched the scar. "I'm glad you're okay."

I stared into her profound eyes and loved her, all her imperfection so perfectly measured together with a brand of goodness she shouldn't have, given her history with pain and struggle. I couldn't stop the words from tumbling forth.

"I love you."

Her eyes searched mine; even her thoughts were speechless. She felt treasured. She felt honored. She felt the same.

Her fingers traced my jawline. "There should be something stronger. Some word or gesture. Then I could express it." Her voice was a whisper as loud as time, wrapping its fingers tight on our souls. It was the measure of us. The measure of Levi and Roxy and their son. Time had tested us in ways we didn't expect, and here we were, in the middle of a war inside a war, and time had not been able to conquer it—the love that breathed and lived in the space between our souls.

I held them both, and kissed her with silent words that insisted on climbing out of my thoughts and reaching into hers.

We barely noticed the light at first. But it became brighter until all the shadows we were hiding in had been swallowed up.

Morris stepped out of the light that seemed a doorway to nothing. He smiled in apology, which made me dread what he was going to say.

"I'm so sorry, Roxy. Levi. I need to take your son."

THIRTY-SEVEN

Roxy stared at me in desperation. *Giving him up would be the same as ripping out my heart and handing it over.*

I grabbed her arms and held them both close. "I know, babe." My emotions swelled up in my throat, but I wouldn't let her see how much it hurt me. I'd be strong.

Please tell me there's another way, she begged.

I saw her eyes, dark and pleading. I glanced at Morris, whose face twisted in empathy.

"Joe is close," Morris confirmed what Roxy had felt and I had known. He eyed an arm band on his forearm that seemed a combination of computer and communicator, much like my WristCom, but of plainer design and better technology. "Joe has tech you should know about. Leona brought a teleportation device. As soon as he figures out how to use it, he'll be standing next to us. We won't have any warning."

My eyes found Roxy's. "You know I would never try to force you to give up our baby. But as his father, I'm telling you, I can't keep him safe here. Deep down, you know you can't, either."

She choked back a sob that reminded me of the dying soldiers that cried their final words on the battlefield. Morris came closer and held a hand to the back of her head. He watched her in peace. I was thankful for his calm. It made it easier to think. Possible to breathe.

"I promise you both—your son will live. He'll be fine. You just need to trust me and let me take him."

"How can I just give him to you? I don't know where you came from. I don't know where you'll take him. Why can't I go with you?" Roxy resisted.

"It's not the right time. There is more you need to do. Get back to Sophie. She'll take you where you need to go." Morris kneeled next to her and held out his arms for the baby, who cooed in contentment. "Roxy, I raised you. You know you can trust me. Let me take him to safety."

Roxy searched her son's features as if she was memorizing every detail of his perfect baby face. He reached a fist to bat at her hair.

"I can't," she whispered. Morris smiled, the palm of his hand sliding down to her cheek.

"I know you can, Roxy. I know it because you already did."

A seed of a thought took root in my mind. It may have been buried in my psyche for a long time. I stared at the man, unable to shake the strange notion that gripped me.

The tech beside us surged with protest at the amount of power being drained from the surrounding area. Any moment Joe would appear, and the baby would be stolen from her arms before any of us could react. Roxy heard my thoughts and took a long, ragged breath. But something suddenly caught her eye. She reached to push aside the gathers of Morris' shirt. I saw it, too.

"The mark," Roxy whispered. "You were just branded by Leona at the citadel."

I shook my head, unable to fathom it. But the burn radiated, still smelling of burnt flesh.

"Aw, it's just a scratch," Morris said with a shrug.

"That was almost two years ago," she said, touching the wound. He winced. I leaned over and healed it.

He smiled at me. "Thanks. For me, it was about ten minutes ago. Which is why I had to cut this so close. I'm sorry about that."

"You were just portaled?" I asked, and he nodded.

"Technically. But I have ways to control the wormhole."

"Who are you?" Roxy said the words like she knew exactly who he was, but couldn't accept the truth. But as she stared at him, she suddenly handed the baby to Morris in one quick movement and shuddered at the emotional toll it took to do it.

"Thank you," he said softly to both of us. He stood and turned toward the doorway that seemed to lead to nothing but light.

"Don't worry," he turned around. "I'm taking this guy to the place he needs to be. He'll be fine."

"Will I ever see him again?" Roxy didn't cry. Her breathing was fast and her throat sounded swollen, but she wouldn't give in to the tears. I helped her stand.

"You will. You'll have many years together. You'll teach him how to be great, Roxy." Morris' voice had gone very soft and his eyes were misty. "You're going to teach him courage, and responsibility, and you're going to show him what it means to be a family. He's going to learn all that from you."

"When?"

"When the time is right," Morris said, with all the feeling of someone who knew what he was saying. Like he'd already been there and seen it.

"But how do you know for sure he'll be okay?" Roxy persisted.

Morris watched us. Watched Roxy fight for control, watched me hold her. He stared at us with emotion spilling so even I could sense it, or I could hear the echo from their minds. Either way, I knew what he was going to say before the words came from his mouth.

"I know he'll be okay, because *I'm* okay."

Time seemed to stand still. None of us spoke.

As if he knew we would have trouble believing it, he held the baby in one arm and used the other hand to unzip and pull apart the gathers of his uniform. Below his branding scar, on his chest, he pointed to a horizontal scar across his heart. Then he patted Baby Morris's chest.

We didn't have to see the baby's scar to know that they matched perfectly.

In that moment I looked on my son, both present and future, and realized everything that spanned centuries in the space of a heartbeat.

His time-traveling device hummed to life as he gave me one last look. "I'll see you soon, Dad. Love you, Mom."

I gulped. Roxy laughed as she gasped a sob, a sound that was exultant and heartbroken, as much a paradox as the sight in front of us. Morris winked as he took a step back into the light.

"Don't believe everything you read in science fiction. This little guy and I have a few minutes before worlds start imploding."

With that, our son in both his forms faded from our eyes.

THIRTY·EIGHT

We had no time to mourn. As Morris faded, Joe appeared. I saw his frustration when he realized the baby was safe. He charged me.

I had to fight to stay conscious when he knocked me over. His body seemed like it was made of steel. I was intimidated. My head hit the ground and my brain wanted to check out. Instead I pushed him back an inch or so and reached for my weapon. He was quicker. He pulled out his sword.

"You know the only scar I have, even after all the fights I've been in?" Joe casually held up his hand. It was the same hand I'd shot to disarm him in Central Park in 1874. A jagged pink and white scar covered the length of it. "You did that. And every time I see it, I remember to hate you. And now that we're here, a hundred years before you did it, I'm thinking maybe if I kill you now, this scar goes away."

I tried to scoot backward. "I don't think it works that way."

He came at me with the sword, but Roxy jumped on him from behind. Her arms went around his neck and a small knife appeared at his jugular. I saw a flash of fear in his expression.

"I wouldn't move," I advised. "I've been in exactly that position before. She's not afraid to cut."

Roxy leaned her mouth close to his ear. "You just made me

give up my baby," she said in a lethal tone. "I don't care what powers you used to have over me. They ended the moment you took my son away from me. Get ready to die, Brant."

She pressed the knife into his neck and blood started spurting. But he swung her around hard enough that she lost her grip and fell hard. I sprung up to hit him while he was distracted by his cut, but all he had to do was extend a rock solid arm and I was back on the ground.

Roxy tried to get back up, but she was knocked back beside me. Joe dragged us both to a wagon, where he tied us together and tossed us in the back like we were one big sack of grain.

Where are we going? Roxy's mind searched for answers. *Where is Morris? Levi, where is Morris?*

I don't know. I hated not having the answers to her questions. *But he's safe. We have to believe that. And I think Joe is headed back to the ship. He needs it to get out of here, which is bad news for him and good news for us. Just relax. We have a long trip ahead of us.*

Hours later, I knew my suspicion was correct when I saw the ship through the rough wooden slats of the wagon. Joe jumped off his seat and dragged us off the edge of the wagon into the dirt. He pulled us by our feet across the rocky path and up the hangar walkway. There he dropped us in a helpless heap near the center of the main bay. I saw Greer at the helm. Roxy called to him for help, but his expression was blank.

He's being controlled by Joe. I explained.

The last thing I remembered was being hit in the head with the butt of Greer's laser rifle.

Wake up!

I don't know how long Sophie tried to get us to open our eyes, but her voice in my head sounded desperate.

I tried to make my eyes focus. Joe was at the main console with Sophie next to her. He stood with a rifle pointed casually at her head, and I realized the ship was moving.

I heard a strange murmuring and shuffling sound. I pulled myself to the edge of the bay floor and peered over the side.

Hundreds of British soldiers stood below the deck, staring at nothing as they awaited orders. Joe had brought them. It wasn't hard to figure out his next move. We were headed back to 2077 so Joe could take over the city I was supposed to protect. He must want us there to watch his victory.

They might as well write it on my gravestone. I was a major failure. I'd let my family ruin everything.

Levi, your integrity doesn't depend on the actions of the people related to you. Sophie wasn't looking at me, but I recognized her voice in my head. *Everything will be as it should be. You must trust me. But we need to take control of this ship.*

I noticed her words "as it should be" instead of "okay." I wondered if I would like the way she thought it was supposed to be.

Roxy woke up, and her first thoughts were murderous. She searched for a weapon before she even considered how we would get our binds off.

"Joe," I said. "If you take that army out of their own time where they are creating history—OUR history—how can you be sure the future will be the same?"

He sneered at me. "Whatever we find, I'm taking it. And I'll find your spawn. I'll kill him, and then I'll kill you, and then I'll kill Roxy."

"That's not going to happen," I promised, trying to keep my voice calm. "You aren't going to win this. Did you think you could? You're just a bully from somewhere in time who spent his life killing for a mother who wanted him hidden. That's not preparation for leadership. You have no clue what it takes to be in charge, and you know nothing about our time in the future."

"You'll be like a fish without water," Sophie added softly. Her voice was delicate. Refined. I watched her with sudden curiosity. Who was she? First dogging Roxy in the bunker, then dying in the chair at the citadel. But here she was again. She'd come with Morris. He'd spoken to her as if he was the authority. But he'd done it with affection. Was it because he thought of all the bunker kids as his own?

I am Sephora of the Transient. I was born to save the past. She caught my eyes as she thought the words.

I shook my head. *You aren't scared. You already know how this is going to end and you're at peace with it.*

I waited for her to admit it. Finally, she gave me a small nod.

Whoever you are and wherever you come from, I'm still glad you're here, I said.

She turned and stared out into the sky of stars, smiling just enough to pull the edges of her mouth upward.

Seeing stars meant we had left the atmosphere. We were hurtling through outer space. *I hope this isn't the first time you've flown a ship in space.*

She glanced at me, and her grin grew bigger. *It's not.*

"I'm going to kill you, Joe," Roxy said into the silence. "Nobody will remember you. We'll clean up your mess and it will be like you never existed."

"Tall words from a little brat tied up on the floor of a time ship." Joe didn't spare her a glance. He nudged Sophie with the barrel of the rifle. "Take this thing to the future, little sister."

Sophie didn't have much of a choice. She could stall, but eventually she would have to enter time coordinates or Joe would start executing us, one by one.

"How does the ship travel in time?" I asked Sophie as I felt jerking on the ropes that bound Roxy and my hands together. Roxy had started rubbing her side of the rope against the handle of a hatch to the lower deck.

"Just get it done," Joe said, wiggling the rifle against Sophie's neck as a reminder.

I had to give her credit, the girl was brave. She didn't even flinch. And she took my bait without hesitation.

"It uses the wormhole from the portal, but only as a general guide, like a GPS signal. The ship's computer in the future finds our signal and compresses our matter into a smaller space. Our mass will shrink as we are pulled through the vortex."

Joe didn't acknowledge her words, but I could tell he was listening. Was Sophie trying to intimidate him with explanations of technology he would have no way of understanding?

Roxy managed to break through two of the ropes, and the rest fell to the ground. We kept our hands together in the same place behind us, hoping he wouldn't notice. Her mind honed in on Joe's sword he had stuck behind his belt.

"What do you think of that, Joe? Ever heard of vortexes? Compressed matter? Is it making you nervous?"

He scoffed at me, and Roxy used the distraction to make her move. She lunged for the sword, pulling it against his belt until the leather split and fell away. He turned, but not before she caught him with the blade across the arm. He cried out in pain.

She held the blade to his chest, but just as the tip cut into his flesh, she was stopped.

He smirked at her. "Go ahead, Roxy," he said in a smooth, soft tone. "Kill me."

She breathed fast, pushing against the handle of the blade as if she was trying to slice through a brick wall.

"Aw, too bad. Looks like you love me too much to kill me." He laughed at her.

"It's not love when you're the one controlling it," she said through her teeth, as if it was difficult to force out the words. "We had this discussion already."

Sophie wore a worried expression. *He's using his powers. This shouldn't happen in this ship. There are measures to prevent it.*

Joe took the handle of the sword and easily turned it from his chest to mine. His arm snaked around her waist and he pulled her against him with one jerk. Greer came out of the corner where he'd been standing and pointed his rifle at Sophie.

"I haven't forgotten about you, little sister," he said to Sophie. "You get this thing to the vortex in the next five seconds or we're going to make corpses of your friends."

Roxy hadn't moved. Her mind screamed in protest, but her body and her voice were frozen.

I'm sorry, I told her. *I should have believed you when you said he was manipulating you in 1874. Stay strong, Roxy. We're going to figure this out. Do whatever you can to fight him.*

Joe brushed his lips along Roxy's neck as she tried to fight off his control. He tilted her chin back and kissed her the same moment he lifted the sword and pressed it to her neck.

I started toward them to kill him with my bare hands. But Greer's rifle moved closer to Sophie's head and Joe eyed me with challenge.

"Stand back or they both die," he warned me.

"Let. Her. *Go*." I wasn't playing around. The pressure of my anger built up inside like a bomb about to explode.

Joe didn't bother to look at me. He continued to take from her, running his free hand down her side. A harbored tear shone in the corner of her eye. "I don't think you understand my power, Little Bro. Back in 1874? I wasn't even trying. If I tell her to do it, she'll take this sword and kill you."

"Never," she said in a strangled whisper. He smiled and inflicted another kiss on her. Then he put the sword in her hand and she swung the blade in my direction, wild fear in her expression.

"Now, then," Joe turned back to Sophie. "Turn it on and get us out of here or Little Brother dies a painful death being hacked to pieces by his one true love."

Sophie was pale. And angry. "How are you doing this? The ship is supposed to block your abilities. We programmed it to keep you unarmed."

He shrugged with an arrogant smile. "Turns out I have a knack for tech. I took apart the communication device I had in 1874. I studied it long and hard. Sure, your ship here is a little more advanced. But it follows the rules. It's predictable. It's what I would expect you to be able to do a few years down the road. And that makes it easy to reprogram."

Sophie looked directly at me. *I should have been prepared for this. I'm so sorry. He wasn't supposed to catch me off guard.*

She turned around and placed her hands purposefully on the console. She closed her eyes. Moments later, the ship shifted violently as the space full of stars we inhabited shifted and rotated in a circular motion, like a drain.

It wasn't like the portal. Inside the portal, the journey went in slow motion. It seemed like centuries. In the portal, my mind would slow and I wouldn't be able to think coherent thoughts.

This was quick, violent, and the most terrifying and exhilarating experience of my life.

The force of time pressed all around us, shrinking us, narrowing us. It forced our matter into something tiny and fragile. I spent the moments staring into Roxy's eyes, watching her fight with all of her being to keep that blade from cutting into my flesh.

THIRTY·NINE

We came through somewhere over Ohio. I saw the wall. Sophie almost hit it, but she managed to pull us over it. It was a good thing. The electrified tech would have caused the ship to explode.

She steered up and headed east with jerky motions. Where before she had been calm, now she was obviously rattled by what was happening, and that made me nervous.

"Put it down in Central Park," Joe demanded, digging his fingers into Roxy's waist. His attention was taken with seeing 2077 from overhead. Warring factions in barren fields. Fires and camps of soldiers.

This broken America closely resembled the America we had just left behind.

Only minutes later, Sophie maneuvered the ship awkwardly toward the middle of New York City. My heart seemed to twist inside my chest. My city. I was bringing an army of automatons to destroy her. What kind of leader did that?

"No tricks, girl," Joe nudged her with the toe of his boot. People scattered below as Sophie prepared to lower the ship to the ground.

There must have been some moment in all of those quickly passing seconds when Joe forgot to keep a short leash on Roxy's will. Either that or she overcame it herself, which wouldn't have surprised me at all. Either way, the sword dropped. I didn't waste the second she gave me.

I lunged and landed on top of Joe. I managed to get him to the floor, but the guy was made of iron. He fought back with a growl that made me feel like a weakling, especially when he hit me in the stomach so hard I had to fight to stay conscious.

Sophie tried to back up the ship. But as her frantic recalculating continued, Joe came at me again, and both of us flew into the console.

Joe landed on Sophie and knocked her to the floor. The ship shifted and turned viciously, as if it was a rearing bear, angry with us for breaking its connection to Sophie.

I tried to get Joe off me. I knew we both had to get out of the way so Sophie could save us all. But it was no use. He wasn't thinking about surviving, he was maniacal and distracted with hatred as he held my neck with his steely grip.

"Joe!" Roxy screamed. It was the only warning we had before the impact. The sound of metal careening against metal screamed in my ears as all of us were thrown at the ceiling.

In the space of the next few seconds, all we could do was fight to grasp onto something fixed. There was nothing but the sound of destruction and the screams of hundreds of soldiers who had no idea where they were or what was happening.

Sophie summoned some kind of bubble that wrapped itself around us and kept us from dying as the ship tossed us and burst into flames.

I imagined the souls outside, screaming, diving for cover. Families. Civil workers, bravely saving those they could before their bodies were hurled out of the way. The grinding, heaving, shuddering of the ship against the falling city echoed in my chest, and I cried with the pain of my people.

A lifetime or a few seconds later, everything went still and quiet. The ship extinguished the flames before it allowed us out of the bubble.

Sophie was crying. "I'm so sorry! I couldn't hold on."

I shook my head. "It's not your fault. It's mine. It's all on me."

I heard a guttural cry behind me as if Roxy expelled the power of Joe's manipulation by ripping it from her mind. Her determination and her strength of will reminded me of the Roxy I had watched give birth.

I grabbed the sword when the bubble deflated, and Joe regained consciousness to find me with a blade resting against his chin.

"Too late, Roxy." He grinned savagely. "Your city's gone. And we're going to die together like family."

His words made us look up, out of that twisted and shattered window in the front. We couldn't see much, but I could tell it was very, very bad.

Sophie activated white, alien-like robots that zoomed around and started cleaning up and making a way for us to get out of the decimated ship. After a time, they made a window for us to be able to see out. As they continued to work, I stepped into the path and went to the window. I motioned the others to stay. I needed to see it by myself first. I needed to take account of my people.

Nothing could have prepared me for the sight. It was devastation, as far as the eye could see. Buildings were leveled. Everything was left black and smoking. I saw no signs of life. Only a skeleton of twisted metal reaching up out of the island as a last testament to the city that had once thrived. That had been free for just a moment of time.

I had no time to mourn the people I had lost. The ship had scraped away the city to the very end of old Battery Park. I realized we were teetering on the edge of the Hudson, and our situation was about to get worse.

"We're going to fall in," I said, my voice breaking. "The city is gone, and we're next."

"Joe … will … not … win."

I heard Roxy speak behind me. I turned and saw her dark expression.

Stay!

Joe suddenly flew back against the wall, his arms spread as if he was attached. He tried vainly to move, cursing angrily until his mouth suddenly closed, as if against his will.

Roxy glared at him, then turned away from him. She held her side as if she was injured, but when she stepped closer to the window she held both shaking hands to the sky. Her eyes closed, and I felt her encompass the wavering ship with her beautiful mind.

Rise!

The ship squealed and protested. It wanted to fall off the edge and sink to the bottom of the river. But Roxy insisted. The force of gravity was no match for the force of her will. The ship inched backward above the wasted city, above the treacherous waves of the bay.

We saw sky.

Sophie handed me the sword Roxy had held and tried to help. She coaxed the dying system to life so she and Roxy could direct the ship to a deserted pier in New Jersey.

When the ship gently touched ground, Roxy fell in a heap at my feet. In the moment it took me to reach for her, Joe shot past me.

He grabbed Greer, unconscious on the floor, and pulled him through the hatch to the lower deck and sealed it behind him, probably by shoving something in the handles on the other side. I watched from the window as he marched his troops out the hangar door.

"Greer!" Roxy held up a weak hand toward the hatch.

"The robots must have got it open," Sophie sighed, covering her face with her hands. "We can't go out there. All of those soldiers had guns. And I don't think they were muskets."

"We'll go to the citadel as soon as they're gone," I said, hearing the panic in my voice. Trying to disguise it. "I have to get my army to the citadel. I have to stop him before he takes everything."

Sophie caught the trail of my thoughts and stared at me, wide-eyed. It made me realize how young she was. Just a teenager. Her features still wore the faint mark of childhood. There was fire in her eyes that reminded me of Roxy, but she was inexperienced, even with all her knowledge.

We finally got out, the sunshine of our own time hitting our skin like an old friend we had missed. I couldn't explain how another time could feel cold and uncomfortable, but standing back on my own soil with my own sun, everything felt right again.

Seeing the rubble from across the river was another thing.

Roxy gasped. It was a feminine reaction that caught me off guard. I reached for her hand. She was different lately. Becoming a mother had taken her through a metamorphosis. Everything meant more. She suffered more. It made me think of the times I had told her love couldn't make her weak. Maybe, in some sense, I had been wrong. Love was powerful, but that power had the potential to make us vulnerable.

I looked to her. To my heart. "What am I going to do?"

She held my hand tightly. "You're going to go fight for what's left of it."

I stepped forward to the bank that overlooked the ruined city. The image of George Washington, knees in the snow, came to mind.

What if I knelt here? What if I leaned my head down and offered my hands toward the sky? Would it mean anything coming from me? Washington had talked to God like he was a father.

The one thing I'd never had.

I could imagine what I'd say if I knelt there on the bank. I'd be letting go and giving up and asking for strength all at once.

I don't know you, I'd say, unsure, but feeling the release the words provided, anyway. *My mother never taught me about God, but I've seen evidence you're there. I don't know that I deserve to speak to you, but I need what Washington had. What he got from you. I don't know how to put this city back together. Maybe they all would have been better off without me, but I'm here, and I'm ready to do whatever it takes. I can't do this alone.*

I looked up at the sky and closed my eyes, smelling the ash and destruction, imagining the cries of those who had lost people. I felt the word with every part of my soul. "Please."

I felt Roxy's arm around my waist and I turned into her embrace.

Sophie joined us and we loaded up all the weapons we could carry. We set out for Manhattan.

The British army was marching a half-mile or so ahead of us, and they were headed the same direction as us—toward the closest bridge still standing and connected to the island.

"Maglev," I called to the girls when I saw a closed docking station behind a building. I blasted the control panel with a laser rifle and tried to force open the door.

"This may take a minute." I swore at the mess of wires I'd made, trying to make sense of them.

"We don't have a minute," Roxy said, looking out toward the bridge. The soldiers were close to it. "If Joe gets to the citadel before we do—"

Her gaze became thoughtful. *What if I could stop them?*

I took in the dark, deep circles around her eyes. She was exhausted. If she tried to stop that army, she could spend every last bit of strength she had. Knowing it didn't stop her from raising her hands toward the bridge.

"Don't," I said, standing up and grabbing her hands. "Don't, Roxy. It's too much. Let me do this."

"I know how to do it now," she said, though I saw the reservation in her eyes. Knowing how to do it didn't mean it wasn't costly.

"Not now, babe. Just trust me."

Sophie was staring at me with wide eyes as I got back to trying to open the door. She looked like she needed a distraction.

"Can you do it, too? What Roxy does?" I asked her, my eyes on wires and more wires in front of me.

"Not large things. Only small."

"I'm still impressed," I smiled, and in the time it took me to glance at her, I heard the lock disengage and the door swing open. I looked back, wondering what I had done to open it.

"It was Roxy," Sophie said.

"Roxy, you have to take it easy." I didn't want to think about the strength she had used jarring open the door with her mind. I used my citadel security pin to open the maglev that waited in the dark building.

We got in the car and I pressed my thumb against the scanner, pushing two buttons under the console at the same time. A set of controls opened out of a hatch under the floor. I pushed the accelerate control as far back as it would go and turned the maglev toward Manhattan.

We moved toward the water. Fast.

"Uh, Levi, water isn't made of magnetite," Roxy said, holding on to the seat with white knuckles.

"We don't need magnetite. This cruiser can fly."

"Only the hybrids in the citadel fly," she said, staring at me like I was insane.

I smiled. "Trust me. I'm the one who invented the tech."

We flew out over the water, almost skimming the surface as we raced down the river, dodging the remnants of skyscrapers, trying to see through the fog of ash and smoke.

Roxy stopped being impressed with my genius. She forgot all about me. She thought about the dead. She thought about the ones the dead had left behind.

Sophie reached for Roxy's hand. She had tears in her eyes, too. But there was no surprise in her reaction.

"You knew this would happen." I didn't mean for the words to sound like an accusation, but they sort of did. Why hadn't she stopped it? She could have crashed our ship in the middle of a field along the way. Why were our three lives more important than a vast metropolis filled to the brim with people?

Sophie must have heard my thoughts. She looked away from me, out her window. "I was not allowed to change this chapter. It's important."

FORTY

"It's important for thousands of people to die?"

"I didn't know this would happen now. I didn't know we would be the cause—I would be the cause—but it's an Unalterable."

"A what?" I asked the question, but I could guess what it meant. I slung the cruiser low over the city streets covered in debris. I switched back to automatic maglev controls when we passed the point where the destruction began. We were close to the citadel.

"It's still standing there. Like nothing happened," Roxy said. "Of all places, this has to be the one that's still here."

The maglev pulled into my private docking station on the roof. We climbed out as Sophie answered my question.

"An Unalterable is a fixed point in time," she said. "So much hinges on it that it cannot be changed. We wouldn't be able to if we tried. Unalterables will always find a way. If you tried to stop it, you would end up causing it."

"So this is an *Unalterable* moment, but George Washington and the Revolutionary War weren't?"

I was a little disgusted with Sephora and the Transient. They were supposed to be all about saving the past, whoever they were. And yet they had let Leona and Joe bulldoze 1777. We all had, and

I was most disappointed in myself over it.

"Think about it," she said as we ran down the hallway. "Would the citadel and New York, and everything you see, be the same as it was when you left if 1777 wasn't an Unalterable? It couldn't have been undone no matter what Leona and Joe did."

I stopped running and turned to her. "Sophie, do you hear yourself? We have a good portion of the British army HERE in 2077! How can you say nothing has been altered?"

She shook her head. "No, it was the same history when we got here. It had to be."

"How can you possibly know that, Sophie?" I had no idea what she meant, and I didn't like that expression on her face. She wasn't quite sure she believed everything was as black and white as she had been told.

"You're doubting yourself," Roxy said simply to Sophie.

We were at the stairs that led to the portal. I realized it when Sophie turned suddenly and climbed them, two at a time.

"Sophie!" Roxy called to her, but she didn't look back. It was like we didn't exist to her anymore. She disappeared into the portal chamber a moment later.

"Come on," I said and pulled on Roxy's hand. We ran to the throne room where I would be able to get a new WristCom and speak to all the army officers on their coms.

"This is General Levi Koenig," I said in what I hoped was a confident, authoritative tone. "We have an emergency, as all of you know. All officers are to report to the citadel within the hour, if it is within your power to do so. Enemy combatants are approaching from New Jersey at this moment. I repeat—if you're alive, get to the citadel to defend whatever we've got left!"

Minutes later, they started shuffling into the citadel complex. Wounded, grieving, battle-scarred soldiers who had only experienced a taste of freedom. But the flavor made them hungry for more. Willing to die for it.

Wounded men tried to ease themselves up the large stone steps of the citadel promenade. When they saw me approach, they stood at attention.

"Governor," a young woman said, saluting me with her left hand because her right had been blown off. "Reporting for duty."

I didn't hesitate. I put my hand on the bleeding, smoking stump on the end of her arm and allowed the surge of energy. She watched in amazement as her hand grew back, whole and uninjured. I was amazed, too. I'd never done anything like it before.

"Get ready to fight," I said. There was no time to explain to them. They seemed to understand, and lined up, one by one, so I could heal them. I unburned flesh and set broken bones. I reversed impalements and removed embedded metal until I was more tired than I'd ever been in my life.

Even then, I saw the ones that couldn't make it up the steps. The ones carried by friends. So I went to them. I healed them all. I summoned strength I didn't know I possessed and went to the furthest edge of myself to restore them.

I knew I was fading, but I didn't care. It didn't matter to me if my life was lost restoring theirs. I kept healing, kept using up the tiny bit of life I had left in my being. But for some weird reason it didn't get used up. Whenever I felt it circling the bottom, something replenished it, like someone poured more water in a well I was trying to run dry.

Finally it occurred to me. I whirled around, and I saw her there. Roxy was sitting on the steps that led to the huge arched doors of the citadel, surrounded by a group of servants and unhurt bystanders. They had joined hands and had their eyes closed.

Mind your own business, Roxy demanded. *You do your thing, and we'll do ours.*

I smiled. *I don't know how you're doing what you're doing, but you keep right on doing it.*

She opened her eyes and lifted an eyebrow. I smiled and went back to my task. By the time we were done with our collective healing, we had an army ready to defend the citadel.

It wasn't a moment too soon. Joe and his stolen army marched down the SmartStreet the same way he had come with his gang in 1874 to stop us from escaping into the portal.

"Peace Implementers," I said into my WristCom. I tried to sound more energetic than I felt. My army didn't need to know my feet felt like cement blocks and the idea of standing up seemed a monumental task. "Your enemy is one man. Joe Brant. The rest of his army is being controlled by him. They belong in another fight, in another time. We have to get them back there, and I ask you not to hurt them unless you absolutely must. Protect them. Keep them whole. You don't know if you might be saving your own grandfather several times removed."

The truth of what I was saying hit me. I heard awe in my voice when I spoke again. "Give yourself for the redemption of your ancestors."

I waited until Joe climbed the steps before I tried to rise. I reached for my laser rifle, but realized the only weapon I had on me was a sword from 1777. I had given my weapons to soldiers. I walked with weak steps to meet him as swords began to clash all around us. My army kept their rifles at their side, engaging in hand-to-hand combat some of them might not have attempted since they were eleven year olds in Leona's army camp. I heard calls to preserve lives and take prisoners. Some were bound and led away to safety.

I also saw too many of my people giving their lives. On my orders. The weight of it stuck in my throat like a rock.

I smelled fire. British soldiers had formed a frantic formation around the citadel. With terrified expressions, they concentrated fire upward until the palace of crystal and iron was engulfed.

The grandeur of my mother's kingdom melted away behind me, and it happened fast. One minute it was there, flashing in elegant remembrance of a tyrant. The next it was a pile of ashes and twisted metal to match the rest of the city. It reminded me of Arabella's story about the Crystal Palace on the same spot, which had burned the night she first traveled through the portal.

"Oops." Joe scoffed, waiting for me to make a move. "I guess we burned down your house. Actually, Greer was the one who showed them all how to do it."

I shrugged. "It's about time someone did."

He shifted, content to wait me out. He held his weapon, but he didn't point it at me.

"I can't let you level the island of Manhattan and live to tell the story," I said, hoping he wouldn't know I was talking to stall, to gather some ounce of strength I had in reserve.

"You think you can finally work up the guts to kill me?" Joe's voice taunted. His eyebrows were drawn low over his eyes. His smug expression didn't falter. "Anyway, I didn't touch Manhattan. That was your other little girlfriend."

"None of it would have happened without you," I said and lifted the gun. "You have to be accountable for your actions."

He lifted his gun, unconcerned. "You've never been able to kill me before. Looks like you can't even protect your precious city. You're weak, Little Brother. Time to face facts."

"I don't have any choice," I said. "Because of you, Roxy and I had to give up our son. I lost my friend, Greer. You created a time paradox I have to fix. You destroyed my city. You destroyed whatever hope I had of fixing my mother. You have to be stopped."

Joe smirked. "I think you're still talking because you're afraid to come over here and make good on your promises."

As he laughed, overconfident that I wouldn't be able to make good on my promise, I lifted my sword from the past and disarmed him with one swipe.

FORTY-ONE

Joe drew his own sword, also a souvenir from 1777. I recognized his super-strength as soon as the swords collided. I wondered, as I countered each strike with a fumbling attempt to defend myself, how he managed to have two abilities. The vaccine had only given Roxy and me one gift, based on our personalities.

It made me suspicious. As I deflected another jab, I decided there was only one explanation.

Maybe his two gifts were really one.

I almost lost my footing at a hard jab at my chest, but I managed to knock his sword back and jump up a stair, putting me on a more level field.

Maybe it wasn't so much that he was stronger than everyone else. Maybe he had the power to make others think he was stronger. Maybe he caused the illusion of strength. I considered the possibility as I fell back toward the rail and felt pain radiate through my back.

I thought about it long and hard as I kept myself alive, deflecting his attempts to make me fall. I analyzed my thoughts, because I knew Joe possessed the power to influence them.

You will fall. I heard the words in my mind. *Just fall and let him kill you. Get it over with.*

The urge to obey the voice was strong. I held my ground and tried to steady the sword even though I felt unnatural fear as he advanced.

"What's the matter, Little Brother? You look scared." He chuckled.

"You never had any superior strength," I scoffed, though I had to fight to get the words out. "All this time, it was only an illusion."

"That doesn't mean I'm weak." He proved it with a hard scrape across my arm. Blood seeped through my linen Revolutionary War tunic. I blocked his move before I jabbed him in the shoulder. He grunted in pain as blood quickly soaked through his own shirt.

"The difference is, now I know I'm not weak, either." I advanced, striking again, my blade cutting through the air with the sort of "whoosh" that sounded a lot like freedom. The black cloud of nonspecific fear I'd always felt around him, that maybe he was undefeatable, and maybe there was no use trying to fight him—it all dissipated like a cloud, and I saw clearly.

He managed to counter my moves. But he was used to depending on his mind control to get him through fights. He was soft. Well, relatively speaking, anyway. Eventually, my determination not to fail gave me an edge. I focused my mind on all the pain he'd caused, and the need for him to be responsible welled up inside me like one giant black spot that covered up his power. I yelled and ran toward him with my sword outstretched, all my strength ignited. He rose to defend the strike, but it was too late.

My sword ran him through. His hands went instinctually to cover the wound and he fell, a wide-eyed look of terror and surprise in his eyes.

I was surprised, too. I waited to feel some kind of remorse. Some emotion that told me I was wrong to be glad at the death of a man who was technically my brother. But I only felt satisfied. He should die. He deserved to die.

It wasn't until I tore my eyes away from Joe and saw my soldiers on the ground that I managed to see past the bitterness. They were bleeding. Dying. All because I asked them to protect their enemies.

I looked back at Joe. I didn't feel differently about him, but it wasn't about him, really. It was about me. It was about whether I could look my people in the eyes and tell them I was worthy of their trust. It was about whether I was going to choose to be noble enough to attempt to deserve the love of Roxy Eisen.

I didn't want to live the rest of my life with guilt because I had felt good about killing a man.

I kneeled next to him and tied his hands. I threw his sword across the promenade. Then I put my hands on his wound before I could second guess my decision. I let healing energy flow.

He didn't speak. He just stared at me as if he waited for the catch.

"Don't read into this," I said, dizzy with exhaustion. "It only means you'll stand trial. You're going to be punished, Brant. I don't let the guilty go free."

"You better kill me now, Little Brother," he said in a weak, mocking voice. "Because I'm just going to find a better way to kill you."

The battle was winding down. Most of the British troops had been rounded up. The moment Joe lost his hold over their minds they started screaming in panic. I had the remaining Peace Implementers get them in a circle and stand around the edge of it.

"Listen up," I tried to yell over them, but I finally had to resort to using my WristCom as a loudspeaker. "Please calm down. This is a bad dream. You will wake up soon enough in your own war, so you might as well conserve your energy."

They started to quiet until the air above us roared with the engines of a large, invisible craft. The atmosphere bubbled as the ship broke through and shimmered into view. It was the same spacecraft we had left in New Jersey in a heap of burning metal.

It didn't look much better than it had when we left it, but it was running. The ship remained in a loud and disconcerting hover over the ruins of the citadel.

The citadel continued to burn. I wondered about fire control, but it seemed pointless.

Let it burn, Levi. Let it all burn.

I felt a small hand in mine. I looked, and Roxy stood next to me. Morris stood behind her with a sad smile.

Something inside my chest seemed to constrict when I saw my son. It didn't matter to me that he was physically decades older than me. He was my son, and I loved him like he was that baby in Roxy's arms. I reached for his shoulder and held it firmly.

"I'm sorry, Dad," he said softly. "I know this isn't what you wanted."

I glanced at the remnants of my city, clenching my jaw. I could feel the loss, the pain. It vibrated as a tangible tension in the rubble. I imagined I could hear the cries of the dead cast in the ash and smoke that hovered in the air.

"It's not your fault," Morris said. "You couldn't stop this from happening."

"It's an Unalterable." My voice sounded dull. "I heard."

He nodded. "I know that doesn't mean much to you, but from our perspective, it's everything."

"What are we supposed to do now?" I asked him.

"Survive. Rebuild. Give your people a reason to get up out of the ashes and start again. It's not the first time this city has known hardship. It won't be the last. But some fires burn as a cleansing. Sometimes they give us a clean slate." He gripped my arm.

"Where's our baby?" Roxy asked suddenly.

Morris smiled. "We're fine. He's fine. Sophie will take you to him soon."

I noticed Sophie stood back, away from the circle we had made. She gave us a wistful look before she turned to start herding British soldiers into the shimmery passageway leading to the ship above our heads. An anti-gravity field?

Morris reached for Joe's arm and hauled him up.

"Where are you taking him?" I trusted my son's judgment, but I wanted to hear that Joe would be held accountable.

"He's had his trial in my time. His sentence has been given by the Arena Council. He is to be banished."

"Banished where?" I didn't want him in the same world as Roxy. I didn't want him in Morris or Sophie's time, either.

"I'm taking the British soldiers back to their time, then Sophie and I will see that he is sent out in time and space on this ship, and he will have no way to return. He will live out the rest of his days alone, where he can't hurt anyone."

Joe snarled, but I didn't miss the fear in his expression.

"So be it," I said.

Morris dragged Joe toward the lift.

I went to the wounded. I didn't have much energy in reserve, but I used enough to make them comfortable until medical help could be given. Even so, there were many who died simply because Roxy had soldiers take me away when my exhaustion reached a critical level.

Many more were dead than alive. As I was being carried away, I saw the young woman I had healed before the battle. Her restored hand lay perfect and still at her side.

She wouldn't need it anymore.

FORTY·TWO

I found Greer in the gardens after Joe was taken away. He sat on the ground, his head between his hands.

"Greer! We've been looking for you," I said, reaching a hand to him. He shook his head.

"I burned it, Gov. I burned your palace." His eyebrows were drawn together in remorse.

"So what?" I shrugged. "It was an eyesore, anyway."

Greer didn't laugh as I'd hoped. "I kidnapped George Washington out of one of the most important battles he needed to win."

"You didn't do any of it, Greer," I said, sitting down next to him. "Joe did it, and he's paying for his crimes."

Greer sighed. "I don't like to think that Brant could have control of me like that. I should have been strong enough to fight it."

"He has an ability he abuses. You aren't responsible for what he made you do any more than Roxy was in 1874. We won. End of story."

He stared over at the rubble. "What about the portal? Do we need to worry about the black hole pulling us out of orbit now that it's in ashes?"

I honestly didn't know the answer to his question, but if my son was in the future and he had a world to live in, I figured we at least had some time to figure it out.

"We'll manage it, Greer. We know how it works. If we need to, I can build it again. You can help me."

His frown began to ease. "I wish I could say how sorry I am, Gov."

"There's nothing to forgive. But if you're still available for that chat about Roxy, I think I'm ready to talk about it."

He smiled and gestured to the space next to him. "I'm all ears."

It would take years to clean up all the destruction caused by the path of the spaceship. There was nothing to do but roll up our sleeves and do the work. I required everyone healthy enough to start work immediately, and run in shifts. Committees were organized to begin finding food and rationing it at food stations. I called Lon to head up a team of tech experts to see if power could be restored, and Greer and I began looking into what we needed to do to protect the portal.

Until we could figure it all out, we were in survival mode. We lived in tents around fires and common water sources. Some went on journeys to hunt and gather food, some protected the remnant. We eventually found a new normal as we attempted to rise out of the ashes.

Again.

Only two days after the battle, we heard the sound of copters. The antique kind from before the blackout. The kind that were only still used in Ohio.

Edan Avihu stepped out of the first one that landed on the remains of the citadel. He glared at me so hard I thought he might be there to finish what Joe had started. Which is why I wasn't prepared for the words that came out of his mouth.

"We heard you had trouble, son. Came to see if we could help."

Four huge choppers landed around the first, and people in camo uniforms, with large weapons strapped to their backs, began unloading crates of supplies.

"I don't know what to say, President Avihu," I said. "I didn't expect this. This is going to help so much."

"Don't have to say a thing. It's what neighbors do, right? Just tell me whether you found your friend."

I smiled as he held out his hand to shake mine. "I did find her. I brought her home."

"Good, then," he said gruffly. "Guess everything worked out, then."

For a few days, Roxy and I both lived in a state of constant exhaustion. We shared a tent on the marble of the citadel promenade, but we didn't see much of each other. I could tell she was avoiding me. It gave me plenty of time to think about us. And one night when I came back to an empty tent, I made the decision.

I was nervous Roxy wasn't going to like what I'd decided. But it was long past the point where we needed to define our bond. Nothing was going to be right between us until we had an understanding.

I made the arrangements between meetings about territory disputes and quarantining hospitals for an influenza outbreak. And one day when all my plans were in place, I stepped out of our tent and grabbed her hand before she could hurry off to her relentless work with our people. I took in the sight of her. No longer burdened with stays and gowns and silk slippers, she looked herself. Comfortable and completely Roxy in her black pants, dark green jacket and beloved boots. Her hair was in a ponytail. She was the Roxy from my dreams. The Roxy I had fallen in love with.

"Come with me."

She gave me a suspicious look, but she let me lead her away. We walked from our tent on the citadel foundation to the steps leading to all that was left of the palace.

I sat and pulled her down next to me. She had been mid-story about a new group of volunteers for an army she was trying to organize. They were scavenging for weapons, and she should be helping them.

Sure she should.

"Let's just breathe, Roxy. Just be with me and breathe." I closed my eyes and filled my lungs with the cool morning air still heavy with dew.

"Finally, an idea with merit." She also took a deep breath.

"You say that like none of my other ideas ever had merit."

She shrugged. I chuckled and slipped my arm around her waist. Instead of pulling away, as I half-expected her to do, she leaned against me, resting her head on my chest. I loved the way she fit perfectly in the circle of my arms.

I decided to push my luck when I introduced my topic. "It was my idea for us to bond."

"Yeah, like that worked out great," she huffed. She didn't speak of the images in her mind. Of the terror of giving birth in a dark shed during a battle in a dangerous war. Of giving up her baby for his own protection.

We sat in quiet thought for a long time. Eventually I glanced behind me, all the way past the citadel mount to the gardens where I could see a group had gathered.

I cleared my throat, trying not to think of my surprise because I knew she would hear me if I did. I pulled her up as a smile—a super-nervous smile—played at the corners of my mouth.

"It may not have all worked out yet," I said, "and I miss our son, too, but you know as well as I do that he's in good hands. Trust Morris. I'm sure you'll be with him soon."

I reached for her face, cradling her chin in my fingers. "It wasn't a mistake, you know," I said in a quiet voice, one meant only for her to hear. "This incredible thing that exists between us *created a life*. He's not something we should regret, Roxy. And knowing everything he's done to protect us, I think we should be thankful."

I saw her tears before she blinked them back. She let me know with a thought that drawing attention to them would result in a punched nose.

"What are you saying, Levi?"

I took a breath and put my hands on both sides of her face. "I'm saying what I've always said. I want to be with you, by your side, every day of whatever life we have left. I'll be your best friend. I'll be anything you let me be, just as long as I can always be with you."

She twisted her mouth to hide her smile. "Are you saying you want to marry me or something?"

I shrugged and reached for her hands. "Not Leona's version. Not anyone's version but yours."

"Mine?" She knew what I meant. She was stalling.

"Bond with me, Roxy. Bond with me for the rest of forever and beyond if we can help it. No Madelines, no Nathan Hales. Just you and me. Always."

"Nathan Hale was pretty hot," she said. "And my son is a time-traveler. It could still happen."

I laughed and grabbed her around the waist. I kissed her. And kissed her again. "Bond with me, Roxy Eisen."

She wrinkled her nose. "I already did."

I nodded. "So we're agreed? You'll stop avoiding me?"

She nodded and slipped her arms around me.

"That's a relief, because there are a few people waiting in the gardens."

"What did you do?" She narrowed her eyes.

"I didn't do anything. They want to ask a couple questions." I shrugged and caught her hand as she moved back.

She muttered under her breath as we walked through the old gardens. I had put out a call to anyone who could spare the time and resources, that the gardens should be repaired. People had been working on them. They didn't look quite so pathetic.

"You pulled Nathan out of the archives!" She shook off my hand and ran to the statue, reaching an affectionate hand to the smooth stone of the base. She tried to reach higher and touch the toes of the statue's boots. She wasn't tall enough, and there was no way I was lifting her up to do it.

She turned to me with a smug smile. "Now I can stare at him

whenever I want."

"Maybe he'll have to go back," I said, pulling her away. "Enough drooling over Nathan Hale. Look by the fountain."

She did. And then she squealed. And then she ran.

Roxy ran to the small group of some of the bunker kids. In true bunker fashion, they were surrounded by screaming babies and roaming toddlers. Lon, Greer and Miles stood in front.

I hoped the group wasn't small because some had been lost.

Roxy jumped into Greer's arms and hugged him tightly. He had to be relieved to know he was completely forgiven.

When I caught up, Greer smiled at me. "Glad you two could make it to our little gathering."

"When did you get back?" Roxy asked, her voice breathless in her excitement.

"After we took care of setting history right. Morris said since I had taken steps to correct what had happened, I had taken care of my debt." His face went serious. "I can't begin to say how sorry I am."

Roxy shook her head. "Not necessary. Remember my stupidity when Joe had a hold of my brain? It was his doing, not yours. He won't be bothering anyone again."

I admired her fierce protective nature. Roxy was a mother bear.

A mother without her son.

I pushed off the anger. It wasn't the time for it. Soon we would get Morris back. Today was a day for us to be happy. Just this one day. We were taking it.

"So why are we here?" Roxy looked at me. "Out with it."

Greer waited until everyone was quiet before he spoke. "It's come to our attention that you two have ... uh ... bonded."

He smiled while whistles and whoops followed his statement. Roxy glared at me with pink cheeks.

I shrugged. *You know it's true.*

Mudsill.

"So, you know what that means, Captain. You know what I gotta ask. Same thing you asked every person down in that bunker when they wanted to go there."

Greer waited for her response. She drew her arms across her chest and frowned. I smiled at her, raising my eyebrows in silent challenge. After a long moment, she looked back at Greer, and her frown unknotted just a little. She gestured that he should get on with his questions.

"Roxy, do you promise to stay with Levi? No matter what, no questions asked, you'll stay together?"

The corners of her mouth twitched. She looked at me. "Yes."

Suddenly it didn't feel like a joke. The person I loved with all of me agreed that we should stay together. She wanted to be mine. She wanted me to be hers. I felt my heart start to race as I considered it.

"Now let's just clarify," Greer continued in a teasing tone. "This means you don't get to stomp off to Antarctica if Levi makes you mad. You gotta talk about it. It means you don't go dancing with good-looking patriots you come across anywhere in time, even if it's technically three hundred years before you made this promise. You got eyes for Levi only, from now on. Think you can live with that?"

"I said yes, didn't I?" Roxy answered, and everyone applauded.

"Okay, then this part is just formality. Levi, we know you've loved and taken care of our Captain Roxy since she was just a baby. We know how you feel, and we understand it's not going to change. But for the sake of bunker tradition, why don't you go ahead and say it."

"Gladly." I waited until the chuckles and whispers died down, reaching for her hands and holding them. "Roxy, I love you. I don't like breathing when you're not around. So I'm going to be beside you until the whole breathing thing stops."

"I love you, too," she said softly during the applause that followed my statement.

I kissed her. "So, you know we'll have to have a governor sized wedding, right?" I teased. "To appease the citizens."

She hit me. Right in that same spot.

I grabbed her around her arms and lifted her up in the air so she couldn't bruise me. When I set her back down on the ground, I saw Morris. He was leaning on the base of the Nathan Hale statue, watching us. When he saw me look up, he smiled.

"Look," I nudged her. Roxy turned around and I heard her breath lodge in her throat.

She ran to him, jumping into his arms.

"Hey, Mom," Morris held her. "Congratulations. It's about time my parents flew the loop."

"Flew the loop?" Roxy was confused.

"Oh, it's an expression in the Transient Village. It means a bonding ceremony."

"It's not very catchy." Roxy made a face.

I chuckled as I walked to meet them.

"Where's Sophie? Where have you been? It's been days!" Roxy hit him on the arm in exactly the same spot she usually hit me. He made a face at me and rubbed his arm.

"Sophie's on her way," Morris said. "I'm going to get her now. She'll take you to the baby." He waited until she looked at him. "Roxy, I want you to understand, your baby is in another time. You'll have to leave 2077."

I don't know what it was about how he said it. Maybe it was the way he glanced at me. Either way, that's when everything occurred to me, and I felt sick.

FORTY-THREE

I didn't know how to tell her I wouldn't be leaving with her when Sophie came to take her to Baby Morris. So I avoided the topic until that evening.

Night had fallen and Roxy sat at the opening of our tent, staring at the sky. I sat down behind her and put my arms around her, wondering if she was cold. I breathed deeply of her skin. Her hair.

The scent of stars.

She leaned back against me.

"What do you think about when you stare up at the sky?" I could guess, but I wanted to hear her speak.

"The light of the stars is old light. Sometimes I wonder if I'm looking at the same star my mom is staring at, wherever she is. Or if I'm staring at the star our child sees from his bed somewhere in time."

I didn't answer.

"I know that's not really how it works. But it helps me feel like they're out there. Somewhere."

I held her closer.

"Sometimes it feels like everyone I love just gets ripped out of my hands."

I shook my head. "Roxy, I ..."

"You don't want to leave the city. I know it. I know you've

been trying to find a way to say it all day." Her voice was quiet.

I didn't answer for a moment. "It's not that I don't want to. And I know you have to go to Morris. But just like you have a baby who needs his mother, I have a city that needs a leader."

"They'd be okay without you for a while," she argued. "Things are stable. No one has attacked us. Greer could hold it together."

"I can't go." I couldn't explain it to her, not in a way she would understand. But I believed it was right. "I don't ever want to be separated again, and I especially don't want to lose you to time. But you have to go, and I have to stay. We'll figure it out. We'll figure out a way to be together again. And this won't change our bond. It's strong enough to hold up."

I saw the images she dreamed about. I knew her arms were aching for a baby who wasn't there. She was watching for Sophie, living for the moment she could leave this time for wherever our baby was. So I would swallow my fear of losing her. I would let her go. Because I loved her.

"There's never been a baby born to any mother in the history of humanity as safe and as loved as ours," I whispered next to her ear.

It was something she didn't see in herself. I recalled the way she'd huffed at everyone for expecting her to live up to her mother's legacy. She hadn't understood why Morris would leave her in charge of the bunker when he died. She couldn't see what was so special about Roxy Eisen.

But I could see it, just as I was sure Morris could see it all those years he raised her and prepared her for her task as the Daughter of Hope. She was a protector by nature. She was fierce, but her empathy was the driving force behind her nature. It went before her almost as a living entity, determined to keep everyone safe. Determined to stand in the way of monsters so bunker kids and ornery toddlers and citadel soldiers turned spies could sleep in peace at night. She was born to set people free, whether she would ever see it or not.

"You're amazing," I said. "I've never known anyone like you, Roxy. I'm sure I never will again. You care more about your people than you do yourself."

"So do you," she said simply, shrugging. "Get over it."

She turned to face me and reached to kiss me. I kissed her back as I picked her up and carried her to the makeshift bed in the corner of the tent. I wished our first night together since the snowstorm was more comfortable, but after a time, neither of us cared about the arrangements.

I held her until she slept. And I tried to lock the moment in my memory so I could remember her when she wasn't there. It hurt. It felt like someone was taking a knife and cutting us apart—two so bonded together nothing but blood and pain could separate us.

Our bond had survived centuries. We would only get stronger. We'd only love harder, even if we had to be apart for a time while Roxy went to Baby Morris and I stayed to hold the city together.

But little did I know the next chapter, the final chapter of our story, of the story of our people, would be the hardest.

RELATIVITY

ONE

I could only hear faint sounds after the electricity hit me. I felt out of myself, unable to move or breathe or think. Eventually, the room became fuzzy and faded to black.

I was sure it was the end. And I was okay with my life being over, even if I was only twelve. I was doing what I was born to do, by dying on the electrified chair in Leona's citadel. How could I not be satisfied with it?

To my surprise, I felt a jolt just before I lost consciousness. I opened my eyes.

"Sephora," a familiar voice said, but it sounded like it was underwater. Muffled, distant.

"Papa?" I tried to speak, but my words were slurred. I tried to remember.

I can't remember.

In my next conscious thought, I opened my eyes. I was in a small, bright room with a clear view of blue sky from the window that covered most of the wall. I smelled juniper and wood smoke. My eyes searched for and found the familiar blue curtain, shining in the sunlight with a thousand glittering stars, waving as the breeze passed through the open window. I heard the voices of people, calling to one another in greeting. I heard the sounds of workmen building. I heard tapping at the data center downstairs.

I was home.

I went to the window, my eyes searching. They quickly found the small hill, surrounded by baby oak trees that swayed idly in the morning sunshine.

I opened the window and slid down the waterspout as I had done a hundred times before. I ran across the field, down to the meadow, sliding across the black rocks. Beyond the ridge, I found the pond next to the little hill I could see from my bedroom window. I fell before the ancient stone marker, covered in moss and worn away by time, though it was lovingly kept free from weeds and had been cemented into the ground in more recent days.

I sat before it the rest of the afternoon. I stared up at the sky and wished I could float up into the cool and pleasant blue sea that stretched from horizon to horizon. I wanted to touch the clouds. To wave to the sun. To race the eagles over the island as far as the sea.

When my stomach started to rumble with hunger, I sat up. I kissed the cold stone and let my fingers trace their names.

Here lie Levi and Roxy
Parents of freedom and of the New Age
Oh stubborn love that does not die
Keep together the bond

The sound of the drumbeat in the arena brought my attention back to the present.

"Sephora, your father seeks you!"

I stood and gave a wave of acknowledgment to the neighbor who made everyone's business her own. I returned to the house with slower steps on feet that did not yearn so much for the sky. If my father was looking for me, it could only mean one thing.

It was time to say goodbye again.

I knew it was his duty, and it was my duty to let him go, but in a moment of selfishness, I hoped he would not return older.

Sometimes, when he left and returned a moment later, he appeared to have aged years, with the creases around his eyes deepening and flecks of gray in his dark hair and beard turning to white. I always felt sorrow when I realized I had missed a piece of his life. That our time had been stolen. But it was a selfish thought and I pushed it to the back of my mind.

I must not complain. I must think of the collective. I must think about the oath I would one day take, in the Arena.

"I am Sephora of the Transient," I whispered as I walked. "I was born to save the past."

What I didn't realize—what I couldn't have known—was that the past would save me, too.

TO BE CONTINUED . . .

ACKNOWLEDGMENTS

Thank you to the brave people we are honored to call our ancestors. Thank you to the founders of our freedoms who didn't love their lives more than those who would come after them. This story couldn't exist without you.

Thank you to future freedom lovers who will put others first and continue the fight against tyrants and dictators, who are sure to rise when people forget what freedom is, and what it costs.

Special thanks to Kent, Caleb, Andrew, Jordyn, Jace, Lexi, Winston, Melinda, Jo, Savannah, Dalina, Paris, Sadie and Daniel. I cannot tell you how thrilling it was to sit down with all of you as young adults and get your perspectives and ideas. To see how much you grasped of Roxy and Levi's story and how excited you were about it. You all helped me much more than you probably realize. Thank you for being an inspiration.

Thanks to my talented editor Tanya Dennis (tanyadennisbooks.com.) You demand the best from the story and the characters, even if it inconveniences the author. I am thankful for that fact, especially with this book, since I struggled so much with Levi's perspective. Thanks to Kathy, Jared and Emily for your feedback and/or your encouraging enthusiasm.

Thank YOU. If you weren't willing to step away from the business of this life and find a quiet corner to devour the words of a story about freedom, we would have no deep thinkers and empathizers who see what needs to be done and have the courage to do it. You are the true heroes and heroines of this story.

ABOUT THE AUTHOR

M.K. Parsons is an asker of questions, a thinker of thoughts, and a fangirl at heart. Her word-loving obsession developed early and she has always been a storyteller.

Besides her husband and children, she is also in love with questions disguised as books, goose bump-inspiring music, and of course, the crafting of worlds and far off people and places, where the only limit is the size of the imagination.

Connect with M.K. Parsons online at:

mkparsons.com
facebook.com/authormkparsons
https://www.goodreads.com/authormkparsons
twitter.com/MK_Parsons
pinterest.com/QuirkyAuthor/ (check out the Transient and Paradox boards!)

Keeping in mind this is an Indie project dependent on word of mouth, please leave your reviews for *Transient* and *Paradox* on Amazon today and spread the word.

Sephora Koenig has been raised in a strict community committed to the task of protecting the ancestors. In the Transient village, it is considered an honor and a duty to give yourself to the cause of time travel with this singular purpose.

But she secretly wonders if she was made for more than blindly following the Council's rules. She longs to be free to use her abilities and discover the dreams that seem to call to her in the quiet moments she is alone. Though devoted to her father, she begins to wonder if he is keeping secrets that could alter her destiny.

When Sophie is sent to protect Levi and Roxy, and they travel to meet the early settlers of Manhattan Island, she will be tested. She will find herself in a dilemma—of choosing love or her mission.

When time demands a sacrifice, can she really do what her upbringing demands?

THE FINAL CHAPTER
NOVEMBER 2016

Printed in Great Britain
by Amazon

39381079R00170